The sexy Ethan Blackstone is in fine form, ladies. Erotica with heart has never been so lovely!

Rare and Precious Things captivated me from beginning to end. Raine Miller spiraled me into her web and I was consumed with her magical writing. These two characters that I love so much have come full circle. Ethan and his beautiful American girl, now husband and wife, and awaiting the beautiful moment when they will get to see their child. I lived every single moment of happiness, tears, fears, triumphs, successes, anxiety, and elation.

I wish I could give **Rare and Precious Things** more than 5 stars. I felt the emotion as each event played out, and I hope you do too!

Just finished this absolutely breathtaking story. **Rare and Precious Things** is the fourth installment of **The Blackstone Affair**, that follows the Fabulous Filthy-Mouthed, Ethan Blackstone, and his Beautiful American Girl, Brynne. I have thoroughly enjoyed it every step of the way!

Ethan Blackstone is the most swoon-worthy male character I've ever encountered.

Rare

and

Precious

Things

THE BLACKSTONE AFFAIR

BOOK 4

RAINE MILLER

Rare and Precious Things

ISBN: 1494751534
ISBN-13: 978-1494751531
Cover Design by Marya Heiman
Strong Image Editing www.strongimageediting.com

Rare and Precious Things

DEDICATION

TO

Valor —and to soldiers fighting the good fight.

All things excellent are as difficult as they are rare.

~Baruch Spinoza, 17TH century

CONTENTS

ACKNOWLEDGMENTS

Thank you, dear readers, for your continued support and love.
I am, as always, humbled by the words and gestures expressed
to me along this journey. My blessings to you.

PROLOGUE

7th May, 1837

I visited J. today. I talked to him and shared my news. More than anything I would wish to have his understanding of my regret, but I know it is out of the realm of possibilities until such a time as I meet my maker. Then I may know his feelings on the matter.

What shall be the price of Guilt? Just five letters in a word which buries me with its weight. I live, but yet I do not deserve the gift. I can go through the days, and the motions of daily life, but for what purpose? What good can I bring to those I love, and who would love me in return, if they should know my secret? I did not act with correctness when the ability was within my power to do so. I kept silent because I was afraid to curb the one whom I loved more than any other. My bitter regret now must always be born in an endless silence that has broken the hearts of all those I ever loved.

Today I also gave my agreement to marry a man who says he wants nothing more than to care for me and to allow him to cherish me. He looks into my eyes and touches a part of my soul in a way that terrifies me, yet at the same time draws me in deeper to understand his motivation. I believe he can see into part of my secret. He understands me, because his words cut right to the essence of my problem, leaving me no choice but to give in to his demands.

So I will go to live at Stonewell Court and make my life with him...but I am very afraid of what awaits me. How will I ever rise to the standard of what is expected of me? I am not worthy, and I fear my carefully guarded heart is in great danger of being shattered beyond the ability for it to continue to beat within my breast. Darius Rourke doesn't yet understand that I do not deserve to be cherished by any man. I am torn, and yet he is persuasively persistent in continuing to assure me all will be well, and to trust in him.

I find myself unable to deny Darius in his wishes for me, just as I was unable to deny my beloved Jonathan...
M G

Part One

SUMMER

So shine bright, tonight you and I
We're beautiful like diamonds in the sky
Eye to eye, so alive
We're beautiful like diamonds in the sky

Rihanna ~Diamonds

CHAPTER 1

24th August
Somerset

"I can hear the ocean," she said up against me, her hand on the back of my neck lightly caressing back and forth, the soft floral scent of her driving me crazy.

"Mmm hmm." I stopped at what I felt was the perfect place for the unveiling. "We have arrived at our nuptial destination, Mrs. Blackstone. I'm going to set you down so you can get the full effect," I warned, before tilting her down to stand on her own. I faced her toward the house and covered her eyes carefully with my hands.

"I want to look. Are we sleeping here?"

"Not sure how much *sleeping* we'll be doing...but we will be here tonight." I kissed her on the back of the head and took my hands away. "For you, my beauty. You can open your eyes now."

"Stonewell Court," she said softly as she took in the view of the great house all lit up from entryway to roof. "I thought this is where we were. I remember the smell of the sea and the sound of the gravel when we walked here that day. It's so beautiful. I—I can't believe we get to actually stay here." She opened her arms wide. "Who did this, Ethan?"

She still doesn't understand. I brought my hands to her shoulders from behind and kissed the side of her neck, my need to have my lips on her skin ruling me for the moment. "Hannah mostly," I murmured. "She's been trying to work a miracle for me long-distance. Thank Christ for virtual meetings and e-signatures on legal documents."

"What?" she asked, turning to face me with a puzzled look breaking over her beautiful face. I loved surprising her, and so far this one seemed to be something she was going to be pleased about. Making Brynne happy made me happy. End of story. We'd both done the second and third shifts manning the check-in desk at Heartbreak Hotel in the last months, and anything that could ease some of that suffering, was long overdue. That's how I rationalized it at least.

"The house is for us tonight," I said, bringing a stray curl of her silky hair to tuck behind her ear as I inhaled some more of her intoxicating scent, and allowed myself the acceptance and contentment of knowing we'd really up and done it. We'd actually managed it. We'd survived and made it to this point right here, right now.

Married. Husband and wife. Baby on the way. Homeowners of a big fucking house in the country. Hard to believe all of those things could be written under my name, true, but I was standing here looking at the tangible proof of it.

One thing was for certain. I wanted it all. No doubts. Not a one.

All mine.

Brynne pulled her bottom lip in between her white teeth and bit the side of it. I had to stifle a groan at the sight of her when she did it. That luscious mouth... I needed that mouth on me. Badly. As pornographic images rolled through my head for how the next hours would play out, she said softly, "Well, I think your sister has succeeded, and then some. It takes my breath away, Ethan. This is the perfect place for us to spend our wedding night...nothing could be more perfect to me."

"You're more perfect." I took her face in my hands and leaned in, putting my lips on hers, pushing my way in for a sweet taste as we stood in front of the house surrounded by the glow of torches and the summer nighttime sea breeze. I coaxed her to open up for me, and of course she did. I took a good, long, and thorough taste of my girl, staking my claim of possession as I had always been driven to do with her from the very start. *My wife.*

So. Goddamn. Sexy.

"You like it?" I asked when I could manage to pull my tongue out of her. It had been far too long since I'd had the pleasure of getting carried away without having to rein it in. And my balls were the perfect shade of blue to prove it. She'd been sleeping at her Aunt Marie's house in preparation for the wedding. I was left wondering how in the goddamn hell people managed to be celibate and still function normally. Well, actually I did know. It sucked massive bollocks and I was barely able to.

"I more than like it, Ethan. I *love* it here." She turned back around and faced the house again, fitting her luscious curves right into my hips. *Oh, fuck yes!* She was going to feel how rock hard my cock was against her lovely arse beneath the lace of her pretty wedding dress in another minute, too. I was beyond the ability to curb things by this point. Two weeks was a fucking long time to go without her...especially when I had grown completely and utterly addicted to her being in my bed. I didn't sleep well without her anymore. It just didn't work for me now if Brynne was not right beside me in the bed...to breathe in, and wrap myself around.

And if I had one of those motherfucking dreams.

As much as I hated for her to be burdened by my emotional train wreck of fucked-up personal baggage, the vulnerable part of me realized that only her presence beside me would ever do anything for soothing away those cocksuckers. Brynne was my only comfort, and yet, as I agonized over scaring her with all that horrible shit, I tried my damnedest to prevent the night terrors from happening. Sometimes I got away with it. Sometimes I didn't. So far I'd managed to avoid another bad one like the night before she was taken by Karl Westman.

Him. I felt my blood boil at the merest suggestion of him. That wankstain wouldn't ever be back to hurt her, or anybody else for that matter, but even the thought of how he'd tried to take her away with him made me physically ill—

"Ethan? What's wrong?"

I shoved my thoughts away and shook my head, holding her a little tighter. "Sorry. I was—I—nothing's wrong, baby." I nuzzled behind her ear.

"I was telling you how much I love that we get to stay here tonight and you didn't answer—"

I cut her off before she could delve any further. My girl was very intuitive with me. She would sense where my head was at and worry. Brynne knew more about my dark place than anyone else, but at the same time, I couldn't bring her into it any further than I already had. I just couldn't do that to her—not my sweet, innocent girl, now my lovely wife, and the mother of my child. And certainly not right now, not with our honeymoon before us. I was going to enjoy our time together. Or die trying. Most fucking definitely.

So I smoothly distracted her instead.

"I'm very glad about that, Mrs. Blackstone, because after we were here together, I couldn't get this place out of my head. I wanted to bring you here. The inside needs some attention, but the bones are good and the foundation rock solid, perched up here with the sea below. This house has been here a very long time, and hopefully it'll still be here a long time from now."

I slipped the small envelope from my pocket and brought it around to hold in front of her so she could see it.

"What's this?" The gentle sound of her voice when she asked the question made my heart thud inside my chest.

"It's your wedding present. I want you to open it."

She lifted the flap and tipped the odd assortment into her hand—some modern, some very old. "Keys?" She whipped back around to me again, her face transformed into one of awe, her lips parted. "You bought the house?!"

I couldn't hold back a grin at her reaction. "Not exactly." I turned her to face the house once more and drew my arms around hers, resting my chin on the top of her head. "I bought us a home. For you and me, and for peaches, and any other raspberries or blueberries that might come along later. This place has plenty of rooms to put them in."

"How many blueberries are we talking here, because I'm looking at a really big house that must have a lot of rooms to fill."

"That, Mrs. Blackstone, remains to be seen, but I can assure you that I will give you my very best efforts at filling a few." *Oh, yeah I would.*

"Ahh, then what are you standing out here for? Hadn't you better get cracking?" She sounded very smug now and I sure liked the sound of that.

I swooped her up, and started walking. Fast. If she was ready for HoneymoonLand then I was not the bloke dense enough to be delaying matters. Again, *not* a moron.

My legs swallowed up the rest of the path quickly, and then the stone steps of our new country house. "And the bride goes over the threshold," I said, pushing the heavy oaken door with my shoulder.

"You're getting more and more traditional all the time, Mr. Blackstone." She laughed softly up at me.

"I know. I kind of like it."

"Oh wait, my package. I want you to open your gift too, Ethan. Set me down. The lighted foyer will be perfect for you to see it with."

She handed me the black box tied with silver ribbon she'd been clutching so carefully, looking very happy, and very lovely in her wedding lace, wearing the heart pendant at her throat. I had a small flash of what she'd endured with Westman when he took her, because I remembered she was wearing it when I got her back and checked over every inch of her body for any sign of injury or abuse. It was the only thing she wore by the time I took us into the shower. Just a jeweled heart on a chain adorning my beautiful American girl... I mentally kicked myself and shook it off, angry that I had allowed bad thoughts in again. I pushed the memory down as far away as possible into the recesses of my psyche. There was no place here for anything ugly tonight. This was *our* night. Only good and wonderful was going to be allowed in with us in this special moment right here.

I lifted the lid off the thin box and pulled back some black tissue paper. The photographs revealed underneath stopped my breath. Brynne beautifully naked in many artistic poses, wearing nothing but her wedding veil.

"For you, Ethan. For your eyes only," she whispered. "I love you with all of my heart, and all of my mind, and with all of my body. It all belongs to you now."

"The pictures are beautiful," I whispered as I studied them in detail. I think I finally understood her as I looked at the images. I was really trying my very hardest to understand her motivation at least. "They're beautiful, baby, and I—I think I can see why you want to have them now." Brynne needed to make beautiful pictures with her body. It was her reality. I needed to possess her, and take care of her in order to fulfill some dominant requirement within my consciousness—my reality. I knew I couldn't help it, either. I only knew that there was no other way for me to *be* with her. I was who I was and couldn't change myself to fit into any other slot in regards to Brynne.

"I wanted you to have these pictures. They're for you only, Ethan. Only you will ever see these pictures of me. They are my gift to you."

"I hardly have words." I looked through the poses more slowly, soaking up the images and savouring each one. "I like this one where you're looking over your shoulder, and your veil is down your back." I studied the photograph some more. "Your eyes are open…and they are looking at me."

"They are, but my eyes have only really been opened since we met. You gave me everything. You made me really want to open my eyes to what was around me, for the first time in my adult life. You made me want you. You made me want…a life. *You* were my greatest gift of all, Ethan James Blackstone." She reached up to touch my face and held her palm there, her clear brown eyes showing me so much of what she felt. *She loves me.*

I covered her palm on my cheek with my hand. "As were you…for me."

I kissed my bride in the foyer of our new, old, stone house for a long time. I wasn't in a hurry and neither was she. It felt like we had the luxury of forever.

When we were ready, I picked her up again, loving her soft weight against my body, and also the tensing of my muscles as I carried her up the stairs. *Holding onto her in order to hold me up.* The concept just made sense for me. I couldn't explain it to anyone else, but then, I didn't need to. It was something for only me to know.

Brynne was *my* greatest gift. She was the first person to really see inside me. Only her eyes seemed even capable of doing it. Only my Brynne's eyes.

CHAPTER 2

Ethan carried me up the stairs, his strong arms holding me securely. The spicy scent and hardness of his muscles filled my senses with his maleness, making me ache terribly with wanting. Wedding night jitters? Maybe a little, with some healthy emotional exhaustion sprinkled on top. We hadn't been together in over two weeks and I missed the intimacy. After all, making love with Ethan was part of our grounding connection. I was honest enough to admit that our first explosive attraction to each other had been all about the sex…and there was nothing wrong with that.

The expression on his face right now was different though, as he carried me along. I wondered what was going on in that head of his behind the carved handsome face. The man behind the mask. My man. My *husband*.

I wasn't concerned though, because I knew he would tell me exactly what that was. Ethan usually had no trouble telling me what was on his mind. Part of his special charm. I had to smile at the thought of some of the crazy things he'd said to me since I'd known him.

"What's that sexy smile about?" he asked without barely a hint of labored breath despite hauling me all the way up one impressively carved oaken staircase. The inside of this house was gorgeous and I couldn't wait to see more of it, but had a feeling I wouldn't be seeing much beyond our bedroom for the foreseeable future.

"I was thinking about your special brand of charm, Mr. Blackstone."

He cocked a brow and gave me a wicked grin. "Does my charm have anything to do with you and me naked on our wedding night, *Mrs.* Blackstone, because I'm dyin' for you here."

I laughed at his veiled complaint about the recent lack of sex. I was dying for him too, but figured this had been a good test for us. Regardless, the anticipation of the moment was so much more intense because we'd taken the sex break before the wedding. I planned on making it up to him very soon. "Of course, *naked* and wedding nights go hand in hand I'm pretty sure."

"Anything else grinding around with the cogs, my beauty?"

"Oh nothing much besides remembering how my beautiful *husband* looked standing at the end of the aisle waiting for me to walk down to him," I paused, "and how

I'm going to reward him for being *so* patient with me for the last two weeks."

He sucked in a quick breath and took faster steps.

I brought my hand up to his cheek, feeling the stubble of his beard, remembering how I'd told him under no uncertain terms was he to be clean shaven at the wedding. I loved his scratchy whiskers abrading my skin when he kissed me and dragged his lips over my body. It was, again, one of the many parts that made up my Ethan. I loved him as I'd known him from the very first, and wanted him just that same way when we said our vows.

He'd listened to me apparently.

When we reached the top of the stairs, he took us left, down a long hallway. At the end of that was a room. Our wedding night suite, I assumed.

"We have arrived, my lady." He muttered the rest. "Thank fucking hell."

I stifled another laugh.

Ethan carefully set me back onto my feet but he kept his body close, his hand brushing up and down my upper arm. Always touching me. He needed to do it, and for me, his constant contact was something that helped me to flourish. I'm sure it was one of the reasons we connected so explosively from the first. He did those things I needed in order to awaken the part of me that was so very broken down. But now? I didn't feel *broken* defined me anymore as a woman. And I had Ethan alone to thank for that.

"Yes, I see. It's very beautiful here." I skimmed the room, taking in what looked to be at least fifty white candles flickering in glass containers of all shapes and sizes, their warm glow reflecting over the walls and furniture, making everything look a little otherworldly. Or, as if we had just slipped back into a time and place that existed many long years ago. As I took in the surroundings, I felt like I could be walking into another century, especially wearing my long formal dress. "I still can't believe you bought this house, though," I said, glancing back. "I love it so much, Ethan."

I couldn't help wondering about the people who had lived here before us either, and what they might have done in this beautiful room, in times past. Had there been other wedding nights like the one Ethan and I were about to have?

I took in the size of the bed situated right in the middle, intimidating every other piece of furniture in the room. A massive carved four-poster with white linens and gauzy drapes shifting ever so gently in the summer breeze floating in from the open window. The oak glowed with the fine craftsmanship of artisans from a lost era.

"Believe it…and I love *you* so much."

Ethan's deep voice behind me broke the quiet stillness.

I stood still and waited.

My veil was lifted off my neck, and then the sweep of my hair was brushed aside. Then I felt his soft lips touch my nape firmly, as if to brand me. I felt his warm tongue roll over the spot in a swirl, rendering me breathless and shivering with wanting all in a second. Ethan barely had to touch me and still I was reduced to a wanton creature desperate for his touch. But he was well aware of that about me.

"You didn't have to buy it though," I whispered. "Just you, Ethan. You're all I really want or need."

He stilled and then spoke softly. "And that...is why you are the only girl for me." He kissed soft sweeps up the side of my neck. "You don't care about all the other trappings. You just see me, I knew that about you from the very beginning."

He turned me and held my face in his big hands, thumbs brushing back and forth, blue eyes searing me with intensity. "I need you like I need air to breathe. You are my air, Brynne."

And then his mouth engulfed mine, deep plunging swirls of his tongue took me over as he struck his claim. I felt my lower body pool with instant heat, desire and craving sparking to furious life. Ethan showed me how much he did indeed need me.

My hands dove into his hair and gripped it in handfuls, edging the passion up a notch. I heard myself moan as he swallowed me up with even deeper kisses that had me literally shaking with desire. I knew I had to slow things down before it became impossible to stop.

My hands left his hair and found their way to his chest where I barely managed, with Herculean effort, to press him back enough to break our kiss. It was not easy, neither physically nor emotionally. I wanted nothing more than to be wrapped up in him all night long, but I also had a plan and I intended to see it through.

We both stood there panting, our faces so close, but yet, not touching; him in his tux with the purple brocade vest, me in my vintage-inspired lace wedding dress, the sexual tension crackling in the air between us like a raging electrical storm about to go nuclear.

I told Ethan what I wanted.

"I n-need to get ready for you... Please?" I managed on a shaky breath, hoping he understood this was something important to me.

He swallowed hard, making his Adam's apple flex at his throat. "All right," he said evenly, as if it were a calculated effort for him to respond to my request without showing me what he really thought of it. I had the feeling he didn't like being asked to wait some more, but he was agreeing for my sake, because he was sweet like that with me. "I'll do the same then, Mrs. Blackstone."

"Thank you, Ethan. I'll make it worth your

while." I stood on my tiptoes and planted a kiss on the side of his bearded neck.

"Oh, I have no doubts about that." My lips felt the vibration of his growl as he spoke his thoughts. "Everything you do is worth my while, baby."

I released him and looked back to where the glow from the en-suite bathroom showed me the way. "Where will you go to get ready?" I felt more than a little guilty about kicking him out of the bedroom, even if for just a short while.

"The adjoining bedroom is also very nice." He gestured toward a door in the wall to the left of the bed. "These old manor houses always had lord and lady connecting bedrooms so they could meet up for the really important, private stuff that happened in the night." He drew a finger across the low neckline of my bodice, moving especially slow over the swell of my breasts sitting against the lace of my gown.

"Oh? The *important* private stuff, you say?"

"Undoubtedly,   baby.   The shagging...is...very...very...*very*...important." He gave me soft, seductive kisses between each of the words.

"Which room are we in right now? Lord's or lady's?" I asked breathlessly, feeling like all the air had suddenly been sucked out of the room.

He shrugged. "No idea. Don't care, either. I shag and sleep wherever my *lady* is, and I always will.

Pick a room, Mrs. Blackstone."

He picked up my hand and kissed the back of it in his gallant way, his eyes slipping up seductively to capture another slice of my heart. Who was I kidding? He already had the entire portion…and he always would.

I sighed with need and forced myself to take a step backward, creating some distance between our bodies. My arm stretched out as I slid back, my hand still clasped in his much bigger one. "Okay…how does this room in fifteen minutes sound?" I stepped backward again, moving closer toward the bathroom door, my eyes never leaving his blues as they tracked my movements.

Those same beautiful blue eyes also glittered with all the shuttered heat of a man who would be ravishing me very soon. He allowed my hand to be released from his grip; the heat of his skin noticeably absent the second contact was lost.

He gave me the serious Ethan-stare, the one I'd seen many times and was well familiar with by now—the one raw with male prowess…and the overpowering sexual dominance that made me burn.

"Like fifteen minutes too fucking long, my beauty."

I had to suppress the slight moan that escaped my throat at the effect his words had on me. I was just a mortal woman after all. Ethan was the one who looked and acted like a Greek god to me.

He seared me with another look dripping with the promise of the molten sex to come, before turning away, walking through the door, and closing it with a soft click.

Once he was out, the room was instantly quiet and I felt more than a little bereft without him. I just stood there and absorbed the reality of where I was in the moment. *I'm getting ready to make love with my husband.* The idea jolted me out of my stupor and sprung me into action pretty fast.

I fled for the bathroom and worked myself out of my dress, which gratefully was not difficult at all with its easy access placement of a side zip. I hung it up carefully on the boudoir hanger which had been arranged, for what I assumed, especially that purpose. I would have to remember to do something nice for Hannah. She'd thought of everything.

I set my veil aside while I brushed my teeth and drank a glass of water. I stripped out of my lingerie, except for the stockings and garter belt in pale lavender silk, and looked at my side profile in the mirror. I had a bump. Not much of one yet, but it was definitely there. I gave our sweet little peach a caress and reached for my veil again. I reattached it and stepped back out into the bedroom. I climbed up onto the raised bed and sank down into the downy softness of the duvet on my knees. I was careful to arrange myself with my back facing the same door Ethan had used when he left the room. He would pass through it again when he returned, and I wanted him to have a first vision of me as I'd planned it out in my head. I was ready even though my heart was racing.

I closed my eyes.

And waited for Ethan to come to me.

THE sounds of the door opening and then closing told me when he was back in the room.

I sensed him staring and the idea gave me a thrill to know what he was seeing of me. I turned my head and found him with my eyes.

"I just want to look at you for a moment," he said, remaining still, a few feet away. I could tell he was affected—his hooded eyes and the set of his jaw—and that knowledge emboldened me.

"Only if I can do the same."

My Ethan had prepared for me as well. The beautiful tuxedo with the purple brocade vest had gone the same way of my wedding dress probably. In its place just one garment. Silky black pajama bottoms slung low at his waist. The contrast of the black fabric to his skin displayed his golden muscled chest and carved abdomen to perfection. And I got to drink him in. The muscular cuts which tapered into a spectacular V below his waist made my mouth water, forcing me to swallow. One of the most beautiful parts of my man. I needed my mouth there.

So gorgeously made in body, so full of male power and strength…it almost hurt to look at him sometimes.

I lowered my eyes to the side.

"Turn all the way around."

The deep command of his voice heated me instantly, rendering me completely enslaved to his unrelenting dominance when it came to this part of us. Ethan's control of our sex. His control over me.

It made me hotter than hell.

He stepped closer, his body radiating power and desire, as he waited for me to comply with his directive.

I rotated my body until I was facing him full on, my body completely bare except for my stockings and my wedding veil. I set my hands flat on the bed and made my arms straight, in effect thrusting my breasts up and out. They tingled under his intense perusal, my now ultra-sensitive nipples hardening from arousal almost to the point of pain. My gesture of offering myself to my husband as a bride on our wedding night had aroused me to an incredible level of anticipation.

"Just for you," I said softly, lifting my eyes to his.

I saw the muscles of his neck tense as he moved forward. "Baby…you are so sexy-beautiful right now.

Don't move. Just stay as you are and let me touch you."

I knew how this game played out. The one where I was blissfully rewarded for following directions.

The edge of the mattress dipped as he joined me on the massive bed, kneeling right before me, so close I could feel the radiating heat his body was throwing off.

I remained still, but I tensed in anticipation of what he would do first.

He hung there before me, for a moment, just studying me, claiming my body with his eyes. Ethan liked a splash of voyeurism in our encounters. A little kinky at times, and a lot dominant, but I welcomed it from him.

Finally, after what felt like eons, he dropped his head to my sternum and inhaled deeply against my skin. Then I felt his tongue draw across the curve of one breast until he reached the tight bud of my nipple. He took the whole thing in his mouth and pulled it inside of him. I gasped in some air and steeled myself to remain still for his onslaught.

"Just feel, baby. Let me suck on your beautiful, perfect tits for a while. I've been starved for them."

He took his time getting his fill as he worked me up with need.

Swirling his tongue in relentless circles over the tender flesh, until he felt like giving me a rewarding jolt of sensation by clipping my nipple between his teeth for a gentle bite.

I shuddered against his mouth, desperately aching for more, but knowing I would have to wait until he gave it to me. Those were the rules. And I was always a good girl.

Despite that, I moaned, "Ethan…"

"What?" he asked, busily working one nipple with his mouth, and the other one with his hand and two fingers to deliver the delicious pinch that made me nearly incoherent. How Ethan had known just how sensitive my breasts were, I do not know, but he'd figured it out from the first time we were together, and he used that knowledge to his advantage with me every chance he got. *Please and thank you, Mr. Blackstone.*

I moaned, throwing my head back, pushing my breasts out and harder against him.

"You want more than just my mouth on your beautiful fucking tits?"

"Yes."

"Thought so," he chuckled darkly. "My beauty, I've been dying for you for weeks," he purred, as he dragged his mouth up to my neck and nibbled, "and I have to warn you, that I'm probably going to be a beast the first time I fuck my beautiful wife with her perfect tits."

"Yes, Ethan…"

"You'd like that?" he asked teasingly, as his hand left my other breast and slid down my ribcage, over my belly, to right between my legs.

I flexed my hips forward to meet his hand, dying for some glorious pressure to relieve the ache blooming at my core. "Yes, I do. I love when you're a beast," I rasped.

He laughed wickedly, his finger sinking in between the lips of my sex to slide over my clit, causing me to jolt sharply. "Oh, God…I've missed touching you," he warned with an eyebrow up, gently scolding me for thrashing around when I was supposed to be controlling my movements.

"I need you, Ethan," I protested as way of an apology, panting against the rising vortex stirring to life within me, struggling to stay still as he'd demanded, even though he was working my clit into a bundle of pleasure about to explode.

"Oh, I need you too…so badly, and right now, I want to see my wife come for the first time. So many firsts…"

He stared me down and worked magic with his fingers as I slipped over the edge, tensing and arching in gulfing waves of pleasure owning me from the inside out.

"Ahhh…Ethaaaaaan," I shuddered as my body's responses took over, and I was helpless to do anything but accept.

Ethan swallowed my mouth in an engulfing kiss as I climaxed, almost bruising from the pressure, but yet, very deeply sensual and romantic as only he can express himself to me. It was the most glorious feeling to be held like that as I came.

As the wave of orgasm rolled over me, the aftershocks still sparking, he started talking. "I love you so much, and I'm going to give you *everything* I've got tonight, baby. *Every* part of you will be claimed and touched by me tonight. Every part. Taken. Everywhere your body can have me, I want to be there…filling you up." He looked into my eyes then, his own intensely penetrating, asking for my permission, making sure I was totally comfortable with what he was asking of me tonight. *I was. Completely.*

Moments like this made me love him so much, it was really too hard for me to process all of it. Even though Ethan was a demanding lover, he always put me first, with care and respect. And love. The domination in the bedroom was just sexual preference, with nothing to do with him and me as individuals. Ethan was no male chauvinist in the way he conducted himself in our life together. He was just male.

All male, and all mine.

My lack of a response must have spurred him because he said more to me. "Because if I don't, Brynne, I'm not sure I can function another day and not be a madman." He nipped at my shoulder and neck. "I love you so much it burns me. Let me show you how much I do." He roamed his hands all over my body, my breasts, my stomach, over my garters and stockings. "So beautiful…waiting here for me like a goddess…"

I answered him on a shaky breath, "I—I w-want you to show me. T-take me how you want me."

He groaned his response at my answer, the rough rasp of his beard stubble at my neck again, teasing and sucking over the spot with his lips, making me shiver with need.

"Do you know why I have to?"

"Yeees I do…"

"Then tell me. Say the words I want to hear coming from your pretty lips."

"Because I'm yours, Ethan."

My declaration caused him to act immediately. I was pressed back into the soft bed with him looming over me, blue eyes searching mine, hooded with the dark desire of sexual power. And it was all for me. I could see the love in his eyes, too. Again, all for me.

"Yes, you are," he answered smugly, sitting back on his knees. "But I have to make sure you're ready for me first, baby. Open up and let me see that spectacular pussy I love so much. I've missed it."

My voyeur was back.

I reached back and pulled the combs of my veil out of my hair and lifted it to the side, before pushing it off the bed to land on the floor with a soft swish.

Ethan's eyes widened as he watched me, the front of his silk pajama bottoms tenting from his erect cock. *I need that cock.*

Slowly, I slid my legs apart, first one and then the other, keeping my feet flat on the coverlet with knees bent. The urge to squirm under his bold inspection had to be forcefully suppressed, but I managed it, understanding his fantasy to have me spread before him, ready to be taken, at his will and desire. The idea of it just served to make me even more of a wanton creature.

"So beautiful. So perfect. So…mine," he said, bringing his face closer to my sex.

The intense hunger, the anticipation that had brought me up to this point, now had me burning up with craving and lust. If he didn't help me soon, I might be dead in an hour from now.

"Oh, fuck, yes," he growled on a fast descent, plunging his tongue inside me sharply.

I shouted his name, unable to stifle my volume, terribly grateful we were alone in this house tonight, because I couldn't help what I said, or did, after Ethan put his mouth on me.

He devoured my sex, using his tongue to penetrate, and his fingers to build me up to the pinnacle of another explosive orgasm that would undoubtedly leave me screaming more than just his name in a minute.

To the point I was frightened of my ability to

endure any more, Ethan consumed me, bringing me to the peak of climax again and again, just to draw back and make me wait. But he knew what he wanted, just as he was very skilled with what he was doing to me.

I felt him shift his body, and then the rustle of silk as he ditched his pajamas bottoms. I watched him position his heavy cock at my entrance and slide in just enough to lubricate the tip.

Ethan paused, his beautiful straining cock right at the edge of my gate, pulsing against me. I was delirious for it. For him. The pagan sex-god come to mate with me and take me to heaven. The sight of him, so erotically potent, nearly caused me to orgasm right then and there.

"Not yet, my beauty. You have to wait," he warned.

"I can't wait anymore." I thrust my hips up to take him into me.

He dragged his hands up and gripped the sides of my head, fisting my hair, binding me to him face to face, eyes on eyes, as was his requirement.

"You want my cock." Not a question. Just a simple truth.

"I want it." I begged.

"Then, my beauty shall have it," he grunted, as he buried himself to his balls and filled me up. Just like he'd promised.

We both shouted at the intensity of our joining,

staring at one another for a second as he lay encased inside me, pulsing with heat. Our hearts melded together in that moment. I am as sure of it as my next breath.

He filled my mouth with his tongue as he started to thrust, both parts of him moving in tandem to take me. As our bodies connected in a frenzy of sex, and heat, and carnal lust, he told me all of the things I loved to hear from my man.

Ethan held me to him, hands cupping my face, and whispered words against my lips as he ravished me. How much he loved me, how beautiful I was, how much I pleased him when I gave myself up to him, how he intended to fuck me like this daily, how good my "cunt" felt squeezing around his cock…

All of the beautiful, dirty, things he'd said to me before, and would undoubtedly say to me again.

Ethan also kept the promise he'd made to me earlier, just as I knew he would.

My husband *was* a virile beast when he fucked his wife for the first time.

CHAPTER 3

I woke up sharply, breathing in sucking gulps of air. *Brynne.* I hated that the first thought in my mind was what I might have done in my sleep, and what her reaction would be to it this time. Had I shouted out angry things that frightened her? Thrashed around in the bed, disturbing her sleep? Tried to fuck her like a madman as a way to bring me down?

My fears were very real. I knew they were real because I'd done all of those things before in front of her.

I dared a glance over at her lying next to me, trying to slow my racing heart. There she was, on her side in all her naked glory, hair spilling wildly over the pillows, and smelling of the floral perfume she used, combined with the unmistakable essence of sex and cum. Her chin tilted in my direction as if she was breathing me in. Peacefully asleep.

Thank motherfucking hell.

Disaster averted. Again. I didn't remember

anything about what I'd dreamt, but the sharp waking did happen from time to time, and I fucking hated it almost as much as the dreams I sometimes did remember.

I turned onto my side, facing toward Brynne and revelled in the gorgeous view she made for me. I loved to watch her sleeping after we'd fucked each other senseless. And I had most surely enjoyed every pounding, orgasmic second of the fucking we'd done on our wedding night. The urge to get up and step out for a smoke tickled my brain, but I told myself that it was just my brain wanting the nicotine my addiction of choice delivered. My body sure didn't need it, and neither did my wife and child.

My wife was beautiful when she slept. She was beautiful all the time, even though she didn't flaunt her beauty like other women I'd known. Brynne was different from every single one of them. A subdued type of beauty. Not flashy to bring attention to herself, but naturally beautiful, drawing interest without any effort at all. I had known it the instant I'd seen her at the Andersen Gallery that night for the show where I bought her portrait. My mind knew she was special before my body did. Now, I held onto the first glimpse of her in my head. It was a defining moment in my life. The place where I returned to when I needed the leveling down from the demonic tortures living in my subconscious. I'd just remember that night when our eyes met across the room. It was a very safe place to go to in my mind when I needed to.

Just watching her right now was enough to make me want her again, but it was the *knowing* that she now belonged to me totally, both emotionally and legally, that really did it for me.

I knew some would say I was completely pussywhipped for marrying off so fast and knocking her up, but I didn't care what anyone thought. If the term fit me, well then, it was exactly what I needed to be, because my life before Brynne sure hadn't been working for me. At least with her by my side, I felt like I had some small chance of being normal…

THE second time I woke, I knew it was morning, and I knew somebody else was awake too. I knew this because she was stroking my cock with her hand and flicking her hot tongue over my nipples. "Good morning to you," I sighed in contentment.

She picked her head up and grinned at me. "Morning, husband."

"I love the sound of that, baby. And I love how you're waking me up on our first morning as man and wife." I thrust my hips toward her hand to create more friction.

"I'm just getting started on you though. You had last night to be in charge. Now it's my turn," she said.

"Well, I am one fucking lucky bastard then." I dragged her fully on top of me so I could have her mouth, and kissed her thoroughly. After a moment, I pulled back and held her face, searching for any signs of trouble. "Everything all right, my beauty?" I just wanted to make sure I hadn't gone overboard with her the night before. I did worry about fucking too roughly, especially now that she was pregnant. I knew we'd have to tone it down as she got closer to the end of the pregnancy, but Dr. B had assured me, that for now at least, everything was on the table.

"Yes. Very much perfect I think." She smiled at me, her eyes sparking a beautiful golden brown.

"Last night…was so amazing." I kissed her again. "You were completely amazing."

She got that shy little blush that happened when she thought about some of the really filthy stuff we did in bed. It made me just that much hotter for her. She allowed me to have her how I wished to and trusted me to treat her right. Her trust in me brought me to my knees, and I would never take that for granted. "So were you." She stroked my length with a firm grip, pulling it into a little twist at the bell-end that got me painfully hard.

"…feels so fucking good," I grit out.

"I know," she said mischievously, and then scrambled down to take me in her mouth.

"Ahh…fuck yes! Yes, that's it…" I lost the ability to form words so I just shut up and took what she gave to me so generously.

Brynne knew how to suck my cock to perfection. She had all the moves down. The long drawing pulls that brought me to the back of her throat, down to the licks around the vein that fed it, to the squeezing of my balls at just the moment I needed to feel the pressure.

I let her work her magic, threw my head back and allowed her to take charge of my pleasure.

For a little while.

Until I was driven to make the switch and take control of things.

She was working me over skillfully, her wet, warm mouth sucking me deep into her throat when I felt my cock swell and my balls tighten. I wanted to be buried inside her sweet cunt when I came this morning, I decided.

So I pulled her off and up my body to straddle me. I lifted her quickly and found my target. She understood what I wanted without me asking and guided my cock home, bearing down to swallow me all the way to the root.

Beautiful. Fucking. Perfection.

She cried out at my invasion, throwing her head

backward, making her hair fall behind her, arching her spine so I could get a really good view of my cock piercing her cunt over and over as we fucked as if our lives depended on it.

She knew. She knew exactly what I liked and how I liked it. My perfect sexual goddess.

As she rode my cock, she made sounds that were so fueled with sex it only served to push me harder. Gripping her hips, I worked her wickedly fast until the little cries she made changed their tone, flattening out in desperation, told me she was very close to coming.

"Look at me, baby. Give me those beautiful eyes of yours when you come all over my cock. Let me feel you cream all over me. I want to see your face when it happens."

What passed between us after that was the stuff that makes memories you'll never forget. I knew I would never forget how Brynne looked to me in that moment of complete possession—faced flushed with pleasure, nipples budded up tight, quivering above her ribs, hair settling over her shoulders and flowing down, eyes fiery with the look of satisfaction. Absolutely breathtaking.

She brought her head forward and looked down at me. Her smoky brown eyes flared and held onto mine. I felt the convulsions start within her, reflexively gripping around me as she went off. I felt my cock harden and swell, preparing to blow me into oblivion, on such a ride of pleasure, I reacted with hardly a thought of what I'd do to her when the explosion hit. My cock in her cunt, my mouth on her skin, my hands in her hair... Ethan inside Brynne. There *was* nothing else in existence in that moment.

I don't know how much time passed, but when I could coherently take stock of the present moment, she was lying on top of me, still holding me within her body, breathing deeply. My mouth was glued to a spot on her neck, sucking softly and soothing with my tongue.

I pulled back and focused. Quite the mark on her elegant neck that I'd just made. It looked like I'd bit her, which I'd done before, and would probably do again. I couldn't help some of the things I did to her when I lost myself in her. Thankfully, she never seemed to be bothered at all by the marks I made on her skin. I always felt guilty for losing control with her though, but realized the capability for it to happen was unique to her specifically. Brynne was my only experience with losing control like that during sex. She was the only one who had ever brought me to such a level of soul-baring exposure. She was the only person I trusted enough to even dare to take a step toward that place.

"I've given you one huge love bite this time, baby. I'm so sorry for marking—"

"—I don't care, you know that," she cut me off, lifting her head up to me.

"You might care this time," I hedged, "because we have to go down to the big house and greet all those overnight guests that stayed at Hannah and Freddy's." I brushed my thumb over the sucking bruise that bloomed between the base of her neck and her ear, wondering what she would really say when she got a good look at it. "I'm a beast, what can I say?"

"You're *my* lovely beast and I'm sure whatever you branded on me is fine. I'll just cover it over with my hair." She laid her head back down and nestled against me with a sexy yawn.

"Somebody is sleepy."

"Well, yeah, that happens when you don't spend much time actually sleeping the previous night," she returned without a pause, bringing a hand to my ribs like she was going to go for another tickle.

I took her hand in one of mine and neutralized her potential attack, grabbing a lovely handful of her prized arse with my other, and squeezed. The feel of her soft curves in my hands made everything feel right with the world. "But we should probably get moving, baby," I reminded gently, annoyed that we couldn't just stay here in bed together and sleep for a few more hours.

"Now wait a minute, am I hearing you correctly? Whose idea was this wedding weekend extravaganza with a morning-after breakfast anyway, because I sure as hell know it wasn't mine."

She had a point. Our wedding had been much more of an *event* than either of us would have preferred, but when the plans were put into motion, the reasoning behind everything was very valid. As the ideas were laid down, I'd wanted as much exposure for her as possible; the higher profile the celebrity of a society wedding would bring, the better the insulation at protecting Brynne from her stalker. At the time none of us had known he was a rogue crazy named Karl Westman. I'd feared much higher levels were involved…and they were on the clean-up end. Of that I was certain. Westman had been taken down by US Secret Service. Threat eliminated and extinguished…by expert professionals who could make a person just disappear if they want to.

By the time Westman was out of the picture, our wedding plans were already deep in motion, and press releases gone out to the gossips rags. Too late to call any of it back, or change the guest lists, so we'd just gone along with what had been originally scheduled. Big wedding, numerous parties, weekend guests, a noisy send-off to our luxurious Italian honeymoon—all carefully constructed to publicize Brynne's status as the wife of elite security, connected at the deepest levels to the British government.

And apparently, the trend of inviting select members to stay overnight to wish the happy couple off the morning after, was the "in thing" at the moment. I suppressed the urge to scoff at the idea. I couldn't wait to get away with her. Just us. Alone in our own little world where everything was safe and peaceful and we could catch a breath.

I smiled at her and kissed her on the tip of the nose. "It was mine, my beauty. Blame me."

She tilted her head up and cracked an eye open. "Blame you for the fact I'm sleepy due to a very busy wedding night, or the big hectic wedding neither of us wanted?"

I laughed at her logic. "Both. Guilty on all counts, Mrs. Blackstone."

"Okay, so your punishment is getting the shower ready and carrying me in, because I don't think I am capable of walking just yet. You know what your orgasms do to me."

I did know very well. She usually fell asleep for a few minutes. "I don't know if I can either after that epic shag, but I'll give it my very best." I carefully rolled her off me and hauled myself up to sit at the side of the bed. "More than just a little motivated here, baby. My plan is to whisk you away where I can keep you all to myself." I picked up my mobile from the bedside table and checked the time. "And to make that happen, I have exactly five hours to get you on a plane with me bound for the Italian coast. If I must have breakfast with a slew of people in order to get us the hell out of here, then so be it, but know this…if I could manage it, we would've already snuck away and been long gone by now."

Brynne's only response was to observe me from the bed as I left to go get the water started for our shower, and she hadn't moved at all by the time I'd returned; just lying there tangled in the sheets, looking soft and flushed from shuddering in my arms only moments before. So beautiful to me, I had nothing else to compare her against. Brynne *was* the definition of beauty when she looked like this after I'd just had her.

Her eyes drew over my body, seeing and evaluating as she often did when I was naked. My girl liked a little leer when the opportunity presented. And if we hadn't just shagged to within an inch of our lives, my damn cock would've been standing at attention begging right now, with the way her eyes were on me. Brynne could express so much without ever saying a single word. How in the hell she managed to be so off-the-charts fucking sexy by just giving me a look, I will never know. I was just the lucky bastard who reaped the benefits, I suppose.

We stared at each other, neither willing to look away, when she gave up one of her barely-there, signature smiles. The kind of smile that shows just the hint of gladness, but with Brynne, it tells me she is happily content with sunny skies in our immediate future.

"You are absolutely adorable right now, Mr.

Blackstone."

I shook my head at her. "I can think of few other words to describe me at the moment, baby, and *adorable* is definitely not among them." *Barking mad maybe, but no fucking way "adorable" fits the bill.*

"But to me you are," she said. "So frustrated at being forced to be social, and having to put on a show for those *people*, as you call them, who just happen to be our closest friends and family, and only want to wish us well and send us off on our honeymoon in style."

"I know," I admitted. "I just don't want to share you right now...with anybody." And I didn't. At least I was honest about it.

Brynne held her arms out to me, and I reached down to pick her up, settling her against my chest, cradling her bum in my hands as she wrapped her legs around my hips. I walked us into the bathroom, kissing her sweet lips the whole way, counting the hours until my wish would be granted.

OF course there were jibes and catcalls when we showed up to Hallborough for the morning-after breakfast-slash-brunch. Ethan would've had us climb out the window and slip away if he could've gotten away with it, but I'd convinced him we didn't have a choice but to show up. I reminded him how happy it would make everyone to see us this morning, and in the end I'm pretty sure he agreed with me, because I had my methods of persuasion, and felt it was my prerogative to use them if I needed to. But as we walked in to join everyone, the knowing looks on their faces, the inner speculations about what Ethan and I had been doing the night previous was a little too invasive for my tastes. I loathed for people to think private thoughts about me. I understood very well why I had hang-ups with that particular idea; it didn't change anything for me. I still felt that way.

As I tried to smile and look happy, realizing the people in the room were imagining all the sex I'd just enjoyed with my husband, put me on the defensive. I had to agree with Ethan's earlier suggestion. The window escape plan sounded pretty damn appealing right about now. He must have sensed my reluctance, because he gave my side a little squeeze and whispered, "Four more hours, my beauty. We've got this." He pressed a kiss to the side of my head and in we went.

Duties to our guests aside, I was very aware of how Hannah had gone over and above in her efforts on our behalf, along with our wedding planner, and the perfectly timed assistance of Elaina, had ensured our gig had gone off without a hitch and I couldn't be more satisfied with how everything had turned out.

Only one thing was missing. Well, one person…but there was nothing to help me with that one. *Love you, Dad.*

The formal hall at Hallborough was casually set up with several tables dressed in cream linens, purple flowers, and old silver, that had to be worth a small fortune. The fact that Ethan and I would soon be country neighbors with Hannah and Freddy, and their three beautiful children, was something that made me very happy. Having a family to love and support you meant everything to me. They had done so much for us already. I looked forward to being closer and spending more time together.

So I found myself standing amid all the splendor, with my *husband* beside me, making the rounds, thanking everyone who'd stayed over at Hallborough to celebrate with us. He looked gorgeous as usual without barely any effort, his damp hair curling at the neck of his thin creamy sweater, paired with faded jeans and buttery-soft loafers in camel. Ethan did casual just as skillfully as he did suits. Mouthwatering.

After our shower, we'd dressed quickly and driven over to greet our guests one last time before taking off. We'd insisted on a very casual and informal gathering this morning, thus our simple outfits of jeans for Ethan, and a white eyelet sundress with leather wedges for me. I ended up wearing my hair down, because he had indeed laid a significant hickey on the side of my neck, and I certainly didn't feel like sharing it with others the morning after my wedding night. It would only serve to feed more fuel to their imaginings of how I'd earned it. Nope. I was too private for that kind of nonsense. And Ethan's remorse later over marking me up, after the fact, always struck me as a little surprising too. For a man so dominant during sex, he sure worried about me a lot. I had told him over and over that if he ever went too far, I'd let him know, but I'm not sure he really and truly believed me. *Oh, Ethan, what am I going to do with you?*

He never took his hands off me the whole time. As we chatted from place to place in the room, he always had an arm tucked around my waist, or a hand at my back. He would press kisses into my hair and brush up and down the side of my bare arm with his hand if we were idle. He just seemed to need it, and for whatever reasons, the idea that he needed to touch me in order to feel comfort, was extremely powerful in my own journey of emotional healing. I felt much loved and very cherished as we made our way around to thank everyone.

Even my mother managed to be happy for us.

"Oh, darling, what a pretty dress you've chosen to go away in. I love the cutwork at the hem," she gushed.

The cutwork at the hem? Seriously? "Ahhh, thanks, Mom. You know me, I like things brutally simple," I told her as I accepted a hug. It wasn't lost on me that Ethan and my mother didn't really acknowledge each other. They had a wary truce of sorts for the moment, both of them intelligent enough to get through the wedding without adding to the drama. Poor Ethan; he'd inherited a monster-in-law, and now had to tolerate her for life.

My mother frowned at my answer, just a tad mind you, but still qualified as a frown by my standards, her unlined face not even hinting to her true age of forty-four. She looked much younger. "But you could wear anything right now, Brynne. You should take advantage of it while you still can." As soon as the words were out of her mouth, my mother realized her mistake and started fidgeting with my hair. She'd managed to bring up my pregnancy, and avoid it like the white elephant in the room that it most definitely was, both at the same time. Bravo, Mom. Why couldn't she be even a little bit more like my Aunt Marie? Marie didn't judge, didn't make me feel like an irresponsible slut for getting pregnant before I was married, and didn't pretend she wasn't going to be a grandmother in another six months. "I don't know why you don't wear your hair up, darling; it would give just the right touch of elegance to that neckline—"

Mom's eyes widened. And then she dropped the bun of my hair she'd been arranging like it was radioactive waste. As my hair settled back down around my neck, she shoved Frank forward to give his congratulations. Guess the giant hickey had freaked her shit right out. Was it bad I had to stifle the urge to tell her how good it had felt when Ethan gave it to me?

I wished for a tiny moment I could indulge in one of those mimosas people were drinking with their breakfast.

My stepfather, Frank, kissed me on the cheek and told me I was a beautiful bride. As much as I tried to appreciate his gesture I felt a sudden clawing ache for my own father, who wasn't here. And whom I'd never see again.

Ethan thanked them both for coming and sensed my need to move on. He was so good with reading me. I felt nothing but relief when we made our way over to Neil and Elaina.

"You're still walkin', mate," Neil teased, delivering a hearty clap to Ethan's back.

"Indeed I am." Ethan returned a half hug, half back-slap to his friend and partner.

But Neil wasn't done with the tongue-in-cheek I was pretty sure. I'd seen these two in action for the last months and they went 'round and 'round all the time. "So, how did he do, Brynne?" Neil asked me, before breaking out in a snickering laugh. "You look absolutely glowing this morning by the way."

Elaina smacked her fiancé's arm and told him to shush.

I laughed back and told Neil a lady never tells,

before accepting hugs and kisses from our closest friends as a couple. Neil worked with Ethan as partners in Blackstone Security, while Elaina and I had hit it off from nearly day one. They lived right across the hall from us in London and we spent a lot of dinners and down time together.

"In six weeks or so we'll be doing this again, only then it will be you two that are fielding all the wedding night innuendo comments," I said to Neil, reminding him that his own special day was right around the corner.

Neil grinned widely and pulled Elaina up against his big body. "I know, and I'm counting the days 'til I can make this one an honest woman."

"Ha, more like Elaina making an honest man out of *you*, my friend," Ethan shot back.

"That's true, but you'll finally get to bring Brynne up to Scotland so she can see the place."

"Trust me, Neil, I would give just about anything to be up there in beautiful Scotland right now, seeing your place and enjoying your post-wedding breakfast," I told him truthfully.

I looked over at Ethan and we shared a co-conspirator smile, because it had been originally their idea to have the overnight weekend thing in the first place. Neil owned a great estate up in Scotland, and since people were coming all the way up there, they had organized a guest sleepover for their wedding, too. It'd sounded like a nice idea at the time.

"Why's that?" Neil and Elaina asked together.

"You'll find out," Ethan and I answered innocently.

"AND Gaby, is where? I need to say goodbye." I'd scanned the room repeatedly for my best friend but she was nowhere that I could see.

"That's a really good question," Ethan answered. "For that matter, where in the hell is Ivan?"

I shrugged. "Looks like our best man and maid of honor have ditched this party for greener pastures." I giggled. "Maybe they're off ditching *together*. That would be interesting."

"I know, right? Gabrielle is Ivan's flavor for sure."

"I could swear I was picking up on a vibe between them last night when I was with Ben, and we were stalking them as Simon was snapping candid pictures. Do you think your cousin and my friend just might have a little somethin'-somethin' going on?"

"If they do, Ivan hasn't said a word to me about it. But, there was that night at the Mallerton Gala when the alarm went off. I always wondered what happened with the two of them, because I saw them both within seconds of each other coming from the same direction, when we were all running out. Like maybe they were together…"

"You never told me that, Ethan." I shook my head at him in disbelief. "Honestly, you men just don't tell details very well at all."

"Well, it wasn't important at the time, baby. I was a little preoccupied on finding *you*." He pulled me against him and kissed me firmly on the lips, making me forget we were in a very public room of people watching us, until the tinkling of silverware on crystal rang out to remind us. I felt my face flush, and heard Ethan groan as we pulled apart, muttering something under his breath about "four more fucking hours."

"There they are. Mr. and Mrs. Blackstone have arrived finally." Ethan's dad, Jonathan, opened his arms and embraced us in a three-way hug. "You did it, my dears. And very well too, I might add." He kissed me on the cheek and clapped Ethan on the back, meeting him eye to eye, man to man, in a moment of silent communication, which they both understood without a shadow of a doubt.

I could only guess as to what they were both thinking, but I had my theories. They were acknowledging Ethan's mother as being here with them, for this special occasion along the road of his life's journey. Jonathan looked up at the ceiling for just a split second, before nodding to Ethan. I saw Ethan return the gesture to his dad, and then I felt a squeeze to my hand from him.

My hand which had remained clasped so very tightly in his because he'd never let go of it.

And so we began our marriage, on a summer's day in late August, just barely four months after laying our eyes upon one another for the first time. It had all begun across a crowded room one night in the spring—at a gallery tucked away on a London street—when fate had stepped in and forever changed the course of our lives.

CHAPTER 4

30th August
Italian Riviera

The Italian sun shining down upon the village of Porto Santo Stefano warmed me, and although the view of the rock islands in the small cove was stunning, I didn't want to open my eyes and see it. I was too warm and sleepy, too perfectly content to even think about anything but letting myself indulge in the peace we had finally found. What a difference a little under a week made.

Ethan and I were in a very perfect place at the moment...where we didn't have to panic about what we needed to do, or what bad thing could happen to us, or be shocked about what already *had* happened to us.

Yes, my life couldn't compare to any resemblance of what it had been four short months ago, but then again, I was blissfully in love with my new husband and, after the initial shockwave of finding out we were going to be parents wore off, very much in love with that idea, too. I reached for my belly and rubbed over it gently. We had a peach for about two more days. After that? It was onward into lemon territory. My next appointment with Dr. Burnsley wasn't for another month, and even though the scans might be able to show the sex of the baby that early, I was determined not to find out. I wanted to be surprised, and nobody was changing my mind on the matter. I'd told Ethan he could find out if he wanted to, but he'd better keep the knowledge to himself. He'd just given me a slightly bewildered look that probably meant something like, *I love you, but you are downright scary right now, baby*, and changed the subject. Such a man. But he was *my* man, and that was the important thing. We'd get through this frightening process of becoming parents together.

And so here I was, sunning on a private Italian beach at an exclusive villa, expecting that my man might bring me a cool drink when he finished his swim. *Not bad, Mrs. Blackstone.* I still hardly believed the name was real. The *Mrs. Blackstone* part was something Ethan took to heart because he sure said it a lot.

I squinted at my wedding ring and spun it around on my finger. *I'm married now. To Ethan. We're having a baby sometime toward the end of February.* I wondered when, and if, the disbelief would ever wear off.

I turned my head the other way, readjusted myself on my side, and closed my eyes again, prepared to soak up some more of the glorious Italian sunshine, so abundant here, as opposed to where we lived. Autumn was just around the corner, and then the dreary days of winter in London would be fast on its heels. The time to enjoy the lovely sun was right now, so that's what I did.

I let my mind wander, going to a place where everything was happy and easy, and tried to put all of the other things that were not happy and easy, away on their respective shelves, locked up tight in that scary cabinet I hated to open. The one for all the bad stuff to sit and gather some dust for a while—the worries about the regrets of life, the losses and the grief, the desperately poor decisions that had been made, and the consequences that resulted from those choices...

ICY drops falling onto my shoulder brought me out of my floaty sleep on the beach. Ethan must be back with my drink. I opened an eye and looked up at him blocking the sun from my body, not appreciating the shocking greeting, and taking in his stern expression. God, he was a beautiful man with his hard lines of muscle and golden skin. I could look at him for years and never be content with the looking. And the complete unconcern with what others might think of him made the combination all the more attractive. Ethan was no pretty boy who got satisfaction out of fawning admirers. And they were frickin' everywhere. And not only women, either. Plenty of men admired my husband, too. He was oblivious to it all.

"What did you bring me?" I muttered.

He ignored my question and handed me a bottle of cold water. "Time for more sun block, you're getting a tad pink."

"You're just saying that so you can roam your hands all over me," I said.

He dropped down next to my towel and raised a brow. "You're fucking right about that, my beauty."

I sipped some water and closed my eyes as he applied sunscreen all over my shoulders and arms, and relished the feel of his hands on my body. His hands. His touch. The feel of Ethan's hands on me still rendered me weak. No wonder I was unable to resist him when he pursued me in the beginning. It had been like that from the first for me…with Ethan. His searing gaze across the room at me that night in the Andersen Gallery, the coercion on the street to accept a ride home from a virtual stranger, the way he steered me with a firm hand to my back into his Rover, and demanded I eat the food and water he bought for me, that first demanding kiss in the Shire's Building hallway, how he took those rights to touch me as if they were his due, with no apology for overstepping social boundaries. That was how Ethan has always been with me.

Ethan's "claiming" of me had occurred in a way that I understood right from the beginning, even if it seemed ridiculous and unbelievable such a man would be in pursuit of me personally, it still made sense to me when I accepted my fate with Ethan James Blackstone. He had a way of asserting his ownership of me whenever he touched me. Felt like heaven.

"That feels so good."

He grated under his breath. "I agree. Now turn over."

I rolled for him and brought my arm over my face to shield the sun. He worked in the sunscreen carefully, making sure he covered every area. When he got to my chest, he dipped his purposeful fingers below the bra of my suit and brushed over my sensitive nipples—back and forth until they budded up high and tight, making me shiver for more.

"Are you taking advantage of me out in public view now?" I asked.

"Not at all," he answered, scooting onto my towel to kiss me, "I am taking advantage of you on a very *private* beach, where nobody will bother us."

He moved his hands up to take down the straps of my top. Open it fell, and then the glorious rasp of his whiskers brushed the area around my nipple as he teased it. There was a sharp internal zing at first touch now; due to the pregnancy I was sure. My nipples felt different when he started, but after that first jolt faded away, his sucking and nipping felt just as good as it always had. I ran my hands through his hair as he rained kisses over my breasts, loving his attentions.

"Just so you know, Blackstone, there won't be any sex happening on this beach right now."

"Awww, baby, you've just gutted me. I've been planning to have a hot beach shag with you for the whole honeymoon."

"Well, if you have any shot at it you'd best try me once the sun goes down. It's the middle of the day and we're out here where anyone could come by and see us. And I'm not putting it out there for public consumption. Didn't you ever see those shows about the hidden cameras filming beach sex?"

He rolled his eyes and shook his head. "But there isn't a soul around here for miles. Just the sand and the sea…and us two souls." He wiggled his eyebrows.

"You are absolutely crazy, do you know that?" I pulled at his chin and kissed him on the lips.

He laughed at me, watching as I pulled the straps of my top back up and covered myself once more. "You're absolutely crazy beautiful lying on that towel in your bikini. Pretty sure you ought to be illegal wearing that."

I smiled at him for the praise, hoping it was true,

and brought my hand to my stomach. "Pretty soon I won't want to wear a bathing suit."

He covered my hand with his. "But you are perfectly beautiful like this. Even peaches thinks so." He spoke to my stomach, "Peaches? Dad here. Tell Mummy how beautiful she looks in her bikini, would you?"

I laughed at how sweetly adorable he was being, loving him even more than I did before, if that was even possible.

He pushed an ear up against my stomach and paused as if listening, nodding his head a few times in emphatic agreement. "Right. Peaches agrees that you look beautiful, and I would say that I have it on very good authority, that to argue with a baby who has yet to be born is completely useless."

I sighed in happiness. "I love you, crazy husband."

"I love you, beautiful wife," he said with a wicked grin, "but I still think we should shag on the beach at least once before we leave this place."

"Oh my God, you have such a one track mind now." I shook my head slowly back and forth. "We need to find you a hobby."

He threw his head back and laughed. "Baby, my *hobby* is shagging you, in case you haven't realized it yet."

I tickled him in the ribs. "I think you should take up gardening, or maybe grouse hunting, or something."

He easily caught my hand and blocked my tickling strategy. "I'll play in your garden any time," he muttered between soft, quick kisses to my lips, "and hunt your grouse, too."

I snuggled against him and put my face right into the groove of his upper chest, breathing in his scent, close enough to feel the tickle of the hairs sprinkled there. "You make me so happy, Ethan."

My words did something for him because I'd never seen him move so fast.

Ethan scooped me up off my towel and said, "Wrap your legs around me."

I did as he asked and got myself adjusted around his waist, crossing my ankles behind his back.

We kissed the entire time he walked us off the beach, as if our bodies depended on it for sustenance. Ethan's strength had always left me breathless, and having him carry me in his arms back to the villa, had the same result. Breathless and so turned on. Again.

The next couple of hours were spent tangled in bed, where he made love to me, slow and unhurried…

"WHAT do you want to do about dinner? Shall I cook?"

"Nope," he answered.

"I really don't mind, Ethan. It's a lovely set up in

the kitchen and everything's stocked."

Ethan played with my hair, dragging his fingers through the strands over and over. He liked to do it. It seemed to be a mindless task, something he did when we were awake in bed together, but I sensed it meant more to him. Soothing. It seemed to sooth him, and was a way to touch me without being sexual. Ethan liked to touch me *all* the time, sexual or not.

"You're hungry."

I nodded against his hand at my scalp. "My appetite is back. I need food to grow this child we made. And dessert." I ticked him in the ribs to get him moving.

"So feisty you are…and impatient," he teased. "Far be it from me to be stupid enough to deny food to a pregnant woman—"

"—don't forget the dessert," I reminded, with another go at his ribs, which he blocked easily.

"I'm taking you out tonight. I don't want you to cook. And…without a doubt, there should be a decadent dessert for my girl."

"Aww, thank you, baby, you are too good to me." I offered my lips to his for a kiss.

He didn't kiss me though, instead, his eyes lit up with a gleam that could only be described as wicked, when I felt his palm smack me on the ass with a playful clap. "You'd better move that divine fanny of yours into the shower before I decide to have it again."

I scrambled off the bed, but before I left him there, I leaned over my very loving, but controlling husband, in all his bared male magnificence, and placed one fingertip at the middle of his chest to keep him down. I gave him the sultriest look I could summon up, cupped my breasts and drew on the nipples slowly, with little twists to the tips. I licked my lips exaggeratedly, using my tongue to curl along the edge of my mouth.

He was mesmerized by it all, and so still, he didn't even look to be breathing as he watched my little sex-show, slash, lap-dance. I put my finger back on one of his nipples before dragging with my nail all the way down, ever so slowly, over his six pack of muscles, his belly, between his V, and finally, right to the base of his cock.

His torso tightened and flexed as I scratched him, teasing him without mercy. Ethan was my sexual minion in that moment and he and I both knew it. I couldn't resist what I did next.

I winked at him. "I win," I whispered, before dashing for the showers.

He chased me down, of course, tickling me, making me laugh as we washed up for our dinner date—but not before paying me back for what I'd done to him on the bed.

In orgasms.

"SOMEBODY is enjoying their dinner tonight." Ethan watched me eating with a huge grin plastered on his handsome face.

I moaned at the flavor of the rich pasta in my mouth. "Oh me, oh my, this is the most delicious baked ziti I've ever tasted in my life. I wish I could make it like this."

"Maybe you can. Take a picture with your mobile to help you remember some of how they prepared it."

"That's a great idea. Why didn't I think of it?" I reached for my purse.

The gleam in his eyes turned to teasing. "Probably because you're too busy cramming it in."

I kicked him in the foot under the table. "Jackass."

"Only kidding," he grunted. "I'm just grateful that you're able to finally eat. I was concerned about you wasting away before, so now it's just one less thing worrying me."

I blew him an air kiss. "Number one, you wore me out earlier today, and number two, I think my body is making up for lost time when I couldn't keep much down. If I allow myself to get over-hungry, then you'll find you have one very cranky gorgon of a wife on your hands." I made a face. "Trust me, you don't want that to happen."

The ziti did agree with me, but mostly it was the fact I could now eat and not feel ill afterward. Our baby was definitely making his or her presence known despite being so tiny, and food is what was required to make everything work.

He put down his knife and fork and feasted his eyes on me. "Well, first, I loved wearing you out earlier today, and second, I love seeing you enjoying your food again. I'm not stupid. When my girl says she needs to eat, then she damn well better *eat*." He topped his wine glass off. "And third, you're one hell of a beautiful gorgon, even when you're scaring the crap out of me."

"Am I that scary now, Ethan? You can be honest." I know some of my emotional highs and lows freaked him out, but pregnancy was hard on me too, and I did worry about the change in me. I couldn't control any of it, and yet, I didn't want to be the crazy hormonal wife that made him long for the good ole bachelor days either.

"Never." He picked up my free hand and kissed the palm, his eyes smiling up at me lovingly. "What would be really scary is not being with my beautiful gorgon and our little peach."

"I love you." I managed to say the words without getting teary, but it wouldn't take much. Ethan could pull emotion out of me by just looking at me.

"I love you more," he said softly, reaching for his

wine and taking a healthy swig. "And I think that was evidenced by the fact I let you drive us here tonight." He emptied the rest of his glass in one drink. "I'm still leveling down from the white-knuckle ride."

"Are you trying to wind me up, as you Brits say, by all the comments and flaunting the wine because you know I can't have it?"

He opened his mouth in surprise first and then turned it into a million dollar smile to dazzle me. "You think I'm winding you up on purpose, baby?"

I didn't say anything, just sat back in my seat and studied him thoroughly; the casual blue shirt highlighting his eyes, the simple linen slacks that suggested the powerful legs beneath, his Rolex and his wedding ring, the only adornments he wore. Ethan didn't need adornments because his face and body were more than sufficient. Such a beautiful man was my husband. I wasn't stupid enough to believe this very remarkable trait wouldn't cause me much concern over the course of our lives together. Other women would try to catch him and it would drive me insane when they tried.

"I've discovered that I love to tease you," he offered finally. The way in which he raked his eyes over my body told me the reaction he got out of me turned him on a little.

"What does it do for you?" I asked in a whisper, my body tightening in preparation for what he might say.

"It makes me hard when your eyes start flashing and you get feisty with me." His eyes flared at me and his voice went low. "I can think of only one thing, Brynne." He reached out with his fingertip and brushed down the length of my ring finger, sending a tingle up my arm. "Do you want to know what it is?"

"Yes…"

"How long before we're fucking again and I've got you spread underneath me about to come."

Okay, so it turned him on a lot.

I closed my eyes and suppressed the shiver of desire that zipped through my body to pool between my legs. The Italian crystal glass of water in front of me was drained in one pass, and I no longer cared a bit about having any dessert after my dinner.

Why on earth did I agree to go out tonight?

I cleared my throat and tried to shake off the blast furnace of heat Ethan was throwing off, and attempted to get back to the conversation we were in before. "So, you were alluding to my driving a minute ago…"

He picked up my hand and rubbed with his thumb over my knuckles, his eyes telling me he would make good on his wicked thoughts just as soon as we could get back to the villa. "Yes, my beauty?"

"I—I wasn't that bad driving." I tilted my head. "Was I?" Ethan had indulged my request to drive us again. We were in Italy where they drove on the *right* side of the road, and I had enough confidence to do it here. My California driver's license was still valid and I didn't want to forget how to. In the four years since I'd lived in London I'd not owned a car or driven myself, mostly because of the left-handed driving situation. It was just too scary for me to attempt, and really, not necessary when public transportation was so good in the city. I'd never needed to drive in England. Plus we had a smokin' hot BMW 650 convertible rental in midnight-blue…and I planned on using it.

"Well, no, you're never bad at anything…" he hedged, "it's just that driving on the right is not even slightly in my comfort zone. And I certainly don't want you getting hurt. I'd feel much more at ease with you in a bigger vehicle with better safety features."

"I don't think I will ever drive in the city. Seriously, I don't think I could ever be comfortable driving myself in London even if I live there for the rest of my life."

He smiled thoughtfully at me, the blue of his eyes darkening to a deep midnight. "You'll be living with me for the rest of your life, wherever that is doesn't matter very much as long as we're together. And you don't have to worry about driving around London either, because it *is* a bloody nightmare, and I don't want you doing it. You've got me to drive you." He brought my hand up to his lips and pressed another seductive kiss to my palm.

"You do know…if you want to drive, I can make that happen—"

The waiter who'd served our dinner interrupted right then with a gift from a patron at another table. A bottle of wine—a very expensive bottle of Biondi Santi, that I, sadly, would not be able to drink for a very long time. We both looked in the direction where he pointed us to a man who looked vaguely familiar to me. Tall, caramel-skinned, and very handsome, he moved with the elegance of someone who used their body as an athlete would, every movement calculated for precision, the unmistakable air of confidence exuded in every step he took toward our table.

"Well, hello to you, too," Ethan greeted him, gesturing to the bottle, "and thank you for this. Very nicely done." The two of them shook hands warmly.

"My pleasure," he answered in a sophisticated British accent laced with amusement.

Ethan made the introductions. "Dillon, my wife, Brynne. And this fellow here, my darling, is Dillon Carrington."

"How do you do, Brynne. Lovely to meet you in person. I have only seen pictures of you in the gossip rags." He extended his hand and I offered mine. There was something very familiar about Dillon Carrington but I couldn't put my finger on it, even though it was obvious he and Ethan were well acquainted.

"Nice to meet you as well, Dillon. Thank you for the wine. I'm sure it will be delicious, but I feel as if I've seen you somewhere. Have we met before?"

Dillon shook his head, laughing. "No, never. I would definitely remember meeting you, Brynne."

"Ethan?" I looked to him for some help but he apparently was having too much fun at my expense because he only winked at me.

"You know, Dillon, it's funny because Brynne and I were just having a conversation about teaching her to drive British, being she's a Yank by birth."

"Ahhh, loads of fun that is. Righty learning lefty. You want to borrow my crash suit, mate?" Dillon asked him.

Crash suit? I had no idea who this guy was but knew that I definitely *should* know him, especially since he knew who I was. I seriously needed to pay better attention to the gossip mags. Ethan knew a lot of famous people, and our engagement and wedding had been splashed all over British media.

"Would you like to join us? Are you on your own tonight? Ethan offered out of courtesy.

"No, no thank you. I don't want to interrupt you, but I saw you when I came in and wanted to say hello, and give my congratulations of course. I am meeting someone in a minute, actually."

"Ahh, right, well, I'm glad you did. We missed

you at the wedding, but I know you were just a tad busy that day."

Dillon laughed at that comment. "Yes, slightly. They had me driving 'round in circles the whole weekend. I come down here for a little R & R afterward when I can manage it."

"Congratulations on your win. I watched the highlights and you tore it up. Brilliant performance." I could tell Ethan was suitably impressed by whatever Dillon had won.

"Thanks. And for the sponsorship, too. I hope you got the signed gifts I had them send out."

"Seriously, money well spent all the way 'round. Seeing Blackstone's logo on number eighty-one was quite the defining moment for me. Truly."

I took a stab at a guess and interrupted. "Are you a race car driver, Dillon?"

"I am in racing, yes." He tilted his head. "I could get you driving lefty in no time, Brynne," he answered, a charming smirk lighting up his eyes as he teased me. "You just say the word if you ever want a driving lesson."

"Fat chance of that happening, Dillon. I believe I'll do the honors of teaching my wife to drive British, thank you very much."

"Well, we'll just have to see how well you've come along with your lessons by the time we meet up again in October for Neil and Elaina's wedding, because I will be checking in with Brynne," Dillon challenged with a wink in my direction.

"Oh, you will be there?" I asked him.

"I will be." He gave a slow nod. "Neil and I go back to our school days. Elaina's brother, Ian, too. Good mates of mine." Dillon looked over his shoulder in the direction of his table. "My guest is here, so I should go and leave the two of you in peace. So lovely to have met you finally, Brynne." He bowed his head to me. "And you, Blackstone, have done *very* well, you lucky bastard." He shook his head with a devilish grin.

"Astute as always, Carrington. Thanks again, for the wine, and we'll see you up in Scotland very soon."

Dillon gave us a wave and returned to his table, his striking looks grabbing the attention of the other patrons in the restaurant as he greeted his date, an exotic, leggy brunette with obvious enhancements of the silicone variety, staring our way quite intensely, probably annoyed at us for monopolizing her boyfriend.

"He seems nice," I said. "He's really famous, isn't he?"

"Ah, yeah, slightly. You were just offered driving lessons by a Formula One World Champion, my darling."

"Wow. He *is* legendary. I knew I'd seen him before, I just didn't realize it had been on TV and at the newsstand." I glanced over at Dillon's table. "I don't think his girlfriend liked him talking to us though, because she's throwing off some pretty toxic vibes."

"I don't think that's his girlfriend." The sarcasm in Ethan's comment was impossible to miss.

"Why do you say that?"

"Baby…" The censuring look he set on me spoke volumes. "I can say it because I *know* the man. Dillon Carrington doesn't have girlfriends. He has dates." Ethan nodded his head toward their table. "And *that* is a date."

"You know this how exactly?" I persisted.

"Because I used to be just like—" He shifted in his seat and looked like he wished he could bite off his tongue. "Oh, forget it. I really don't want to talk about Carrington's social life on my honeymoon."

"Me either," I said. And I really didn't need to know any more, because I was confident that Ethan knew exactly what he was talking about, because he'd just let slip the reason.

After all, he *had* been just like Dillon Carrington before he'd found me.

CHAPTER 5

"As much as I'd love to stay swimming out here with you, we'd better go in and start getting ready for the party. I have to wash my hair."

I groaned my protest with plenty of displeasure, hoping it might work. "Not that fuckin' thing, please."

"Ethan, come on, you know we have to go. *I* have to be there. Marco said we are his honored guests, and he's planned around us being here, specifically. How rude would it be to just not show up?"

I pulled her legs around my hips and trapped her against me as I tread the sparkling water of our little beach cove. Maybe denial would be more effective since she wasn't buying my complaints. "I'm keeping you out here in this beautiful sea with me forever." I nipped at the shell of her ear and flicked the lobe with my tongue, tasting the mix of her skin and the salt of the ocean.

"Forever, huh?" she answered, allowing me access to her neck by tilting her head to the side.

"That's right." I took her offer and sucked at her beautiful neck, the mark I'd made on our wedding night now just a faint blush. With her hands gripping my shoulders and her long legs wrapped around my hips, I had her exactly where I wanted her. Now, if I could just get her mind off the motherfucking cocktail party she was demanding to attend, my immediate future would be sorted out perfectly. Floating in the sea and soaking up the sunshine with my sweet girl in my arms. "Yep. Forever here with you, not some sodding party crawling with idiots."

She sighed heavily, most likely thoroughly fed up with me, but she brought her forehead to rest against mine, and rocked from side to side. "What am I going to do with you, Blackstone?"

"I have some good ideas if you're really stumped." I squeezed both luscious halves of her arse and pulled her against my cock.

"So, sex in exchange for taking me to the party?" She thrust up and down my length with a few grinds of her hips under the water, giving me an instant hard-on, and heading for the shore.

I'd done this grab and carry from the beach to the house a few times since we'd come here. It always ended the same way. Volcanic sex. Extraordinary fucking. The ultimate prize in intimacy with the person I loved, bringing me to a place of nirvana with her. A place I'd only ever found with Brynne.

With her pillowed at my neck and nuzzling as I took us inside our villa, I was pretty confident I wouldn't have to worry about that stupid party at all in another few minutes.

"*THAT* is what you're wearing to this thing?"

My question earned me a hearty scowl, and a stiff back turned on me with a toss of her silky hair.

So much for the nice after-swim shag of two hours ago. Might as well have been two years ago, because right then we were getting ready to go to Carveletti's motherfucking cocktail party in town.

"Why, Ethan, are you saying that I don't look nice in this dress?" her tone chilly, as she applied eye makeup at the bathroom mirror.

"You look more than nice, and that's the part that worries me." Brynne was off-the-charts sexy all of the time, but this little dress she had on was going to kill me tonight. Emphasis on the *little*. It was a silky tunic-like creation in yellow and blue, with a print of the Parthenon on it. That part was fine. It was the micro length of the thing, showcasing her long, tanned legs in a manner that would serve to give any man who saw her in it one thought—and only one thought. *How I'd love to get those sexy legs wrapped around my cock.*

"You worry too much. It's just a babydoll summer dress. We're on holiday at the beach for Christ's sake. I am dressed for the occasion."

A babydoll dress? Fucking hellfire and damnation. I was confident tonight would age me permanently. For a few reasons. One was just the casualty of having a beautiful wife who grabbed attention everywhere we went in public, no matter how subdued she was in her personality. Another was the destination, and crowd we'd be mixing with tonight. I couldn't pretend to be happy about it, but knew I was outvoted and undermined when it came to Brynne's modeling.

I imagined what I could say to the people I'd meet at this blasted party, as I sat on the bed and shoved my feet into my shoes harshly. *Hello, Ethan Blackstone, nice to meet you. My wife is one of Carveletti's models. Isn't she lovely without her clothes on? Smashing tits, I know. Oh, trust me, I know. *wink* Which picture of her do you prefer? The one of her tits or this one where you can really see the curve of her sexy arse?* I dragged a hand over my beard in anxious frustration.

Simply absorbing the content of my imagined social greeting was a little more than I could handle, so I tried to distract myself by thinking of this afternoon's swim with her instead. Didn't help much...

Carvaletti, one of her photographer friends, had invited us to his home, which just happened to be in Porto Santo Stefano. Marvelous fucking luck. Brynne was determined to drag us there, so I guess I'd be cockblocking all goddamn night instead of enjoying the beach under the stars with my girl.

I was pulled from my inner rant by her cool hand at my cheek and a worried expression on her lovely face. Wouldn't it be wonderful if I could just kiss her senseless into forgetting about going to this thing?

"Please don't let this party ruin our night. It's just a mixer of industry people who happen to be gathering while we're here." The pleading look she gave me tugged at me, making me feel guilty for not being more supportive of her work.

"I'm sorry, baby. I'm trying to support you here, but am afraid I suck at it. I go mad when other men hit on you. I want to kill first and ask questions later when I see how they look at you." I shook my head at her "babydoll" dress. "And with you wearing *that*, I know I am well and truly fucked for an evening of torture."

"Many of my photographers are gay, Ethan." I could feel her inner thoughts calling me a possessive arsehole, even though I knew she wasn't to that point yet. Not yet…but I might push her there if I kept on.

"Carveletti's not one of them though, is he?"

She sighed heavily and pressed her lips to my hair. I reached for her and drew her onto my lap, burying my face at her neck.

"We don't have to stay very long, Ethan. Just long enough to be polite and greet everyone."

"Promise?" I knew I was acting a bloody dickhead but at least I was being honest with how I felt. "I don't share you very well at all, and I won't apologize for that part," I murmured at her ear.

"I promise, sweet husband." She offered her lips to me. "Just give me a code word when you're done and we can leave."

"Now see? You go and say something like that to me and I feel like an insensitive brute." I tucked a loose curl behind her ear. "You're so beautiful, and I don't mean just on the outside." I brought my finger to her heart. "Here is beautiful."

Her expression softened. "I love you so much, Ethan, even when you're being an insensitive brute." She drew me to her lips with a hand under my chin.

"I know...and I count my blessings every day that you do."

"So what's your code word so I know?"

I thought for a moment and it came to me in a brilliant flash. "Simba."

She laughed and shook her head at me slowly. "Simba it is, then."

"BELLA, you look magnificent, the glow in your cheeks, everything, is utter perfection." Marco, kissed me on both cheeks as was custom, then held me at arm's length for a thorough perusal. "Lovely dress. I can see that marriage and motherhood are both agreeing with you, darling."

I felt Ethan's hand at my back soften and relax at Marco's friendly, but appropriate greeting. Maybe he'd get over his paranoia that Marco was trying to bag me every time he photographed me. Ethan just didn't understand that Marco wasn't like that at all. He was a professional photographer doing a job with me, and nothing more. Well, nothing more than a working, platonic friendship. He'd always been kind to me, and I liked working with Marco Carvaletti very much. I hoped Ethan could see it here tonight as we all interacted.

"It is, Marco, and I don't think I could be any happier." I leaned into Ethan, nudging him to speak up.

"Mr. Carvaletti, thank you for the invitation. We've been looking forward to this all day." Ethan lied smoothly, offering his hand, playing the social gentleman to perfection, which he was well skilled at. I guess he did it out of love for me. I knew he didn't want to be here any more than he wanted me modeling. I mouthed a *thank you* only visible to him. He kissed me on the cheek and whispered in my ear, "Don't forget about Simba, baby." Then he wandered off to get drinks for us.

Marco took me on a tour of his elegantly restored seventeenth-century villa as I marveled at all of the art. He had a whole room set up as a gallery of his photographs. There were a couple of me in there. One where I sat in a formal chair with one knee up, strategically placed, my expression far away and pensive. The other pose was a side view recreation of a vintage Ziegfeld Follies girl with a feather boa and some satin pumps. It was one of the first portraits I posed for and I really thought it was nicely choreographed.

"It is a beautiful piece, bella. I knew when we did that series you had the gift." Marco stood behind me admiring the image he had created with me as the subject.

"I was so nervous posing, but you made me laugh when you told me to imagine Iggy Pop in a dress." I shrugged. "That broke the ice and I was fine after that."

"That one works for me every time, bella."

"Well, Iggy Pop in a dress *is* funny, so good job, Marco." We laughed together and made our way back to the main gathering.

Where was Ethan with my drink? I scanned the room for sight of him, but didn't see his tall form standing out among the crowd anywhere. And I needed water.

"He is talking to Carolina and Rogelio, my friends," Marco said, correctly reading my quest to find Ethan. "I believe they have discovered they are acquainted already."

Really? Ethan knew people at this party? I suppose it wasn't as bad as he'd predicted it would be after all. Couldn't wait to bust him about his whining to come here.

"Oh, well that's great. I look forward to meeting them. But first, I need to get some water. I'm really thirsty after spending a long time swimming in the ocean today. Must be all the salt."

"Come with me, bella, I will take care of you."

ONE hour later and I was so ready to blow this taco stand. Unfortunately, I was the only one who felt that way. Ethan and his old *friend*, Carolina, sat next to each other on a sofa laughing and chatting about the Italian elections and everything in between; from the best ski slopes in the Italian Alps to Ferragamo shoes. Looked like they were having a great time together. I, on the other hand, was stuck fending off the lewdly inappropriate glances coming at me from Rogelio, who apparently wasn't giving up on trying to get a good look at what was under my dress. And he wasn't with Carolina as I originally assumed, either. Rogelio was with another woman who gave her name as Paola—an Italian model I had seen in photos but never met before tonight. She eyeballed me too, almost as much as Rogelio was doing, but for different reasons. Rogelio was just a skeevy creep, but Paola saw me as a threat. She didn't have anything to worry about from me though; I sure wasn't interested in what she was doing—practically sprawled on Rogelio, letting him feel her up. Were they going to start screwing in front of everyone in a minute for an encore? *This lecherous creep and exhibitionist slut are who I get to talk to?* Not fair.

Ethan was oblivious.

I shifted in the seat and fidgeted with the hem of my dress, wishing it was a little longer to cover more of my legs. I wanted to go home and crawl into bed, but Ethan didn't take my subtle hints when I rubbed his leg or squeezed his hand. He just kept flapping away as if he could keep it up for hours. What in the hell had gotten into him? He was not usually chatty, but for all intents and purposes he sure was tonight—at this party he begged me not to drag him to.

It wasn't lost on me Carolina was a very beautiful woman, either. Elegant, and lean, in that Euro way that intimidated the hell out of me and my pregnant curves, which would only grow more pregnant, and more curvy in the coming months.

I patted Ethan on the leg.

He turned to me and smiled, covering my hand with his.

And returned right back to his conversation with Carolina, dismissing me with an affectionate brush of his thumb over my hand.

A server brought a tray of gelato through and I couldn't resist taking one, even though everyone else declined it.

The rich frozen chocolate cream tasted like heaven. At least I could enjoy something nice here, since the rest of it sucked.

Paola clucked at me. "So many calories in the gelato. I never indulge."

Well, you sure do indulge in being a massive bitch, Paola. "Really? I do. In fact, my doctor in London told me to start packing it in. As many calories as I can stand. It'll be healthier for my baby if I gain some weight." I smiled warmly and shoved another spoonful of gelato in my mouth. *Put that in your pipe and smoke it, you stupid cow!*

She narrowed her eyes at me. "You are pregnant?"

I rubbed over my bump, which due to the shape of my dress, was pretty much invisible. "Yep. And married." I held up my left hand and showed my ring.

"I'm so lucky; sometimes I think I must have won the lottery of life." I leaned into Ethan's arm with an affectionate caress of my cheek.

I felt more than a little satisfaction when she rolled her eyes at me and huffed off to get a drink. Rogelio just snickered in his quietly leering way and adjusted his erection, now that it was out there for me to see. Ugh. *Get me the hell out of here.*

Ethan was so unaware of what was going on, the look on his face was blank when I interrupted him and said, "Simba just called and said it's an emergency."

"What?" he questioned with a blink.

I hardened my expression and tried again. "Simba needs us to come home."

"He does?"

"He said *now*, Ethan."

ETHAN drove us home as I pouted in my seat. "You're not feeling well, are you?" he asked after several minutes of quiet.

"Whatever gave you that idea?" I looked out the window at the pretty lights set out in jars in front of the houses. It was a local custom that we'd discovered on our trip here. Wishing jars they were called. You put your wishes inside on tiny slips of paper that burned away from the candle inside the jar. As the words were consumed by fire, your wish was released into the spirit world to maybe be granted. *I wish I never went to that party.*

"Well, you didn't seem to be in a very social mood back there."

"Well, you sure were." I folded my arms and looked over at him.

"What? I was just having a conversation with an old friend. Thank God there was somebody I *could* talk to, or I would have gone mad. Let's remember that I didn't want to go to the fucking thing in the first place, Brynne. It just turned out to be more pleasant than I imagined it would be."

"How do you know Carolina?" I hated that I felt insecure asking him about her. I didn't want to know if they had ever been more than "friends," but had to be pragmatic that it was a strong possibility.

"We met when I was working an important job for the Italian PM years back. She's a cultural consultant for the government," he said a little too quickly, as if he'd already prepared what to say when I asked.

I sensed some hedging on his part. The way he was acting reminded me of that night at the Mallerton Gala when the strawberry-blonde "he went out with just the one time" was vying for his attention.

My heart did a little drop and I felt insane jealousy at the thought of Ethan and Carolina being together at some point in the past. He'd fucked her. I knew it.

"Oh…" I couldn't think of a better response. I just wanted to go to bed and put the unpleasant thoughts out of my mind.

I didn't wait for Ethan to come around and open my door when we arrived back to the villa. I just got out and headed toward the steps.

I didn't make it very far before strong arms wrapped around me from behind, pressing me back into the hard planes of his body. "Where do you think you're going?" He nuzzled at my neck and rubbed thumbs over my collarbones seductively. My body responded immediately, my nipples hardening into peaks that gave me the now familiar sting of pain when it happened.

"To bed, Ethan." I knew that he knew I was pouting. I didn't care. I couldn't help how I felt— jealous, and insecure, and more than a little hurt.

"Not yet, my beauty." He kissed behind my ear, the rough sound of desire evident in his tone. "I went to your party and played nice, and now I get my date with you on the beach that I wished to have in the first place."

My stiffness melted at his words, and I spun around to face him, burying my face into his chest, breathing in his scent of spice and cologne that had captured me from day one. "It was an awful party," I muttered, "I hated it."

He stroked over my hair and kissed the top of my head. "I can see that, but I can make it better now," he promised. "Forget about that pretentious party and come with me."

"So, you didn't want to stay there and talk to Carolina longer? You were obviously old *friends* catching up." My spiteful words just slipped out before I could stop them.

He gave me the blank look again and tilted his head. "Baby, what does that mean?"

I shrugged. "I got the feeling that you and she were past…that the two of you had—"

His eyes grew wide before he started laughing. "Okay, I get it now. You thought that Carolina and I had gone out together." He shook his head slowly at me. "No, baby. We're just friends and colleagues. Besides, she's got at least a decade on me."

"Well, she's still very beautiful. I doubt her age would bother a man much at all."

He laughed at me some more. "The fact that she only does women would."

"Oh…well, that's good. I mean—that makes sense then. Wait, Carolina is a lesbian? That beautiful woman is not into men?"

"Nope. She bats for your team, baby. Why do you think I sat between us tonight? I didn't want her getting even the chance to be close to *my* beautiful wife." He kissed me softly, with nibbles to my lips. "Not that I'm worried that you would ever switch teams on me, but why take the chance?"

"Oh, God. Like that would ever happen." I pushed at his chest and shook my head. "That's the most ridiculous thing I've ever heard in my life."

"Have you not yet learned that I don't take chances with you, my darling? I don't, and I never will." His gaze was unflinching.

"I guess I've learned a few things tonight..." I felt like a stupid fool now, but still, the fact that Ethan had been championing me at the party instead of ignoring, soothed my fears greatly. "One of them being that this dress wasn't a good choice for me to wear to a party." I looked up at him sheepishly. "It *is* too short, and I won't be wearing it anymore when we go out again."

He blew out a relieved sigh. "Well, you look gorgeous in it, but I won't deny that I appreciate your offer." He smoothed his hands over my ass in a possessive caress. "Because this is *mine*," he growled, as he descended for another slow kiss, plunging his tongue into my mouth in a demanding tangle that showed me he really meant it.

I was his.

When he reluctantly pulled his tongue out of me, I realized he wasn't done with his explanation. "I thought I was going to have to scoop out Rogelio's eyeballs at one point. Watching that cocksucker pant over you just about killed me. I had to turn away or he'd probably be blind right now...and I'd be locked up for mayhem in an Italian jail." He shrugged, offering no apology for how he felt. Ethan was a very honest man. It was one of the traits in him I admired, and loved. I had just learned a valuable lesson about trust.

"Oh my God, Rogelio was disgusting. I hated him."

"Agreed." He kissed me on the nose. "Now let's stop talking about that hideous party, and go have the date on the beach I want with you. Off with your shoes, Mrs. Blackstone."

As we slipped off our shoes, I realized that Ethan had enjoyed every moment of my discomfort. The twinkling laughter in his blue eyes told me so. I couldn't deny that Carolina's sexual orientation relieved me, but I wasn't dumb enough to think I wouldn't run into some of Ethan's former lovers in the future. It would happen, and I would have to deal with it when it did.

"What are we doing on the beach?" I asked, as he led me along the cool sand under my bare feet.

"Having our date. Trust me, baby. This is something I have all planned out for us."

"I bet you do. I am well aware that when you say *date* you really mean sex—"

My words were lost as we rounded a turn in the beach path and came out onto the shore. The waves lapped at the sand with the soothing sounds of water moving against earth. A sliver of moon glowed over the water, but the real beauty was the many glass jars lit up with tea lights set out on the soft sand of the beach. What seemed like hundreds of them flickering away around a pallet of blankets and pillows. Off to one side sat a bucket of iced drinks and what appeared to be little dessert cakes on a tray with some fresh fruit.

"It's beautiful, Ethan." I could hardly speak as I realized what he'd done. "How did you do…this?"

He led us onto the blankets and drew me down to sit beside him. "It was my idea," he began, "but I needed some help to pull it off. Franco got it organized while we were at the party."

I looked around behind us, imagining if the caretaker for our villa was lurking in the dark, hoping for a glimpse.

"I know what you're thinking, but you don't have to worry, baby, Franco is not in the bushes watching, trust me."

I laughed nervously. "Well, if Franco is in the bushes somewhere, I am predicting he's gonna get one hell of a show."

"Now that's what I like to hear. My girl accepting the idea of a hot beach shag," he whispered teasingly against my ear, his tongue flicking out for a lick along the shell. "You like my surprise."

My body came instantly alive, needing him so badly. Ethan could get me hot with just the simplest look or touch. He reached up and worked on the messy knot holding up my hair and unpinned it. He was getting good at figuring out my hair. It made me smile to watch him as he found the pins and pulled them, knowing how he'd be fisting my hair in handfuls and using it to dominate when we were deep into the sex.

"You're smiling," he murmured, as he worked over my hair.

"I just love to watch you doing simple things."

My hair fell free.

"This is not a simple thing to me," he whispered, fingering through the tangled length with both hands. His gaze grew smoky as he focused on my lips. "It's everything."

He dropped his lips to mine, seeking entry with his tongue, tracing over my open mouth with great care. Both of his hands gathered up my hair and tugged, forcing me to arch into him, to offer myself.

"You're everything, Brynne," he whispered low, dragging his mouth to my throat, and then moving lower, over the silk of my dress to a breast. He zeroed in on my nipple and found it with his teeth, pinning it between two layers of fabric and his teeth.

"Oh…God." I moaned into the sharp bite of pleasure. So heated by his touch already I was slipping fast. In a moment he had moved me into that place where I didn't want to think about anything but the sensual journey he would take me on. He was so good at loving me—so good at everything. "You're *my* everything, Ethan." My own voice sounded breathless even to my ears.

I felt his hands pulling my dress up, and then the warm air meeting my bare skin as he drew it over my head. And it was off.

"You're my goddess. Right here, right now…like this." He pressed me back into the blankets and loomed over me, arms planted straight, penning me in, devouring with ravenous eyes. "Where to go first…" he muttered, "I want all of you at once."

I didn't care what he took first. Didn't matter. It never mattered. Anything he did was what I wanted. What I needed in that moment.

I moved my hands to the buttons of his shirt and started undoing them.

He smiled wickedly down at me. Ethan loved for me to undress him. Loved to watch me suck his cock. Loved to watch his cock penetrating me. Anywhere.

I pushed his shirt off his shoulders, abandoning it when it would move no farther because his palms on the blanket kept it trapped across his back, and started in on his trousers, growing frustrated when I was only able to push them down over his tight ass.

"My baby is frustrated...tell me what you want," he commanded.

"I want you naked so I can see you," I panted, moving my hands into his boxers to grip his rock-hard cock. Hard as bone and sheathed in velvet skin, I wanted that perfect part of him in my mouth where I could suck and stroke until he came apart because of what I did to him. "I want your cock. I want you."

"Fucking hell," he moaned, his eyes wild with need as he jerked his body up, shrugged off the shirt violently, and kicked off his pants and shorts in a vicious twist that left him breathing down at me with a look of raw, raging possession. "I love you so much."

Ethan pushed up my bra and gripped both breasts in his hands, dipping to suck the tips into sharp peaks that sent a path of molten heat straight to my core. I was completely ready for his cock but knew I wouldn't be getting it yet no matter how much I begged for it.

Ethan took charge of the pace.

Arching my back with his hands, he grappled with the clasp of my bra, detaching it easily, before flinging it to land somewhere on the beach. He growled in pleasure as he returned to my breasts, teasing them relentlessly with his prickly whiskers framing the softest tongue that knew just how to suck and lick me into a frenzied bundle of desperate need.

His hand burrowed into the white bathing-suit bottoms I'd worn under my dress and found my sex with a claiming touch. "All mine," he said forcefully, pushing a long thick finger inside me.

I arched into his hand on a cry when he curled his finger to find my sweet spot, bridging the gap between the clawing building of pleasure and the climax he'd made me want so desperately.

He did all of this to me in mere seconds.

"Ethan, please," I begged.

His answer was to slide over my clit with his thumb as his finger worked my passage to a blinding orgasm. One that left me shuddering and trembling beneath him, winded for breath.

"Don't look away. I still want your eyes on me after I've made you come," he ground out. "I want to see your eyes flashing fire and your legs shaking when I'm inside you, making you scream my name." His fingers stroked slower now, bringing me down from the drenching pleasure, utterly captive to his need to own me.

"I want to make you come." I panted at him, taking his cock in my hand and stroking up and down the velvet shaft, loving the sharp hiss he gave as I made contact.

"You will," he promised darkly.

My bottoms were peeled down my legs and a kiss placed over my mound reverently. It was often the last gentle thing he did before things got really dirty and wicked. Almost like a final affirmation to let me know he loved me, and not to forget it when things got wildly primal. My raging sex god had a worrisome conscience, I'd learned. It only made me love him more, when he showed his care of me.

He need never worry though. I'd take him wicked or gentle…or any way.

Ethan rolled me to my side and turned his body opposite of mine, aligning us so my mouth could have his cock and his mouth could have me. He lifted my leg and took his time kissing up the inside of my thigh, teasing slowly toward my sex as if it were a delicacy he wanted to savor.

I took his thick length in my hand and stroked him, adding the little twist at the top, knowing how it drove him wild. He groaned into my pussy as I brought him into my mouth and closed around the wide crest of his cock. I drew him deep and slid my hand in tandem to match the rhythm I knew he loved. Suck…twist…stroke…slide.

I brought him along, relishing the tensing of his thighs and abdomen, the sounds and words he ground out, muffled by his lips pressed between my legs, building me up to my own peak until it all became just a swirling vortex of sex and pleasure impossible to describe in thought. We both got lost in the beautiful frenzy of finding our pinnacle together.

"So good…oh, fuck it's so good. You suck my cock…so good, baby…" Ethan's gasping moans brought me out of my own swirling pleasure enough to get my body moving.

I love sucking your beautiful cock. I scrambled around and knelt between his legs, taking his hard flesh very deep, in long sweeping sucks that bumped the back of my throat. I cradled his balls in my other hand and squeezed, feeling them tighten up in preparation to give me what I wanted from him.

"Fuck, fuck, fuck…I'm gonna come in your mouth. Brynne—" he choked out, jerking his hips in short bursts, fucking into my mouth. His hands gripped my hair in handfuls, holding me captive on his cock…as he emptied his hot male essence down my throat.

In that final instant, as I had come to expect of him, because it was how Ethan needed it from me; he said my name in a desperate call to look up at him.

I lifted my eyes and found the blue of his own staring down upon me, shattering in all their fiery brilliance, with love…for me.

"I…love…you," he said to me in a roar that could only be described as one of utter, agonized bliss.

I recognized it because it was exactly what he did to me.

Hours later, and more orgasms than I thought possible, I lay cradled in my man's strong arms with the soft lapping of the sea on the sand, and the flickering of candles in jars lighting the night around us with a soft glow. I knew more happiness and love than I'd ever experienced in my life, and now understood how precious it was to have that love.

How could I ever live without it now? What would happen to me if I ever lost him? Could I even survive such a thing?

Ethan had changed me forever and there was no unringing of that bell. Ever.

I closed my eyes and focused on where I was in the moment. On our Italian beachside bed-of-love, with Ethan spooning behind me, his hand cradling my belly as he slept.

Holding us both against his heart, owning us, protecting us…loving us.

Such a beautiful thing…

I was almost frightened to believe it had happened to me.

Part Two

AUTUMN

Did the cold wind bite you, did you face up to the fright?
When the leaves spin from October
and whip around your tail?
Did you shake from the blast, did you shiver through the gale?

Jethro Tull ~Weathercock

CHAPTER 6

30th September
Somerset

As the mother lay dead in the street, the boy cried over her body they'd left abandoned in the dirt. The hours dragged as slowly as the sun moved overhead. It became harder and harder for me to tune him out. The wailing just zeroed in through my ears, and straight to my motherfucking heart. That boy was me. I'd been right where he was. I couldn't stand hearing him for another bloody second. So I swooped in to grab him. A decision I cannot take back, because what I did was his death sentence. He never had a chance. None. They used him like bait to lure me in. No take-backs for what I did…

I crashed awake gasping for breath. Like a film in super slow motion, then fast-forwarded, defying logic, but making acceptable sense to where I'd just been in my dream. One moment I was buried under with the oppressive weight of darkness and despair closing in on me, and then in a split-second, shoved to the surface to face the blinding light of freedom.

I fucking hated it.

The dreams fucked with my head.

I was fucked up because of them.

I was also sleeping in the same bed as my pregnant wife. This is the part I dreaded more than anything. The moment when I had to lie there suspended, too panicked to look over at her and see if she was peacefully asleep…or *unpeacefully* awake. Had she caught me this time? Or had I slipped through the net again?

I dared to look. Turning my eyes toward her without moving my head very much, afraid to cause any movement—which was absurd because people moved around in their sleep all the time—in hopes that she didn't see, didn't hear…didn't know.

Asleep on her side facing away from me.

Blessed Jesus, thank you!

My girl slept less soundly now that she was pregnant, and I dearly wished I couldn't say the same. Trying to rationalize the reasons for my nightmares, attempting to figure out why they'd been triggered so suddenly after being buried for years, wasn't impossible to work out.

Brynne was the reason. Finding her, falling in love with her, had initiated every possessive instinct inside of me. She had switched me on, and that was it. I'd been driven to have her, yes, but it was Brynne loving me back, putting me in a position of being worried over for the first time, it was her offering comfort to me that made her so different.

Before Brynne, I could just bury the bad and horrible, detaching myself from what had happened to me, and not allowing myself to feel. I was disconnected, aloof, emotionless. Not now.

Now when I had a flashback, the sequences of events were even more deranged than usual. In my head, the past and present melded together in a confused clusterfuck that rattled around in my subconscious, but wasn't anywhere close to direct reality. Shit that had happened, mixed up with what could have happened, but hadn't. And then there was the cocksucking future... That bastard would be the death of me, I was certain.

There's a shit-ton of crap to worry about in the future.

Falling in love with a person changes everything. You learn this, after the fact of course, because you quickly realize you didn't really ever have anything to worry about before you had someone to lose. Once you do have them?

Newsflash, motherfucker. You *can* lose them. And in more ways than one, too. You have a lot of fuckin' things to worry about. Like whether or not you'll be able to breathe through another day if some deranged lunatic takes the only person on earth you can't live without.

Brynne was that person for me. I needed her in order to live now.

And thankfully she was sleeping right now, undisturbed by my subconscious ravings and safe in the bed with me.

I breathed in deeply and told myself I could do this. I was getting better at separating the past from the fear of the unknown down the road in the future.

So I focused on her comforting scent and slid over to spoon up against her body, getting my face right next to her hair on the pillow, where I could breathe in the intoxicating smell of floral and citrus that belonged uniquely to her.

I rested my hand over her belly which had grown more since our honeymoon, but still didn't look very big to me—just a curved mound where she used to be very flat. Eighteen weeks along and we now had a sweet potato according to the TheBump.com, which was bookmarked in "favourites" on all my devices. I liked knowing what to expect.

Brynne didn't want to know the sex of our baby. And we didn't know yet anyway because it was still too early to tell, but she amazed me with her ability to wait for something that most people would beg to find out, if the information was available. She said she wanted to be surprised. I had to respect that. Plus, if I did know, I would undoubtedly fuck up and ruin the surprise anyway, and then I'd be in massive trouble. Better if both of us were in the dark about whether we had a Thomas or a Laurel coming.

Either one would be perfect.

I started drifting off again, very loose and soothingly peaceful with her softness against me, when she grew restless. Her breathing picked up and her body tensed. She touched her belly and found my hand already there.

"Ethan?"

The sound of her voice was agitated, almost frightened, in an oddly muffled pitch that told me she was sound asleep and dreaming.

"Shh… Right here beside you, baby." I gently rubbed the swell in slow circles over her nightgown, and nuzzled at the back of her neck through her hair until she quieted from whatever dream had disturbed her.

I closed my eyes, finally ready for my own sleep, when she spoke out again, this time, as clear as a bell…

"Always here for you, Ethan."

My eyes snapped open.

Her revelation floored me, not because of what she'd said, but the fact that even in sleep, even in her dreams where the consciousness is blurred, my girl was right there loving me—showing her care and concern for me all the time.

We were that deeply connected.

No matter what fate held in store for me, I could never let her go.

※

THIS house was really big. Too goddamn big for our needs, I decided. This was confirmed by the size of the modern garage I was parking the car in at that moment. It still retained its original façade, appearing on the outside as the carriage house it had originally been built as, over two hundred years before. As in big fucking coaches and carriages pulled by teams of horses and driven by a coachman. It was more than a little strange for me because I had always lived in the city. Born and bred. But still, we loved this house already, and in my gut I'd known it was right for us to make a home here. We couldn't live here full time yet, but three- or four-day weekends were working out for now. And we couldn't abandon London altogether because the business was there, and Brynne's studies, which she was determined to return to once the baby was born.

The estate agent had shared some history of Stonewell Court with us. The foundation had been laid down in 1761, then several years to build it, before being occupied by a London gentleman who wanted a country cottage to wile away the lazy summer days at the seaside when the heat of the city got too oppressive. And the stink of the city probably.

London of centuries past was not as pleasant as it was now in the modern age, so it made sense as to how all the big country mansions were built in the first place. Funny to think that we were doing the same thing the owners of centuries ago had done. Living in London and visiting the country for a break. We were having fun playing house and that's all that concerned me.

Still made me laugh to think that they'd referred to this monstrosity of stones as a "cottage." I shook my head as I headed around to the back of the house to find her. I'd given Robbie strict instructions to keep her occupied while I was on a stealth errand to pick up her birthday present. Yeah, my girl was twenty-five years old today and had a celebration coming her way this afternoon.

I came out through the arch that led to the gardens and looked for her, and there she was. Playing in the flowers. She wouldn't call it playing, but she looked like she was having a good time, garden gloves and trowel in hand, planting an ancient looking urn with some lacy green vines.

The gardens had appealed to Brynne from the first day we set foot on the property. I thought it was interesting even though she claimed to not know much about plants. She'd been talking about wanting to learn ever since she'd seen my mother's garden at my dad's London house. The place where I'd asked her to marry me.

Robbie James, the gardener we'd inherited when we bought Stonewell, was helping her with the different beds and plantings, getting everything refreshed from some years of neglect when the house had been empty. I was happy to see she had chosen *a lot* of purple flowers, which were her favorites. *I knew that, of course.* I'd sent her purple flowers the very first time…and she had given me a second chance. I glanced up at the clouds and gave a silent thank you to angels who believed in second chances.

So Brynne was really taking to this part of her new life, and that made me glad. If she wanted to play in the dirt then she should. But, she was strictly an observer on the labour aspect though. I made sure Robbie understood no lifting anything heavier than a garden hose for her. If she tried to do too much I'd better hear about it, so I could put a stop to it.

I waved to him from across the turf, letting him know I'd returned and that his Brynne duties were finished. I gave him the thumbs up and he saluted back. Birthday gift was sorted and everything ready to go. I grinned at what she would say when she saw what I'd done.

I snuck up behind her and covered her eyes with

my hands. "Guess who."

"You're very late, you know. We'll have absolutely no time for our lover's tryst now. My husband will be back any minute and he'll go crazy if he finds you here."

Damn, she's quick with the mouth. "I work fast. I'll be in and out before he knows a thing."

"Oh, my God." She spun around and put her hands on my chest, laughing and shaking her head at me. "You did *not* just make that joke to me."

"What joke?" I deadpanned. "If we want to get in a quick shag before your jealous husband comes back we need to hurry up."

She laughed and stepped back from me, making a great show of taking off her garden gloves, enjoying the hell out of this game we were playing. Her hair was up again, just the way I liked it to be, so I could have the pleasure of taking it down when I got her in bed.

The coy and mischievous smile on her face was a sure sign telling me she was up to something though. I held on for her to make her move, both of us doing the stand-off, waiting, plotting, and grinning like fools.

She dropped the gloves at my feet.

My cock woke up.

Her eyes lowered seductively...and then she spun on her heels and took off running for the house.

Yes! I gave her about a two-second lead before I

went after her.

Catching her was going to be fucking heaven.

BRYNNE rode me with expertise, rotating her hips in a circle that made the walls of her cunt grip me so tightly I knew it wouldn't take much longer before I was gone.

"Oh, Ethan…you're so hard," she said breathlessly, "you feel so good."

"You make me hard, so I can fuck you like this." I gripped her hips and angled her back slightly. I liked to see us fucking, our bodies colliding, connecting. It got me off.

But I needed to get Brynne off first, before anything.

"Hold your tits in your hands for me."

And like the perfect lover she was, she cradled one in each palm, like an offering up to me, as if they were a prized piece of fruit. *Perfect fuckin' analogy there.* Brynne's breasts had always been succulent works of art, but they were changing from her pregnancy. In a very good way. They were even more succulent now.

As she pinched the dark pink nipples that were budded up tight and high in the center of those voluptuous beauties, she cried out. I could see the clear signs of her pleasure melding with that fine edge of pain, and made my move to bring her the rest of the way. I brought my fingers to her clit and worked the slippery nub as she continued to take the spearing of my swelling cock.

Nuclear explosion imminent, I waited for the first convulsion from inside her to suction and pull at my shaft. That's all it would take right now. Her going off would bring me to follow her within seconds. I knew what she did to me and it was always fucking magnificent.

"Ooooohhh…I'm coming…" she crooned on a breathy groan.

So beautiful in all her bare, naked glory, she found her pleasure, those wide brown eyes of hers sparking amber fire down at me.

"Oh, yes, oh, yes!" I followed my girl down the path of explosive pleasure the instant her eyes connected with mine, her internal shudders and reflexive gripping drawing every last bit of spunk out of the tip of my cock. I kept on fucking, working it in deep. I know it was crass of me, but I wanted my cum in her. Like that way I could stay inside her even when I wasn't.

She collapsed onto my chest, both of us heaving, the heavy breathing that feels so good after you come. I rubbed her back and closed my eyes. We were a mess of sweat, and spunk, and her arousal. A lovely, sexed-up, dirty, fucking mess.

"That was the best birthday present a girl could

get," she muttered, "but you'd better go before my husband finds you here."

I laughed and nuzzled her jaw. "Glad you liked it. And your husband should keep a better eye on you."

"What he should do is keep a better eye on making sure I'm satisfied," she sniffed. "Being pregnant makes me nearly insatiable."

"I can take care of you, baby. Forget him. He's a fuckin' idiot."

"Yeah, and you have a *much* bigger cock than him, too."

"Damn, woman, you are a feisty handful." I tickled her until she shrieked and begged me to stop.

We laughed and settled down again, just enjoying the moment of closeness together. This was pure happiness for me. I didn't need a lot, but I did know that now that I'd experienced Brynne's love, I would be lost without it. Love. A thing I'd never sought out, had caught me up, completely ensnared me…so that now I was dependent upon it for my emotional survival.

I breathed in her heavenly scent, aimlessly stroking up and down her back, when I felt a prickling on my chest right by where she'd laid her cheek. I brushed at the spot with my fingers and met a pool of warm wetness. *What the hell?* I pulled my hand back to find my fingers dripping in blood.

My heart just fucking dropped to the floor. "Oh,

God, Brynne, you're bleeding!"

"WHAT? I am?" I sat up and met Ethan's terrified grimace with the blood on his hand suspended between us as it dripped down his skin. I lifted my hand to my nose, understanding quickly what was happening. "It's okay, Ethan. I'm okay," I soothed, seeing clearly how my nosebleed was freaking him out.

"That's a lot of fucking blood," he barked. "I'm ringing Fred," he said, reaching for his phone on the side table.

I tilted my head back and pinched the bridge of my nose. "It's just a minor nosebleed, Ethan. Don't call Freddy for this, please." I got off him and stepped down from the bed. And it wasn't easy when I was trying to keep from dripping all over the bedding.

I zipped into the bathroom and found a washcloth to use. It would be ruined now, but I didn't have a choice. I held it under my nose with one hand and turned on the cold water at the sink with the other.

Ethan was right behind me, still panicking with eyes as wide as saucers. "Here, let me do it." He pulled the washcloth away and checked me. "It's still going," he stated, his face pale.

I pressed the cloth back down on my nose. "Baby, this is nothing to get so worked up about. It's just a nosebleed. This isn't the first one I've had."

"It isn't?" he shouted. "When? What other times?" An angry frown had overtaken his beautiful face. Gone was my sweet teasing man from a few moments ago.

"Easy, buster, you need to lighten up—they are nothing serious. I had one yesterday while you were at work."

"Why didn't you say something?! Fuck, Brynne." He dragged a hand through his hair raggedly, gripping the back in a tight handful.

"Okay." I held a hand up, starting to get pissed at his overreacting. "I want you to take a deep breath, and go look at the website and check for 'eighteen weeks pregnant.'"

Glaring, he shook his head at me, but he did step back and reach for his phone. The smears of blood on his hand looking gruesome, as he pulled up the site and studied the information. His eyes moved quickly as he read the "Pregnancy Symptoms" section. He lost some of the tension in his body and sat down on the side of the bed. After a moment more of silence, he read it out loud to me, his voice flat, "Increased pressure on the veins in your nose may be causing nosebleeds." He was clearly upset.

"Are you sure it's nothing to worry about?" When Ethan looked up at me, the expression on his face made my heart twist. He was sad, and scared, and frustrated, and concerned, all at the same time. Poor guy was going to need tranquilizers when I went into labor. "I'm okay, really I am." I turned to the mirror and removed the washcloth. Bleeding stopped. My lip and chin were a bloody mess, but my nose was dry now.

Ethan jumped up and came to me. "Let me do it." I knew better than to argue with him. I stood still for him as gently cleaned away the blood, wetting the cloth and carefully washing it off bit by bit until it was all gone.

I closed my eyes and let him work, feeling very loved and cherished despite the "trauma" my poor Ethan had just endured.

"How in the goddamn hell will I survive the birth of this baby, Brynne?"

I held his face in my hands and made him focus. "You will. You can do it. One minute at a time, just like me." I didn't know what else to tell him. I was scared, too.

He drew me into his arms and just held me against him, kissing the top of my head and smoothing down my hair. We'd shower and get ourselves cleaned up for my birthday dinner with his family in a little while, but right now we both needed this.

He just held me.

"SO we've had cake. Which was really delicious—thank you, Hannah." Ethan gave his sister a bow of his head in appreciation. "We've had presents…except for one." He snickered at everyone, looking far too smug for my liking. What in the hell was he up to? I sensed it might be something big, and that made me anxious. I didn't need extravagant gifts from him. Didn't really want them either. I knew myself. I was a simple girl.

"I want to see Auntie Brynne's present," Zara piped up. My five-year-old niece had absolutely no trouble expressing her opinions about life in general. It was safe to say that *extravagant gifts* didn't bother Zara one iota. Ethan doted on her, and I adored her. In fact, she came over to see us quite a bit. One of her older brothers would walk her over if the weather was nice and she would run around our house and play with her Barbies. Zara was a hoot.

"Okay, let's go see it," Ethan said smugly. "Now, Zara, I need your help with it. Your job is to make sure Brynne doesn't open her eyes until I say she can." Zara stared up at him, her little neck bent flat on her spine.

"Okay," she said, taking my hand in hers. "You can't look, Auntie Brynne."

"Deal," I said. "When you say, 'let's go see it,'

where is that exactly?"

Ethan laughed and the others smiled cryptically.

"To the front of the house we go." He held out his arm and I took it, letting him lead me on one side with little Zara on the other.

Before we passed through the front doors, I made a big show of closing my eyes and allowed them to bring me forward. I didn't need to worry about stumbling because Ethan had me firmly, directing every step. Of course he would make sure I didn't fall. It made a lot of sense to me as to his chosen field for his career. My man had been born to protect and serve, and those hard-wired traits were carried over in all that he did.

The crunch of gravel sounded under everyone's feet as we walked, and I still had no earthly idea what sort of gift he'd gotten for me.

We stopped.

I heard whispers, and then Zara shouted in her adorable child voice, "You can look at your white car now, Auntie Brynne!"

A car? I opened my eyes to a brand, spanking, new, white Range Rover HSE Sport. The full deal, left-handed drive and all. *Holy crap.*

I spun on Ethan. "You bought me a car?!"

The grin on his face was worth having to learn to drive lefty. "I did, baby. Do you like it?"

"I *love* my Rover." *I am so very intimidated by this*

Rover. I threw my arms around him and whispered in his ear because we had an audience. "You are crazy for buying such an extravagant gift for me. You must stop."

He pulled back and shook his head slowly. "Crazy for you is all…and I'll never stop."

I knew he wouldn't, either. The steadfast look in his eye told me so.

I wanted to shake him and kiss him at the same time. He spent way too much money on gifts for me. He didn't need to, but he'd always been so overly generous with me from the first. He spoiled me and enjoyed doing it.

I looked at my new car and swallowed. I had an idea as to its price tag and knew it was a shitload of money. *Jesus Christ, what if I wreck the thing?* Better yet, how would I drive the damn thing?

"What am I going to do with you, Blackstone?"

"You aren't doing anything *with* me, but I think you are going to do something with your new car." He looked worried, like maybe I wasn't happy with the gift. I couldn't hurt him though. Out of the question for me to ever do that to Ethan. Plus, he was still a little freaked about my earlier nosebleed problem. I could tell it had triggered something for him. I wasn't sure exactly what, but sensed it had little to do with my pregnancy, and more to do with his traumatic past. I sighed inwardly and shelved it for now. This was not the time to delve into it.

I stared at him. At Freddy and Hannah, Colin and Jordan, who waited with smiles for me to take possession of my gift. Zara, bless her, broke the tension and jumped up and down. "I want a ride in it. Let's go, Auntie Brynne."

I laughed nervously for a minute, and then figured, why the hell not? I was married to Ethan now. England was my home, and we had a house in the country. I couldn't take a train into town. I would need to go out and get things like normal people did every day. I would be a mom soon, and there would be places to go with my baby. Better to learn now, rather than later.

I gave everyone my best confident smile and went for it.

Channeling Rain Man here, people. "Okay…just real slow on the driveway. I'm an excellent driver."

"Who's coming first?" Ethan asked.

Zara and Jordan volunteered and climbed in the back. I went to the driver's side and opened the door, smelling the new-car leather and finding it hard to believe this beautiful piece of machinery now belonged to me, along with everything else.

Ethan, the house, his family, the baby…just *everything* was a lot to take in for my pitiful self, especially in my hormonal state.

I buckled myself in, the seatbelt being the least of my problems as I looked at the dashboard. More like a control panel for a stealth bomber. I looked over at Ethan in the passenger seat and held out my hand. "The key?"

He smiled at me. "You push here to start it." He reached forward and pointed to a round button.

"Are you fucking kidding me?!"

Jordan snickered. Zara giggled. Ethan rolled his lips as if to keep himself from saying something he would later regret. *Smart husband.* I pushed the damn button.

I only dropped one more f-bomb and two or three "shits" in the course of my first, driving-left, sitting-right lesson, with Ethan as my patient teacher.

The kids in the back thought it was hilarious fun, and loved reminding me I needed to "keep left" on the country road, which was stupid because it was only one lane.

Ethan, wise man that he is, kept his mouth shut.

I gave him a really nice show of my *appreciation* for my very generous and lovely birthday gift, as soon as we were alone.

CHAPTER 7

4th October
London

"There we are. Baby looks a great deal different this time, yes? About the size of a banana now, and at twenty weeks, you are officially past the halfway mark. Measurements are looking to be right on target for a healthy pregnancy. Umbilical cord, perfect. Heartbeat, strong." Dr. B narrated details about what we were seeing on screen. The magical sight of our baby moving erratically all over the place, legs and arms pushing and pulling in breathtaking clarity. I couldn't even take my eyes away for an instant to answer the good doctor. The realism was so sharply improved since the last scan, I couldn't believe it. I was looking at a little person in full form, with no doubt whatsoever about the humanity of what we'd created.

Brynne stared at the screen with me in utter awe, watching a little thumb pop into a tiny mouth for a suckle. Just as quickly as it was sucked on, the thumb was released. "Did you see that?" I asked.

"Oh." Brynne laughed softly, still staring. "Sucking his thumb... Ethan, he was sucking his thumb—or *she was*." She squeezed my hand, the shy excitement in her expression making her glow in a way that was new to me. She looked like...a mother.

"I know." Moments like these showed me just how good of a mum Brynne would be. No doubts whatsoever. I rubbed my thumb into her palm.

"Ahh, yes, I can try to see if I might tell the sex of baby for you—"

"—No! I don't want to know, Dr. Burnsley. Don't—tell me, please." Brynne shook her head at him. Her decision was final. Any fool could see that, and the doctor was no fool.

Dr. B shot a glance my way, and then tilted his head in question to ask if I wanted to know. I thought for an instant about saying *yes*, but I shook my head *no* instead.

"It's fine, Ethan, if you want to know. I'll turn away and Dr. Burnsley can look for you."

Her quiet beauty and utter confidence in her firm decision to be surprised about the sex of our child, was compelling to me. She was so sure about how she wanted to find out. Brynne didn't want to know until the baby was born, and that was all there was to it. Whereas I would've just shrugged and said, "sure, tell me." I would know if we had a son or a daughter on the way, and that would be exciting to me. *Thomas or Laurel?*

"No, I'll be surprised with you," I told her, shaking my head at Dr. B again, giving him the negative.

Nothing but utter respect for my girl. I brought her hand up to my lips and kissed it. We shared a look but no words. None were needed.

The doc interrupted, "Right, then. Surprised it shall be for the both of you." He printed out some pictures for us, and wiped the jelly from her rounded bump, before shutting off the machine that managed the remarkable business of taking ultrasonic pictures of our unborn baby. Good God, the man was stronger than me. There wasn't enough brass in the goddamn world to entice me to do his job. "Well, I will tell you both this much with certainty," Dr. B said dryly, "your baby, will be either a boy, or a girl."

⧓

"HALFWAY to the finish line, baby." Over our lunch at *Indigo*, I accepted that I was trying to do too many things at once, and failing at all of them. Checking messages on my mobile, following the football highlights reporting from the TV in the bar on the level just below us, and making conversation with Brynne. Being an arse is more like.

I set down my mobile, tuned out what the sportscaster was saying about Manchester United over Newcastle, and gave Brynne my full attention. She had that half smile she did to perfection, the quiet observation that told me she was rather amused by my lapse in manners.

"What are you thinking about right now?" I asked.

"Hmmm, just enjoying my view." She picked up her water and took a sip, her eyes peeking over the edge of the glass. "Watching you working, thinking about Banana Blackstone, wondering when you might figure out I wasn't answering you."

"Sorry. I was distracted by crap that doesn't matter very much. So the better question is, how are you feeling about what the doctor said?"

"That I need to walk instead of running?"

I nodded. Sometimes Brynne didn't show much reaction to things. I know she heard what the doctor said about her exercising habits, but I didn't know what she thought of it.

She shrugged at me. "I can do some walking. Besides, I have you to give me plenty of exercise to make up for all the runs I'll be missing. I'm sure I'll be fine." Her half-smile grew into a full-smile, with an added sexy little laugh at the end of it.

She wasn't kidding about the sex, either. Pregnancy raised the libido in a lot of women, and I was really fucking grateful that my woman had a raging one right now. The doc had given his blessing, and so we were shagging pretty much like mad. And loving every minute of it. "You've got that right. Dr. B is my new best mate."

She rolled her eyes. "Is that so? Typical men's club stuff with the 'intercourse is perfectly safe as long as you're *up* for it,'" she mocked the doctor's posh speech with a toss of her head, "with the penis-innuendo thrown in. So clever and original of Dr. Burnsley. I wonder how many times he's dropped that line."

"I don't care how many times he's said it. Giving the green light on the bang time is all that matters, baby." I cocked a brow. "And I always am."

"I know you are," she whispered sexily, a slight flush spreading up her lovely neck making me want to have my mouth on her.

The look she was giving me right now... A sensual, beautiful, fleeting look, from her to me, over a finely dressed table. And I was undone—in a restaurant at midday, having lunch, wishing I could have her instead. It didn't take any more than that with us. A look, a touch, a whispered comment, and I'd be instantly caught up in thoughts of when and where.

So I tried to change the subject back to something

a bit more appropriate for public consumption. "I also liked what he said about the nosebleeds." She had been right. Nothing to worry over, just normal side effects. "I'm sorry for overreacting."

She lowered her head and blew me an air kiss, mouthing the words, "It's okay." Brynne put up with my shit with the patience of a saint. I wasn't under any misconceptions about my rampant arseholery being wearisome a lot of the fuckin' time. And neither was Brynne. She let me know when I was behaving like a prick, but mostly she just loved me, and soothed all my rough edges. A miracle worker. I was even doing well on tapering off with the smokes. I'd really been pushing myself to finally do it. Ending my nicotine addiction was symbolic of several things. A break with the past, a resolve to live a healthier life, and a commitment to at least two other people who needed me sticking around for another sixty years or so.

I was down to one ciggie a day now. Almost always at night, right before sleep. The symbolism of that habit was something I wished wasn't so obvious, but anything I could do to help keep away the dreams and a flashback was useful to me.

Brynne excused herself to go to the ladies, and I returned to the scrolling ticker for football scores and messages on my mobile. It was looking like I would be heading to Switzerland for the XT Europe Winter Games in January. Normally, I jump at a job like that, but this one had some concerns. Prince Christian of Lauenburg's qualification in the snowboarding thrilled the young prince, no doubt. His grandfather—the King of Lauenburg—not so much. Royalty was tricky, and in this situation, more so. The grandson was the sole heir. Heirs are *everything* to royals. If that lad got hurt, it would be my reputation shot to hell. And we couldn't forget the threat of terrorism that gained momentum like clockwork at any high-profile international event that ran. There would be a round of veiled threats put about, I predicted. The crazies couldn't resist the opportunity for some dependable worldwide press.

I resigned myself to making the job work out as I always did, but the spark of interest was not really there for me. As long as my traveling schedule stayed clear for February, I'd be good, I decided. Baby wasn't due until the end of the month, but I wouldn't take the chance of being out of the country when it was Brynne's time. I felt my stomach tighten at the thought. If I was honest, I was fucking terrified about the birth. Hospitals, doctors, blood, pain, Brynne suffering, baby struggling. There were a motherfucking myriad of things that could go wrong.

A text from Neil alerted me that something required my immediate and undivided attention. We had synchronized alert ringtones for emergencies. I read his text.

And felt my blood run cold.

The news ticker on the TV had switched off sports and over to politics.

No. Oh, fuck no.

THE look on Ethan's face when I returned from the bathroom, told me something was very wrong. I followed Ethan's eyes to the TV and felt my knees go weak when I saw *his* face. I listened to what the reporter said about *him*. I read *his* name in letters across the screen.

Seven years was a long time.

It had been seven years since I'd looked at his face. More than seven years, actually. I would be lying if I said I'd never thought about him over the course of that time. Of course I thought about him sometimes. Things like, "How could you do that to me?" Or, "Did you hate me that much?" Or, the very best one of all, "Did you know I tried to kill myself over what you did to me?"

The reporter told the whole story for me with perfect, efficient words that I didn't want to hear, or be faced with having to comprehend.

Second Lieutenant, Lance Oakley, was one of the critically injured yesterday, when outside the Interior Ministry headquarters in Baghdad, a bomb killed five people and wounded eight more, in what is believed to be a terrorist incident. The bombing came at morning, just as workers were arriving for their day at a block of government buildings, where he was stationed as one of the few remaining US troops working in an ambassadorial capacity on the ground in that country. No terrorist organization has claimed responsibility for the attack as of yet, but that is expected to change due to the nature of Lieutenant Oakley's connection to the inner circle of US politics at the highest levels. Lieutenant Oakley is the only son of United States Senator, Lucas Oakley, Vice Presidential candidate alongside Benjamin Colt, in the upcoming US elections held in early November, every four years. Colt's campaign bid for highest office in the United States has been rife with tragedy since its beginning. The death of Peter Woodson, US Congressman, in early April in a fatal plane crash, led to Oakley being vetted as a replacement for Woodson. The Senator is said to be enroute to see his son, who is receiving care at Lord Guildford Hospital in London. Lieutenant Oakley, and the other wounded, were airlifted out of Baghdad to the UK for specialist care and rehabilitation. There are reports that Lieutenant Oakley's injuries have necessitated the amputation of part of his right leg, below the knee. The news agencies are flooding officials here at Lord Guildford for any information on the status of Lieutenant Oakley. Political analysts are already weighing in, considering the effect this will have on the outcome of the presidential election in the US in less than one month. Reporting live for CNN in London…

ETHAN took us straight to the flat from our lunch at Indigo. Both of us quiet on the ride home. I wondered what he thought about the whole thing, but I didn't really want to discuss it with him. He read me well. He didn't ask any questions or make any demands. My man just took me home and let me be.

This was Dr. Roswell territory for sure.

Ethan was working in his office when my phone rang. I knew who it was before I ever checked. "Hello, Mom."

"Sweetheart, did you see the news about Lance?"

"Yes."

"And how are you feeling about it?"

I took a very deep breath and was very grateful that my mother lived in San Francisco and we were separated by an ocean, because I quickly figured out where this conversation was heading, and I didn't like it. "I'm feeling like I don't want to hear his name, or see his picture, or hear about his father running for Vice President, or knowing that it will be everywhere in the news—"

"—Brynne, listen to me. Senator Oakley will want you to go and visit Lance in a show of support and ties to your friendship, and since you live in London I think you should consider—"

"No! There is no way in hell, Mom! Have you lost your mind?"

Silence. I could picture her lips pursing in measured frustration with me.

"No, Brynne, I have not lost my mind. I am thinking of you and trying to make you see that for the good of your happiness and future peace of mind you should go and make a visit to an old family friend."

"How can you ask that of me, Mother? You want me to go visit the man who hurt me and made a video that nearly destroyed me? You want me to do this? Why? Because his dad is running for Vice President and it will look great for our family to be connected to his family? Is that...why?" It hurt me to ask the question, but I had to know. I hoped she could tell me if it was true. I doubted it, though. The tears I wanted to cry didn't come. Instead my heart hardened a little more toward the woman who'd given me life. She claimed to love me, but I didn't believe it anymore.

"No, Brynne. I'm only thinking of you and worried that distancing yourself from this opportunity to let go of the past...is a mistake."

"Let the past go?" Now, this was what you call being blindsided right there. Just bashed to hell, with no warning, whatsoever, of the impending hit about to rip you in two. I found myself reeling in pain and shock, in total suspended disbelief, before I managed to find my voice again. "How could that be, Mom? You—you think I should go visit him in the hospital and pretend he didn't rape me, and let his friends abuse me on that pool table? I—I should *forgive* him?"

"I do, sweetheart. Let the past go, and you can move on with your life. It's not helping you to hold onto it."

Now the tears were coming.

My mother couldn't love me. There was no way she did. I had to suck in a gasping breath at the sharp pain that pierced my heart.

"No, Mom." My voiced cracked as I spoke, but the words were true, and she would understand my meaning. "I wish Daddy was here to help me. He loved me. Dad loved me. You know how I know that, Mom? Because he would *never* ask me to do what you just asked of me!"

I didn't give her a chance to respond. I hung up on her instead and resisted the urge to throw my phone against the wall. As I stood in our bedroom, I was unable to do much more than breathe in and out steadily. I felt curiously numb, and strong.

This would be true if there weren't tears streaming down my face.

The muscled arms of my husband came around

me from behind and pulled me into his body. I brought my hands up to hold onto his arms and...just lost it.

"Ethan—she—she said I should go and v-visit Lance and f-forgive him..." The flooding tears had wet my face to the point where I couldn't even see. "She—she thinks that it will help me to let go of my bad experi—"

"Shh, hush." He turned me around and held me against his chest, the welcome scent of him enveloping my senses, and so very comforting to me in my wretched state. "I know," he crooned. "I overheard some of what you said. You don't have to go anywhere, baby. You don't have to see anyone that you don't want to see. Or speak to anyone you don't want to speak to."

"I—I can't believe she asked me to do th-that...I miss my dad..." I trailed off, my blubbering gaining momentum with every new tear that leaked out of me, until Ethan took over the unpleasant task of trying to settle me down.

"To bed you go. This is not good for you or our child, and you're lying down now." He led me over to our bed and sat me on the side of it. He bent down to take off my shoes, working silently but efficiently, maneuvering me into bed in under a minute. He loomed over me, bringing his face very close. "You can tell me everything if you like, but I want you off your feet and resting when you do. You're exhausted and upset, and that's just fucking wrong." His actions were gentle, but the tone of his voice was anything but. He was also sporting a frown that showed me just how angry he was about the situation. And at my mother. The two of them had absolutely no chance of ever being friends. I scoffed inwardly. *Don't kid yourself. You're not even friends with her.*

After bringing me a cool washcloth to clean my face, and a glass of water, he joined me in bed. Keeping very quiet, Ethan comforted me, spooning his big body behind mine, petting my hair over and over, and listened to me replay the conversation with my mother in all its garish detail.

When I was finally finished, he asked me a question. His tone changing from one of comfort and gentleness to one much firmer and serious. "Brynne, have you ever told your mother about what happened with Karl Westman?"

"No, you said never to speak about him to anyone."

"And you've told her nothing?"

"No, Ethan, not one word. I never even mentioned him to Dr. Roswell."

"Good. That's good." He continued to rub my head and trail fingers through my hair for a minute before he said, "Baby, I know this is hard to bring up, and to think about, but nobody can ever know about what happened with Westman the night he took you. Never.

You have to take that experience and just put it away into a part of your mind as if it never happened."

"I-I know. Because they killed him, didn't they? Senator Oakley's people had Karl killed because he was trying to blackmail them and holding the video as collateral over them, right?"

He kept rubbing my head with his strong fingers massaging my scalp through my hair. It felt divine, and was in such contrast to the unpleasant topic we were discussing. "I think that's very close to what happened, although there'll never be any proof or evidence to show it. His body will never be found. Westman has been wiped off the face of the earth."

I nodded. I couldn't really express my feelings, but I got it. Ethan's choice of words hit me right in the heart. *Wiped off the face of the earth.* Because that's what had happened to my dad. Gone. No longer here for me. No more hearing the love for me in his voice when we talked.

And the reason he was gone, all went back to something I had allowed to happen years ago. Consequences of my actions. Lance was in there too, yes, but it was my decision that made his evil deeds possible. I went to the party. I got drunk and didn't respect my body. I was used and abused, and let the experience take me over to the point I was willing to just go out of this life. *Pathetic.* But in the end, it was my father's life that was sacrificed.

"What are you thinking?" he asked me in a soft voice, for the second time today.

"About how I miss my dad," I blurted, my emotions so raw I felt another crying jag coming on strong.

"Baby…" Ethan put his hand on my belly and started rubbing. The gesture was very sweet but it just made me long for my dad even more.

The words started tumbling out of me and I couldn't stop them. "Today we went to the doctors and saw pictures of our baby. If Daddy was still here I would have shared with him, and he would have wanted to listen…and be excited about being a grandpa. I would have shown him the pictures—he would have wanted to know how I was feeling—I just miss him so much…" I paused for a breath. "I can't talk to him now, and I can't talk to my mother, either. I have nobody... I feel like an orphan—" I finally broke, silently this time, but no less emotionally painful, in sharing my grief about something that would hurt for a very long time.

Ethan felt my silent sobbing shudders, but his response was simply to hold me a little tighter, showing me that even with my great loss, I still had him. The rubbing on my belly must have gotten a little stronger too, because that's when it happened.

A fluttery little tickle from inside my womb. A brush alongside the front of my belly that reminded me of the beat of butterfly wings. I froze, and covered over Ethan's hand with my own, pressing on the spot where I'd felt it.

"What?" he asked worriedly. "Are you hurting—"

"I felt our baby. Moving around inside me. Like butterfly wings flapping." *Like a message from an angel.*

He kept his hand on me, probably hoping he could feel what I was feeling but I doubted it was possible quite yet. As we lay in bed together worrying about bad things that couldn't be changed, I realized something very important. I would never make it through this without Ethan. His strength pulled me through the hard parts.

Ethan never let me give up.

The words that came out of his mouth next, showed me just how much I had been blessed when he'd found me, regardless of my losses.

"I love you," he lulled at my ear, "and this little person loves you…so much." He splayed his fingers wide, swirling them over my stomach in a show of affectionate possession when he told me the last part. "He's there watching. Your father. He loves you from another place now, but his love is still there, Brynne, and it always will be."

OAKLEY didn't waste even a day in reaching out. I'd thought a few days before the request came through. But, no, I suppose not. The Senator didn't have much in the way of time to work with. The US election was less than a month away, and time stopped for no man. I'd played out the scenario in my mind as soon as I saw the news report in the restaurant at lunch. That cocksucker was going to use his son's war injury to propel his running mate into the presidential seat. And it was going to work.

The call came through on my mobile while I was smoking my one cig for the night.

"Blackstone."

"Yeah. What do you want?"

"I want insurance that puts the past to rest once and for all."

"Of course you want insurance. We all want it. How do you propose for that to happen, Senator?" I dreaded whatever he might suggest. Probably because I had an inkling for what it might be. The earlier call from Brynne's mum was a good fucking clue.

"A simple showing of support to an old family friend should do it. Hospital visit. Media will be taken care of."

Bingo. I cringed at the idea. "My wife will never agree," I told him, picturing how I'd left her in bed after crying herself to sleep. Drained and exhausted, and very emotional from the argument with her mother. That insensitive bitch had stretched my patience to its last reserve today. What sort of fucking cow thinks so little of her daughter's emotional and physical welfare? And now this arsehole. I stubbed out my ciggie and lit another.

"Make her agree, Blackstone."

"I know you care for nothing but the success of your campaign, Senator, not even what's happened to your son, but I don't give a maiden queen's first fuck about your politics, or your rapist son."

I'd give Oakley points for laying it all out on the line. He wasted nothing on words. Just went straight to the issue in that tonal American accent of his that seemed almost devoid of humanity. "Don't you think it's better to be a couple of indiscreet teenagers who had a lapse in judgment years ago, and who've put it firmly behind them, than to worry about extortion should their shameful secret be brought to light? If they are still friends, then no crime ever occurred. Simple insurance, Blackstone. I think you should care very much."

As much as I hated to admit it, Oakley's "insurance" scheme was really very clever. But the cleverness of it wouldn't help Brynne. It would hurt her. "I care about the welfare of my pregnant wife, who was made ill tonight by this whole shitstorm blowing up in media. And that, Senator, is not going to help you one iota. I can't make her go and see him. She won't do it."

He responded with, "Within the week, please," and cut the line. *Fucking bastard.* I stared at my mobile, sure the number he'd called from was already deactivated. The tingle of fear scratched its way down my spine. I lit another Djarum and filled my lungs. I didn't know how to fix this problem, and it had grown exponentially in a matter of hours. The US presidential election was propelling this one. How in the goddamn shitting hell did one fight that monstrous beast?

So I got up and left my office. I went to sit outside on the balcony, where I started smoking in earnest. One Djarum after the other, until I was high from the pumping nicotine and spice that fueled the addiction I couldn't deny.

The smoke drifted away on the cool nighttime breeze in lazy, wafting swirls. I had a flash of longing that my problems could magically do the same. Wishful thinking. Real life never worked that way. My hand was being forced in this. Sometimes my experience with poker was a curse...because I knew the odds here. I could see when folding was the only option.

It wouldn't help Brynne to bring her into Oakley's circle, but I feared it was already too late for that. *My poor girl was going to be hurt.*

CHAPTER 8

"I found Ethan outside on the balcony smoking a few nights ago. I'd been upset earlier about…the Lance Oakley situation…and woke in the middle of the night to find the bed empty. I got up to use the bathroom, and then went looking for him. He's been trying to quit smoking, and was doing well from what I knew, but a few nights ago…I could see that he'd fallen off the wagon."

"Nicotine addiction is no less difficult to break than drugs or alcohol," Dr. Roswell said in her non-judgmental way.

"I think it's more than nicotine addiction in his case, though."

"How so, Brynne?"

"Umm, he once told me about his time as a prisoner of war in Afghanistan." I hedged with what to tell her because it felt like a betrayal to share Ethan's story without his permission. I decided my need for information superseded his privacy. "He was held and tortured for twenty-two days. During his time in captivity, he suffered cravings for cigarettes to the point he nearly went mad. He told me that the cigarettes were a reminder that he survived. That he was alive after all that he endured—able to smoke another day. He has terrible nightmares and suffers through them, and when I try to help him he shuts down. He won't tell me very much and I think he feels ashamed. It's horrible…I worry so much about him."

"I imagine it is very hard for Ethan. So many soldiers suffer with Post Traumatic Stress Disorder." I noted that she wrote it down in her book.

"So, what can I do for him?"

"What you have to understand about victims of trauma, and from what you've just told me, Ethan has suffered—and survived—trauma in the extreme, is that they will do almost *anything* to avoid having to be reminded of what traumatized them in the first place. It's too painful."

"So, when I press him to tell me, it's just making it harder for him? Asking him to speak of what happened, hurts him even more?"

"Well, think of it in your terms, Brynne. You have suffered a trauma. It's affected your life in every way. You just told me about how the coverage of Lance's injury in the media this week has upset you terribly." Dr.

Roswell never was one to sugarcoat anything. "How hard do you work to avoid being reminded of what happened to you?"

Really fucking hard, Doctor.

LEN held the door for me as I left Dr. Roswell's office. "Shall I take you home, Mrs. Blackstone?"

I sighed at my gentle giant of a driver. "Len, please. We've been through this over and over again. I want you to call me Brynne."

"Yes, Mrs. Blackstone. Home then?"

I shot him a slow nod, and muttered, "I give up." The man was as stoic as they come, and yet I always felt he was teasing me when we played this little game of ours. I settled into the seat and pondered what Dr. Roswell and I had discussed about PTSD. I had a lot to think about. For Ethan and for myself, but mostly, I just wanted to be a good wife and supportive of him. Letting him know I was there, and loved him no matter what he'd shouted out during a bad dream, or needed from me in order to feel better. If it took some pounding sex to help him relax after a bad dream, then I could do that. The sex was always superb, and right now my body was on hyper-drive with the hormones, so...

My phone chirped and I fished it out of my purse.

From Benny. **You okay, luv?** It made me smile when I read it. Ben hadn't stopped looking out for me just because I was married to Ethan now. We kept in touch religiously. He was a friend I loved with all my heart, and knew I could just be myself when we were together. Ben and I were different in a way that I couldn't be with Gaby. Ben and Gaby were also very close, but she wasn't without her own demons, either. We both teased Ben that he attracted women friends with mountains of emotional problems. He said it gave him "pussy points" knowing what made us females tick. That he may not be into pussy himself, but it did make the world go round, so it was worth understanding. Sadly, his jest was very true. Ben would have seen Lance's story splashed all over the news. Hell, a person would have to live under a rock not to have heard it. So he was just letting me know that he was in my corner.

I shot back: **I will be :) I miss u tho. Take me shopping 4 pregger clothes sometime soon?**

I grinned wide at his quick reply. **Yes, sexy mum. xo** He had the very best taste, in regards to all things fashion and design. Ben would do me right in the clothing department, I had no doubt.

London traffic dictated that the time spent getting me home would be taking much longer than it ought to, so I checked emails and responded to texts until my inbox was cleaned out. Len was not a chatterer, so I didn't have to keep up conversation as he drove the Rover expertly through clogged streets and autumn drizzle.

It hadn't escaped my notice that my mother never tried to call me back either. Not a surprise really. I'd said some pretty harsh things and hung up on her. It would be a while before we talked again. Our relationship was just so messed up. I hated believing that, but the truth was often ugly, and for my mother and me, the truth was a succubus with raging PMS.

My phone alerted me to an incoming text. I dug it out of my purse once again and read it.

It was a media message that included a screenshot of my Facebook profile. I looked closer, feeling my heart sink like a stone when I deciphered exactly what had been sent to me. A post I'd made on my profile, when I'd used the GPS on Facebook to lead Ethan to where Karl had me. I'd also tagged Karl Westman in *Who are you with?* so Ethan would know who had taken me. Below the screenshot was a single sentence: **Karl Westman has been missing since August 3rd and his last known contact was you.**

HYSTERICAL, was the only way to describe her when she arrived at my office. Len ushered Brynne up to the forty-fourth floor and I met her out in reception. From there I took her straight into the *en suite* adjacent from where I worked.

She looked around the studio flat in confusion, probably wondering why she'd never been in it, or heard me speak of it. Telling her this was the place where I would fuck all the women *before* she came along, didn't seem appropriate at any time, but right now? Out of the motherfucking question.

So I held her in my arms instead. "Tell me you're all right, baby."

"Ethan, why are they doing this to me? Are they *ever* going to stop? Her questions broke my heart. As if a meat cleaver was put to my chest and given a hearty whack, shattering bone and obliterating flesh.

"Brynne, I need you to calm down and listen to me." I took her face in my hands and lifted it up, forcing her to focus on me. "Senator Oakley rang me that night after the news hit the wires. He wants you to visit his…*son* in the hospital, and show the world what good friends you are." It made me ill to have to even say the words to her, but I'd realized a few nights ago, there was no other way out of this mess.

"He called you? You spoke to him and didn't tell me?" she shouted accusingly.

I shook my head. "I'm sorry, but I made a judgment call—"

"—But why? I don't ever want to see Lance Oakley again as long as I live. Don't you dare ask me to go to him," she spat. "You're no better than my mother!"

With her eyes flaring wildly at me, I could tell she was ready to bolt, so I shut that idea right the fuck down. "Nope, not true," I said, gripping both of her arms, forcing her to focus on me. "I told him no. I said I wouldn't ask you to do something that would upset you, but they sent that Facebook screenshot today." I lowered my voice and told her the brutal truth. "This shit won't go away until you go on the record as a close family friend."

"No…" she said pitifully.

"Brynne, baby…there are others who know about the video—you told me so yourself. This visit to see Oakley in the hospital will make it *worthless*. I can't risk you any more than you already have been. Please just listen to why."

The look she gave me? The tragic expression on her beautiful face, streaked with tears and devastation…really fucking hurt me.

After a moment she closed her eyes and nodded almost imperceptibly.

I kissed her long and slow. Just to bring us close,

and show her first and foremost how much I loved her. Then I sat her down and told her about my conversation with the Senator. About how important it was to keep any others who knew of the video's existence, from trying to do what Karl Westman had attempted. *Blackmailing degenerate motherfucker.* And, also to neutralize any negative effect of the video by declaring friendship with Lance Oakley. *Rapist dog with two dicks.* How, if they were seen to still be friends, then a crime never could have occurred—just a youthful indiscretion between two kids, in the event the video ever surfaces to embarrass the future Vice President of the United States. *Cocksucking immoral maggot.*

Brynne took it all in, listening to me speak without interrupting or dragging everything down with more questioning. Her clear brown eyes held mine, quietly processing the situation. God, I admired her strength. Never a doubt about my girl's bravery, or her intelligence.

But I was also hurting her right now. I knew about facing the things that scared you. For Brynne, being forced to visit Oakley's bedside scared her.

It's fucking killing me too.

She seemed to think about everything I'd told her, and got up and walked into the bathroom, stopping before the mirror. She stood there and stared into it, with seemingly little emotion, looking, in some ways, nothing like the passionate girl I'd met back in May.

Finally she turned to look at me. Lips trembling, eyes filling with tears that would taste salty if I licked them, she opened her mouth to speak. Her throat swallowing reflexively, her voice cracked, "I—I have to go and see Lance…don't I?"

I cringed at her question, knowing there was only one answer I could give. *Clusterfuck motherfucking load of steaming shit.*

WHOEVER says the government moves slowly is not talking about the people that work for the future Vice President of the United States. Things moved at the speed of light as soon as I gave my agreement to visit Lance Oakley.

You have to do this. I stood in the hospital corridor waiting to go in, the smell of antiseptic and food permeating the sterile air making me want to retch. The bouquet of flowers I'd been given shook lightly in my hand as I tried to pull myself together. *You don't have a choice.* Ethan's hand at my back felt possessive, but I couldn't deal with whatever emotions he was struggling with at the moment. *You have to do it to protect your baby.* I knew why Ethan was freaking. But there was nothing I could do for him right now.

The moment Ethan had sent my agreement to meet Lance via the text message on my phone, a very well-organized media show geared into motion. Limousines, police escorts, secret entrances, personal photographers, gifts for the patient, debriefings on what to do, how long to stay, what to say. Everything arranged down to the millisecond. *You're doing this.* Ethan's hand caressed my low back. He was being forced into being a part of this bedside circus too. My husband was about to meet my past. Everything I wanted to forget about. *He's just a soldier who's been injured serving his country.*

"Mr. Blackstone, you'll stay on her left, until after your introduction to Lieutenant Oakley, then you'll excuse yourself from the room to take a phone call. Your wife will finish the visit alone with Lieutenant Oakley." The press secretary who addressed Ethan blanched at the look her gave her. Make that a wince. I couldn't see him shooting her the *fuck-off-you-pretentious-gash* glare, as he was slightly out of my range of vision, but I could imagine what his face looked like right now. And no, Ethan wouldn't take to her instructions well at all, now would he? Especially as she just told him to leave me in the hands of another man. *Lance is not just any other man.* Ethan might not even follow her instructions. I guess Miss Press Secretary was about to find out.

"We're all ready?" she asked me, pointedly

avoiding eye contact with Ethan.

No. "Yes." *He's just a soldier who's been injured serving his country. You knew him a long time ago...you can do this.*

MY legs propelled me forward. I don't know how.

I felt close to an out-of-body experience to be honest, but somehow I moved in slow steps that brought me into his private hospital room. I don't know what I expected. I knew Lance had been horribly injured and that his leg had been amputated just below the right knee, but the person lying in that bed, was nearly unrecognizable to me.

The Lance Oakley I remembered was a prep-school, west coast society boy. Clean cut and ambitious. He'd been a student at Stanford headed for a law degree when we were together.

He didn't look like Stanford Law now.

Tattoos covered his arms in sleeves down to the knuckles on his hands. His brown hair was cut short as it would be for a military officer, but blended with the unshaven beard, he looked raw and edgy. Big bodied, muscled and inked, dressed in a hospital gown and lying in bed, his gaze straight ahead on the wall. Not at me. He looked bereft, and not at all like the cold misogynist

I'd carried in my head these long years.

I must have stopped short because Ethan's hand at my back pressed more firmly.

I took another step, moving closer. He flipped his eyes up. Very dark brown as I remembered them. Gone was the cocky self-assuredness I also remembered.

Now, I saw something in him I'd never seen before. There was regret, and apology, and shame in the way he appeared before me, in his hospital bed, missing one of his legs. At some point in the past seven years—maybe just since his injury—Lance Oakley had found a conscience.

"BRYNNE."

"Lance."

His face softened. "Thank you for coming...here," he said clearly, as if he had also been briefed by his father's press secretary.

"Of course." I came forward and placed the flowers on the side of the blanket and reached out my hand.

His tattooed fingers gripped my outstretched hand, and miraculously...nothing horrible happened. The world didn't end, nor did the sun go dark. Lance brought my hand up to his cheek and held it there. "I'm so happy to see you again."

The photographer shot the hell out of that moment, and I knew I would see the pictures in print, on TV, magazines, everywhere. I was in it now, and there was no going back. For any of us.

I could feel Ethan beside me, as tight as a bowstring about ready to snap. He was undoubtedly furious that Lance was touching me in an intimate way. Strangely, it didn't affect me much at all. I felt numb more than anything. So I forced myself to continue on with the charade, to propel it forward so we could all end the torture.

Retrieving my hand from his grip, I said, "Lance, this is my husband, Ethan Blackstone. Ethan, Lance Oakley, an old…friend from San Francisco."

Lance gave Ethan his full attention and held out his hand in greeting. "Pleasure to meet you, Ethan."

There was a long pause where I wasn't sure Ethan would return the handshake. Time stopped as everyone held their breath.

After what felt like an eon, Ethan brought his own hand forward and delivered a firm shake. "How do you do?" The greeting was conveyed smoothly, but I knew my man, and he was hating on every bloody second of being here. Of me having to be here. Of him having to pretend.

Then, as if a screen director were calling the

shots, someone came up and tapped Ethan on the shoulder, apologizing for the interruption, but he had an important call that required his attention. And just like that, he excused himself. I watched Ethan walk out, the rigid gait showing me how hard it was for him to leave me there alone. *You can do this.*

"Will you sit down?"

"Yes, of course." I followed the script, astounded that my brain was remembering what to say and do.

Once I was seated beside him, he reached out and took my hand again. I allowed it only because I could hear the camera clicking as it captured pictures of us chatting together as close friends would, when one of them was hurt in the hospital. *You are doing a job and you're almost done. Finish it, and walk out the door and never look back.*

"You look so wonderful. You look happy, Brynne."

"I am happy." And as if I needed reminding, my little butterfly angel chose that moment to assure me of its presence. I closed my eyes and allowed myself to feel the fluttery brushes of my baby growing safe inside me. The beauty of that miracle sort of made all of the awkwardness in the current moment fade out of my focus, enabling me to bear it.

"Brynne…I am so sorry about this…that you had to come here. I'm sorry you had to, but I am so grateful to finally see you again." His voice was so different now.

The way he spoke was different. I sensed sincerity…

I opened my eyes and looked at him, having a very hard time coming up with a response. Eventually I did. "I hope—that you recover quickly, Lance. I—I have to get going." Time for the *coup de gras*, the part which would be the hardest for me to get through. But I knew what I was expected to do. And so I would.

I stood up from my chair and bent down to him.

His face fell, his expression changing to one of displeasure that I was ending the visit. I took a deep breath and pressed my cheek to his in a simple embrace. I held myself suspended as the camera exploded in another round of furious clicking.

Lance brought his arms up around my back.

I closed my eyes again…and thought of Ethan and my butterfly angel to get me through the moment.

My mission was nearly complete, the checkered flag about to drop, when Lance whispered in my ear. The words were spoken in a rush, and audible only to me, but there was only one way to describe how he sounded. Desperate.

"Brynne, please come back to see me again. I have to tell you how sorry I am for what I did to you."

CHAPTER 9

I knew Ethan was in a bad state the second I came out of Lance's room. I could see the lines of worry around his eyes and the harsh set of his jaw. And I most definitely felt the tension in his body when he refused the car to take us home and had Len waiting for us instead. Ethan wouldn't accept another morsel of anything from the senator. He was done.

The moment Len dropped us at the lobby of our building, Ethan propelled me inside with quick steps. No seconds wasted on even a simple greeting to Claude, our concierge, as he usually did. He moved us along with a singular purpose, trundling me into the elevator without ever uttering a single word.

He herded me into a corner and pressed his body up against mine, dropping his head to my neck and inhaling. Still silent, he just pinned me there and breathed me in. I could smell the seductive male spice coming off him. The scent of desire for sex, and the burning drive to mate.

"Ethan," I whimpered his name.

"Hush." He brought one finger to my lips and held it there. "No talking."

I could feel the length of his cock pressing into my hip and a long shiver rolled down my spine. I was already wet and he hadn't even done anything to me except press his body to mine and express his displeasure for conversation. It was all in the power of suggestion in his manner, the way he communicated to me with his mind and his body about what he wanted, that was so compelling.

Ethan wanted to fuck. Me.

I knew he was just holding back the firestorm that would be coming at me the second he got us behind closed doors.

❧

THE click of the door latch sounded incredibly loud against the tense silence.

With my senses on high alert, I braced myself for him to come at me. I didn't have to wait long. In less than a second, I was covered from behind by a very hard body intent upon one, and only one goal. To get inside mine.

Ethan had his hands up my skirt and his fingers sliding over my clit before I could even take a step. His forceful probing of my sex was primal, and sent me into instant lust. It was his animalistic desperation that flipped the switch. Ethan was a ravening beast at my back right, and the erotic images he conjured up in my mind made me go just as wild.

"So drenched already," he purred smugly at my neck, his hips thrusting into my ass while he fingered my pussy, building me up to where my body took over, and my mind didn't have to think about anything beyond this.

He pushed me forward, up to the foyer table. "Put your hands there and hold on," he commanded.

As I took my place, I felt my panties pulled down roughly, one leg lifted out of them and then…his magic fingers were back at my pussy. *Thank you.* This time, he plundered from the front so he could grind into me from behind. Spreading the slickness up and down my slit, he worked it around with talented fingers, stroking and lubricating my flesh until I was nearly ready to orgasm. Ethan was well versed in the signs, and I knew he would change things up because of it. He let me go along until I started to rock into the rhythm he had going, riding his hand like a wanton. Then he stopped. "No," I cried out in protest when his fingers left me.

"I've got you, baby. Hold on." He smacked my ass cheek with a firm slap, the sting edging my pleasure up a notch. I tensed my muscles and shuddered into it, desperate for him inside me. *How does he know?*

The noise of him unzipping was the best sound I'd heard all day. Still shaking, I moaned in anticipation as I felt the blunt head of his cock nudge at my entrance, hot and ready.

Bracing my arms on the table, I looked down at the floor made of beautiful Travertine marble. The scene below us could only be described as sex personified. Creamy-lined stone, created by nature, juxtaposed against the haphazard cluster of abandoned clothing. Ethan's dark grey trousers and leather belt bunched along his shins, the rolled pink lace of my panties still around my left ankle, the wide stance of my Gucci peep-toes propping up my legs. A truly jaw-dropping sight to behold, because of what it represented. Wild, filthy sex between two lovers too desperate to bother with getting naked.

And also that I was about to be fucked senseless.

Ethan filled me up on a steady thrust, his hands at my hips for leverage. He made that breathy groan of pleasure that I loved to hear from him as he sank into me. "Feel that, my beauty. All of it—just for you." He drew out on a glorious slide of his thick cock. "You're so good, so fucking beautiful right now, bent over this table—" He plunged inside me deeply. "—taking my cock."

God, he felt good in me. " Yes…oh!" I couldn't respond to his erotic ravings with any coherence. All I could do was take it.

"You belong to me!" he barked on harsh punctuating thrusts, his pace almost punishing as he pounded faster.

Yes, I do. My man was trying to reestablish his claim over me after having to give me up at the hospital. He needed this. I needed it. Over and over he pumped into me, the hot flesh of him sinking and retreating in a wicked stride that left me barely able to breathe.

"I want to hear you say it," he growled.

My orgasm building, I could barely think, let alone speak, but his demands always pulled it out of me. "Oh, my God, Ethan…yes…I only ever belong to you!"

I felt the first convulsion start, rolling me to the tip of the crest as I clamped down on his hammering cock as hard as I could.

"Oh, fuck, yeah. Squeeze it just like that!" His hand gripped my hair in a huge handful and pulled my neck all the way back. I understood why. Ethan needed that intimacy of our mouths and eyes meeting, no less than the joining of our sexes. He brought his other hand around my throat and held me pinned, cock pounding relentlessly into me from behind as he took my mouth. His kiss was searing, devouring, and ravening. He bit and sucked at me with rough lips and teeth, possessing me in every way, demonstrating that I was, indeed, his.

Just as I needed to be.

As I climaxed into a blissful explosion of intensity, his tongue plunged deep into my mouth claiming my breath, my soul, my everything.

I felt him harden and swell inside me. I cried out his name in a long, low wail, unable to vocalize anything other than that one word. "Ethan" was the only word I knew.

"I love you," he rasped against my lips right as he started to come.

BRYNNE squeezing and gripping around me as she came—was so good. *So—fucking—good.* Every convulsive grasp and shudder coming from her sex, owned my cock. I felt the tightening rush in my balls just as I started to go off. "Uhn…uhn…uhn," I grunted, with every plunge into her tight cunt.

My beautiful girl gave herself up to me in exquisite surrender.

"Fuck, YES!" I ground out, a hot flood of cum shooting out in spurts, spunking her up good and dirty. I kept on fucking through the ecstasy, holding her against me by pieces of her beautiful hair. *Fuck. Love. Mine. Brynne…* Random thoughts filtered through my consciousness as I melded into her, but one idea stayed with me though. No matter how far gone I ever got, I didn't lose sight of the truth: This woman owned me from head to toe, and everything else in between.

And she always would.

I released my hold of her hair, straightened her neck, and buried my face at the back of it. Breathing in her floral scent, laced with the smell of pussy, I traced the top of her spine with my lips, whispering to her, cherishing her, kissing in between the words. I might be calmer now, but I was fully aware that I'd just fucked my wife like a madman in the entryway of our home.

"Are you all right?"

"Mmm hmm," she purred sexily.

I wondered what she was thinking. Even so, I knew there was nothing I could have done differently. After leaving Oakley at the hospital, I'd slipped into a very dark place in my head. I understood the visit was necessary, but I hated every second of it. All I wanted was to protect my precious girl from the things that had hurt her. And I wasn't able to do that today. I had to stand aside and allow him to put his hands on her...again.

Don't think about that cocksucking shit.

Pulling out, I yanked my trousers up, only bothering so I'd be able to walk. They wouldn't be on me in another two minutes.

I swept my hand over her gorgeously displayed

arse and squeezed a cheek, taking in the view. "You're so...goddamn...beautiful." The word didn't even do justice to how she looked right now. There weren't words. And I could never get enough of looking at her.

She rolled her neck like a cat getting a good stretch out of the way. My girl seemed pleasantly sated, but I wasn't done with her yet. That desperate entryway fuck we'd just had was merely a warm up.

"I think I need to get off my feet," she said from her position bent over the table—pink pussy framed between her spread legs, standing long and straight, all the way down to the black heels at the end of her dainty feet.

Guilt speared my gut. Of course she should be off her feet. She was pregnant. *You're a fucking moron sometimes.* I helped her to straighten and turned her around to me. "I'm so sorry 'bout that, baby. Let me make it up to you." I scooped her up into my arms and kissed her, relieved to see the sexy smirk teasing her lips as I walked us toward the bedroom. "I'll rub them for a long time."

"Pretty please," she hummed into my chest.

And that's all it took for everything to be right with the world. I just needed a sign from her. A smile, a word, a caress—something that told me she wasn't bothered by my freak-out, and still loved me. That, and the fact I had at least another blinding orgasm coming to me. Brynne, on the other hand, deserved at least two more, plus a really nice foot massage.

"You will be," I told her when I laid her out on our bed.

IN the SF, Captains lead troops of five men. Small squads for tactical ops that require zero detection. My men were the best the BA had to offer. Mike, Dutch, Leo, Chip, and Jackie. That day we found the boy and his dead mother in the middle of the road was the final day we were all alive at the same time. The last time brothers, husbands, fathers, and sons of Britain drew breath. Twenty days later, that number was reduced to…one.

Mike was the only other besides me to make it out of the ambush in the street. It would have been so much better if he hadn't…

IMMERSED in the bathtub with luxurious scented water warming my body, I processed through the last twelve hours. Jesus Christ, it would take more than a soak in the tub to figure it all out.

Ethan had fallen asleep so soundly after we finished the second time, he didn't even stir when I slipped out of bed. He usually followed after me when he heard the tub filling, if he hadn't been the one to start it in the first place. But not tonight.

I imagined Ethan was exhausted from the pretense at the hospital. I could tell that he was torn up inside about having to ask me to go. We didn't have a choice though. Lucas Oakley was going to secure the presidency for Benjamin Colt because of a twist of fate that made his son a war hero at just the right moment. Handsome young Army officer gets his leg blown off in the war. Oh, and the handsome young officer just happens to be the son of the nominee for Vice President of the United States of America. The polls were already predicting a landslide victory, and everyone knew it.

The really scary part though? Once Senator Oakley *was* the Vice President, he would only be a heartbeat away from being...The President. The very thought made my heart ache. The normal response would be to rub over the area to ease the sting, but I cradled my belly instead—my first instinct to protect my little butterfly angel. I'd done what I had to today. I had to secure some kind of assurance that my sordid past with Lance couldn't do damage to his father's future, or to mine. And I would willingly do it again, too. Anything for my butterfly angel.

Lance... When I had woken up this morning, he was the last person I ever imagined seeing. I wasn't ready to deal with him yet, but I was realistic enough to see that Lance Oakley was not going to go away. Especially now. *"Brynne, please come back to see me again. I have to tell you how sorry I am for what I did to you."*

Which had led me to my second shock. He was sorry? I didn't know what to make of his request, but I understood Lance only wanted me to hear because he asked me in a secret whisper. It didn't matter. I wouldn't go back there to see him again. I didn't need to. Oddly, I was okay with how things stood. All in all, the way the visit had played out, was not as traumatic for me as I thought it would have been. I was strong during our meeting, and I did everything I was asked to do. As did Lance.

I didn't really dwell on the idea of what this all meant in regards to my emotional health, because I didn't have the time or the inclination to delve into it. I had a life to lead, with a husband who loved me and needed my support, and a baby who needed me for everything. All of the past crap with Lance would just have to take a back seat in the driving force that was now my life. I didn't see any other way to move forward.

And I was determined to move forward. I brought my hand to my stomach again and tried to feel for more movement, but baby wasn't in the mood, I guess.

I couldn't let Lance, or his scheming politician

father, stop me from what I needed to do. The meeting had really stunned me in the way Lance appeared so different than he'd been when we were together. Like, complete-one-eighty different. I still had some trouble connecting the man I'd seen today, with the one I'd known before. They didn't even feel like the same person. Maybe he had changed over the course of the years. His body sure had changed with all the tattoos—

"—Noooo! Mike, I'm sorry, brother. I won't do it again! Awww, fuck no. MIKE! God, please no. FUCK! NO, PLEASE DON'T DO IT. NO…NO…NO!"

Ethan. I heard him shouting from the bedroom and understood immediately. My man was having another night terror. I stood up from the bath, water streaming off my skin, and reached for my robe. I drew it on over my dripping body and rushed out of the bathroom. He needed me, and I had to help him. Simple as that.

I bolted up from the bed gasping, both hands around my throat, just hanging there taking in oxygen.

Breathe, motherfucker. In, out, in, out.

That flashback was the worst. My deepest torment—one that could never be erased from my mind. I knew I was doomed to carry that one inside of me forever. *He's at peace now.* I told myself that, whenever the guilt seared into me to the point where I was right then. It didn't help a great deal, but some. And it was the best I could do.

In, out, in, out.

"Ethan, baby…" Her gentle voice told me she was awake this time.

I was afraid to look at her. Fucking terrified to lift my head and face my sweet girl. If I did, she would see my shame and my weakness. Fuck all knows what I'd shouted out. I felt like I would be sick.

But Brynne didn't do what she had done on the other occasions. She didn't get upset or demand I start talking. Didn't judge or question. She just put her soft hand to my chest and brought herself close so I could take in her scent, and know I was in the here and now, and not lost in my past. She let me see that I had her safe beside me. "I'm here, and I love you," she crooned at my ear. "How can I help you?"

Pure, flooding relief cascaded over me at her words. I pulled her into me and held on for dear life. The idiom was a perfect description of me. I held onto my girl for *dear life*.

THE hair at the back of her neck was a little damp. I could mess about in her hair for hours. I loved the softness of it, the texture, the smell, everything. As soon as she'd asked me how she could help me, I'd showed her exactly how.

I think she knew because she had "helped" me before, allowing me to find a small measure of comfort in her body by using sex to drown out the demons. Now came the hard part. The part where I apologized for my beastly reaction of using her like a tranquilizer.

Spooning on our sides, I breathed her in and cradled our little bun-in-the-oven with my hand. I was looking forward to feeling a kick or a fist pump, but hadn't been so lucky yet. Brynne brought her hand to cover mine on her stomach and sighed in contentment. Which made me feel miles better. A satisfied Brynne was a good start.

"I'm so sorry, baby," I finally whispered at her ear. "Forgive me…"

"You have nothing to be sorry about, Ethan, ever. All I care about is that you know I'm here for you and that I love you. That's what's important to me." She yawned sleepily and patted over my hand. "Go to sleep now."

My eyes snapped open. Did I just hear her

correctly? She wasn't going to interrogate me about my nightmare, or demand I go "talk" to some headshrinker about the shit in my fucked-up past? Her actions made me curious.

"Brynne?" I nuzzled the back of her shoulder.

"Hmmm?"

"Why aren't you disturbed by what I—what I did tonight? My nightmare?" I asked carefully, my lips pressing down on her skin with a kiss as soon as the question was out of my mouth.

"I spoke to Dr. Roswell about your PTSD."

My body tensed as I struggled with feelings of betrayal for a moment, but I held off, because I was sure there was more in the way of an explanation from her. Brynne was not the hothead I was. She thought about things before she said them. Most of the time. And if I was in her shoes, I would probably do the same. My *condition* was no secret to her anymore. Why pretend with the only person I could even trust?

"Well, I didn't tell her very much, just that you have bad flashbacks from your time as a prisoner in the army. I asked her how I could help you." She rolled around to face me, her expression telling the truth in her words. "Because I love you, Ethan, and I will do anything to bring you out from that dark place if I can."

"You do already. You have from the beginning," I told her. "You're the only thing that helps me." I traced her cheekbone with my finger, wishing I could tell her I'd never have another flashback, or wake her from a sound sleep with barking-mad ravings in the night. I would do it again. I might never stop doing it.

"So Dr. Roswell told me a little about the way the trauma memories work," she began cautiously, her voice like a soft caress.

"What did she say?" I managed to ask.

"She told me that people with PTSD will do almost anything to avoid having to remember the events. It's too painful and terrifying."

Dr. Roswell is right.

She shook her head slowly. "So I won't ask anymore…I'll just be here for you. Whatever you need from me, I'm here for *you*. Sex? To bring you out of it if that's what you need. With no pressure to talk it out if you don't want to." She swallowed and her throat flexed in the hollow of her neck. The cool touch of her hand on my cheek came next. "I know now that when I pushed you to talk to me about your nightmares I was just making it harder on you. I'm so sorry, Ethan, I thought talking would help you. I didn't know I was hurting you by trying to force you—"

I kissed her, cutting off her words. I'd heard plenty. Beautiful words of acceptance that went further to heal me than anything probably ever could. I knew this was true. My girl had just helped me to take the first step. Maybe now, with her unconditional support, I could find the courage to go out and find some help somewhere.

Brynne brought her hands into my hair and gripped hard, letting me know she was going to be right with me through and through. God, I loved her so much it was beyond what I could ever express. It was just something I would have to hold inside me. I was the only one who could ever know how deep my love went for Brynne.

When I finally ended our kiss, I still held her against me because I couldn't bear to let her out of my arms. Could not fucking bear it. I had to hold onto her for the rest of that night.

CHAPTER 10

19th October
Scotland

Brynne and I were dressed for a wedding, but we weren't the bride and groom. That honour went to Neil and Elaina today. That is if Neil didn't drop dead from anxiety before he could say the vows to his bride.

"You're going to wear a hole in this ancient stone floor if you don't stop pacing like a lunatic. Are you going to sit in the corner and start cradling back and forth, too?" I couldn't help myself, the opportunity to wind him up was just too sweet to pass over.

Neil shot me a death glare and kept right on with the back-and-forth. "Easy for you to say that to me, now that you're already married. I remember how mental you were in that room before you said your vows to Brynne. You would've smoked your Blacks three at a time if we hadn't hidden your stash away where you couldn't find them."

I shook my head. So that's where my smokes

went. Fuckers. "Listen mate, all will be well in a very short time. You're starting to worry me."

Neil stopped with the pacing. "I feel ill," he squawked. "I need water."

"I think you need a fucking bottle of Scotch, but really, it's going to be fine."

He nodded weakly and gulped in huge breaths of air. "What time is it?"

"About two minutes later than the last time you asked." I took pity on the poor sod. He was a miserable wreck. So I walked over to him and slapped him hard on the back, under the guise of brotherly love, and told him a little lie. "I saw Elaina in her dress all ready for you when I snuck a peek at my girl in that side room where they're all waiting." I hadn't really seen Elaina, but he didn't need to know that. I'd seen Brynne in her pale blue dress though. *Delicious.* I'd needed to make sure she was feeling okay because she'd woken up with a headache in the morning.

Neil started rapidly firing questions, too desperate to wait for any answers—which would all be made up, but my blending of the truth was beside the point, I needed to get him to the altar standing and conscious, as opposed to flat on his back. "You saw her? How was she? Did she seem nervous? Did she look worried about anyth—"

I lied well, which wasn't hard at all. Elaina would

be lovely as she always was. "She looked gorgeous and like she couldn't wait to get shackled to you, you big great ape. Do I need to tranquillize you or something?"

My comment did the trick because he came to life and spat back immediately, "I'll remember this, when Brynne is ready to deliver your baby, and you're a quivering mass of jelly on the floor. Don't worry, I'll return the favour with the offer of tranquillizers."

Well, fuck. He has a point. I refused to think about the birth at that moment. If I started down that track, I'd be on the floor along with Neil. I'm sure my mouth looked a lot like Simba's when he wants a krill; hanging open for a moment before I could get a grip and close it. Neil smirked at me and shook his head. I checked my watch and decided to give him the brutal truth. He was my best mate, and deserved to know what was coming. He'd survive it just like the rest of us. "Okay, I'll be honest. The ceremony is a fucking stress ball of bullshit, and I can't help you even a little bit. The good news? In about five more hours, you can start on the wedding night and that part is completely golden." I trolled my hand like an airplane on a smooth ride.

Neil looked at me as if I were the biggest idiot ever to draw breath. I shrugged at him and we both busted into laughter at how fucking ridiculous this was, easing away all the tension. He looked better and that was the main purpose for my confession. Neil would be fine. I knew nobody stronger than him, or more loyal. The two reasons he was my partner and confidant. He was getting his girl after years and years of waiting for her, and I was happy to see it happen. Honored to be standing up for my friend on his wedding day.

A knock sounded at the door, and Elaina's mum peeked in. "Is it all right for me to come in?"

"I'll leave you to it then, brother." I excused myself, leaving Neil and his future mother-in-law in peace. Neil had hit the lottery with her. Caroline Morrison was a sweet lady and a loving mum. The polar opposite of my mother-in-law, I thought with a grimace. *It must be nice.*

I stepped outside and checked my Rolex again. If I made it quick, I had just enough time to get in a smoke before curtain call.

The stunning landscape in all its harsh ruggedness framed the house perfectly. Neil's place up here in Scotland was quite the countryman's establishment. I stood under a flowering tree and lit up a clove. My resolve to work on getting into some kind of treatment for my *issues* had helped with the anxiety of flashback dreams thanks to Brynne, and only her. As far as doing a thing to help me cut back on the coffin-nails? Not so much. One step at a time I told myself as I sucked it down.

I stubbed out my ciggie and looked for someplace

to get rid of the butt. I didn't want to put it in my pocket, which seemed a bit crude considering the occasion, but I might have to.

"Ethan?"

I turned around to find someone I never thought I'd ever see again. My heart dropped like a stone, and then bounced along the pavers, propelled by a momentum that seemed to have no fucking end. My past come for its due notice, I suppose.

"Sarah…" My voice cracked out her name as I took her in, right before me after so long. She was just as beautiful as ever; didn't look like she'd aged a bit. The smile she gave me did things to my heart I didn't want to face up to again. *Don't fucking smile at me, Sarah. I don't deserve it.*

When her arms came out to embrace me, I closed my eyes, terrified of what I'd feel—and also, the irony of fate, that only now, put her back into my path again.

"ARE you all right?" Brynne asked softly, her eyes looking up at me with concern.

Not really. "Yeah. Why do you ask?"

She shrugged and moved her fork around her dinner plate, doing a good job of not eating. "You seemed preoccupied during the ceremony, and now even," she said glumly.

Pull it together. "No, baby." I put my hand around her neck and pulled her under my chin for a kiss to the top of her head. "Still have the headache?"

She nodded against my jaw. I rubbed the back of the top of her neck, massaging deeply on the pressure points.

"Mmmmm, that really helps," she moaned, straightening her neck into my hand so I could work out the kinks.

"Good. I want you taking it easy at the—"

"Ethan, you haven't introduced me to your new bride," Sarah interrupted us from behind, her pleasant expression merely a mask for propriety's sake.

Fuck.

AAAAAND it begins.

So, Sarah was going for martyrdom today. Just throwing herself down on the track before a speeding train. I tried to wrap my head around her motives, but it wasn't working. She wished to meet Brynne...my *wife?* She wanted to know all about our posh wedding and honeymoon? She enjoyed hearing about the baby, and found it amusing we weren't going to know in advance if we were getting a boy or a girl? She needed to congratulate me on my good fortune with Blackstone Security?

Why? How could she bear to do any of it? I surely couldn't. I needed to get the fuck out.

But there was no place to hide here, except for the bottom of a pint. Or four. Best thing I could figure to do given the situation.

A former soldier's wedding with my pregnant bride beside me…

Getting pissed might possibly dull the edge enough I could pull off the nice-and-happy required for a marriage celebration. Or maybe not.

Rather a blessing that Brynne wasn't feeling much in the party mood actually. This way she might not notice just how fucked in the head her husband was.

I thought I'd handled Sarah's surprise visit fairly well, given I had absolutely no time to process, before I was expected to go stand up for my friend in front of a crowd of people. And with Brynne right there, glowing with new life and enjoying the moment. No fuckin' fair.

Don't say that. None of this is fair. Not for Sarah. And certainly not for Mike.

I'd been too distracted during the ceremony to pay much attention to what Brynne might be noticing. My girl could read me so well. She did not need this worry added to her plate, in addition to feeling ill already. I couldn't allow it.

I'd thought I might somehow make it through the evening, until Sarah caught me as I was getting fresh, iced water for Brynne. She came to tell me she had to leave…with tears in her eyes. She said she hoped she could have stayed for Neil's sake, but once she arrived and saw us both, it was just too hard. Too much. Too painful. So she must go.

And I started drinking.

"HOW'S your headache?" Gaby asked.

"Unfortunately for my head, still with me," I answered wryly. "One of the not-so-nice parts of pregnancy, and the fact I can't take anything for it, sucks big time." I lifted the iced water and pressed the side of the glass to my forehead.

"Well, you look beautiful if that helps," she said, picking at the skirt of her chiffon bridesmaid dress, "and you've got a pretty new dress to add to your collection of pretty dresses." She shrugged. "I'm getting quite an assortment." Elaina had asked both of us to be in her wedding, which landed Gaby her second stint as a bridesmaid in just seven short weeks. First my wedding, and now Elaina's—she must be drowning in a sea of lovey-dovey, praying for a rescue.

"You wish you could be anywhere else but here, huh?"

"Of course not. I want to be here, Bree." She gave me the look that told me so much more than the words she'd just uttered. I knew my friend, and thus was privy to information that confirmed why this would be hard for her.

"You're a beautiful liar, darling." I patted her hand affectionately. "But I know Elaina appreciates you being here for her."

"No, I'm not," she said stubbornly, taking a sip of something alcoholic that looked wonderful, and I wouldn't be having. "I don't want to be anywhere else than right here for Elaina on her wedding day."

I laughed at my best friend who never seemed to acknowledge her own beauty. Gabrielle Hargreave was one absolutely gorgeous woman, with her mahogany hair and green eyes, and a body that didn't quit, but she didn't see it. Men panted after her all the time. And there were men here right at that very moment looking at her. Ethan's cousin, Ivan, was one of them.

"So what's the deal with you and Ivan?" I swung a look over to the bar where Ethan and Ivan were chatting over beers. Lots of beers. My husband might just be getting drunk at this wedding reception. We'd both been asked to be in this wedding, just as Neil and Elaina had been in ours. I guess he was letting off some steam, and he was entitled to that. During the actual ceremony he'd seemed a little tense to me. I wondered why. It was a happy time. His best friend had just married the girl he'd loved for years. Ethan's behavior didn't make sense, even for him.

"What do you mean?" Gaby's eyes were now trained onto where Ethan and Ivan were ensconced. I didn't miss how Ivan found her the instant she looked over to the bar, either. "We met at your wedding obviously as maid of honor, and best man. We—we have been forced into each other's company."

"Forced, huh? Ivan is so sweet...and *hot*. Why wouldn't you want to be around him?" I smelled a rat with her lame explanation. And I was also fishing with my best friend. I hadn't forgotten what Ethan had told me about the night at the Mallerton Gala when the alarm went off and everyone had to flee the building in a hurry. Ethan had seen them all mussed up like maybe they had been *together*. Ethan also seemed to know the type of woman his cousin would go for, and he'd told me more than once Gaby had all the right qualities.

"Well, I—I think he is—he's very...um...Ivan is an interesting man." She twisted her cocktail napkin into the shape of a toothpick. "He told me about all of the Mallertons at his estate in Ireland. He wants me to go back there and work on cataloging the entire collection."

Ahhh, there it was. The nervous napkin

destruction, the stammering, the blush in her cheeks, all suggesting Ethan's prediction was dead-on target. "Back there?" I asked.

"Hmmm?" Her innocent look didn't fool me.

"You said, 'back there' as if you've been to his Irish estate already." I tilted my head at her. "Gaby, have you been to see Ivan's paintings and not told your *best friend* about it?"

"Um…yeah, I was sent over there by Paul Langley to check out what was there." She shook her head. "I couldn't stay, though. The timing was—bad for me." She took another sip of her drink and looked down, avoiding eye contact.

"Well maybe you will find a better time to go back then. I bet the paintings are magnificent if they're anything like my *Lady Percival*." I decided to let my probing go—for now. I could tell she was done with confession, and I didn't want to hurt her by bringing up bad memories of things she didn't need reminding.

"Yeah. I hope so." She looked up and asked honestly, "How are you dealing with your political celebrity?"

Nice topic change, Gab. My turn to embrace avoidance now. "I try not to pay attention to it," I lied. "We both had to put on a show, and we did. Now, I just want to move on and let my past stay there, you know?"

"I do know, my friend." She squeezed my hand

affectionately before heading off to find Benny, who was doing the wedding photographs.

✦

"MAY I join you?" a silky voice asked at my ear.

Dillon Carrington was indeed here, just as he'd promised when we met him in Italy. He was one of Neil's groomsmen and had all the ladies swooning. I imagined it was nothing he wasn't accustomed to already, being a celebrated racing champion and all. The dark good looks didn't hurt his chances, either. The man was quite simply gorgeous. But he knew it. "Sure, if hanging out with a pregnant chick cranky from a lack of wine is your thing." I winked at him.

He laughed and pulled up a chair. "Well, you're a stunner, pregnant or not, even if the lack of wine has made you a bit barmy. How can I help?"

I shook my head and smiled. "I'm fine, just sitting back and people-watching. It's my favorite."

"Really? I know people like to look at you in photographs."

Was he flirting with me? And if so—why on earth was he paying attention to me when he could have his pick of any single women in the room. "You've seen my photographs, Dillon?"

He pursed his lips as if he were trying to hold

back a grin. "Yes, Brynne, I have." He bowed his head in deference. "I wholeheartedly approve."

I huffed out a laugh. "Ethan doesn't."

He nodded with a tilted head as if considering. "I think I can see why he would feel that way. Ethan has territorial tendencies. He has to, in his profession, plus he's just snatched you off the market, so I can only imagine."

"Yeah, I know." I drew in a deep breath and thought about it from Ethan's perspective. What if he were the model and women saw him naked in photographs? I wouldn't like it. Honestly, I would hate it. I decided a swift subject change was needed to lift the mood. "Where's your pretty girlfriend, Dillon? Why aren't you out there dancing with her right now?"

"Oh, Gwen? She's not my girlfriend, she's just my date for this weekend." He flashed me a devilish grin that told me more than I wanted to know about Dillon Carrington's sexual skill with women. He spelled TROUBLE in straight shouty caps, and Ethan was right on target about Dillon only having *dates*. "And I'm not dancing with her right now because your husband is."

❦

DILLON laughed at my reaction. Ethan was indeed, with Dillon's "date," the leggy Gwen, who looked like she was really into dancing with *my* husband. He just looked drunk. *Oh, I don't like you at all, Gwen.*

"I was going to ask you to dance with me, but when I came over, you seemed like maybe you weren't up for a spin, and I couldn't face the possible rejection." His amber eyes twinkled naughtily.

My decision made, I snuck a sideways glance at Ethan, and stood up to smooth my dress. "Dillon, I'd love to dance with you."

Dillon's skills were such that he made me look good out there. And it was fun. When he spun me, my skirt flared out in a gauzy wave and I loved it. I felt pretty and desirable for the first time today instead of the awkward preggo bridesmaid who watched everyone else having fun while I sat around on my widening ass.

When the song changed to *Bloodstream* by Stateless, I thanked Dillon for keeping me company, and looked around for Ethan. It was one of my favorite songs and reminded me so much of how Ethan was with me. *I think I might have inhaled you—I can feel you behind my eyes—You've gotten into my bloodstream—I can feel you flowing in me.* Slow dancing to that particular song with anyone other than my man, was out of the question. I didn't even see him dancing with Gwen anymore. Where in the hell had he gone? My husband should be dancing with me at this wedding. Not some random woman who was thin and beautiful... *My body is changing very fast.*

Quite frankly, I was irritated. He'd basically abandoned me to drink at the bar with the guys, and then went off to dance with another woman. I didn't like feeling this way, and for the first time since I'd known Ethan, I could actually imagine he was avoiding me. But why? This morning he'd been fine, and later before the ceremony he'd come to check on me, worried about my headache. My caring, attentive man, as he always was with me. But then, after the ceremony moved onto the reception, he seemed distant, and went off with Ivan and Elaina's brother, Ian, for some bromance time I suppose. Was it possible all the wedding hearts and love blossoms were getting to him?

Well, he was the one who'd insisted on marrying, I reminded myself. I never demanded a ring. All Ethan—all the way, with the—let's-get-married-right-now—ridiculousness. If he was having second thoughts about his new ball-n-chain, then he was just a little goddamn late on figuring it out.

Ethan's game at the moment? Full-blown assholery to the millionth power. And a bitter disappointment for his pregnant and crabby wife.

I kissed the bride and groom, made an excuse to Gaby and Ben about my headache, and figured I'd see the rest of the crowd tomorrow at the brunch. Right now, I was ready for my head to meet my pillow. Growing a tiny human made me require a ton more sleep than usual. As

I steered for the staircase, I treated myself to a mini-tantrum—inside my head, of course—at how un-romantic this evening had been for me. Talk about a buzz-kill.

My decision in favor of sleep, over searching out wherever Ethan had gotten lost was really very easy for me. Because it'd felt like I'd been on my own all night, anyway. When I got up to our room, I changed into a warm cozy nightgown and settled into the lonely bed, feeling bereft, wondering when he would stumble up to join me. But I did *know* he would make it eventually.

That was the thing with us. I trusted Ethan even though he was being an ass. He knew the lay of the land with me. Honesty and trust were required, or there was nothing holding us together.

Good sex wasn't love.

For me, honest devotion and loyalty was love.

If Ethan ever cheated on me I would walk out his door and never look back. I knew it. He knew it.

CHAPTER 11

I gave her half an hour before following her up the stairs. I wanted to wait longer so the alcohol buzz would dull my edge a bit more, making me safer to be around. But I couldn't stand being away from her another moment. I needed my tranquillizer. Neil had said it to me before. *Brynne is your cure.* Nothing could bring me out of my hell when I felt like this...except her.

I breathed easier knowing I wouldn't have to say much. Her new rule of letting me alone to house my demons in solitude helped a great deal. Everything about Brynne helped me.

When I came into the room it was dark and she was sleeping just as I'd hoped. I ditched the tux and slipped under the sheets, settling in behind her. The first inhale of her comforting scent went up my nose and straight to my brain, immediately soothing, giving me hope to make the ugliness fade away. Best I'd felt all night, the instant I notched into the back of her neck and buried my nose in her hair.

Brynne was so generous with herself to me, she never minded when I woke her up and wanted to fuck.

I needed to fuck right now.

Drown out the guilt.

WHEN I moved down the bed and pulled back the blankets, I found her swathed in some kind of nightgown that covered her up from head to toe, and of a style maybe worn by my grandmother…when she was well into her eighties. Ugly thing was a dustbin candidate for sure. Hiding all that beauty away from my eyes only frustrated me. Being half pissed didn't help my judgment probably, but it didn't stop me. I found the place where it buttoned down to about mid chest on her, dug my fingers in between the buttons, and split that fuckin' rag right in two, all the way down to the hem. Her naked tits came into view first, and then the rest of her. I felt instantly better. My cock was bone-fucking hard.

She woke with a gasp and a scream.

"Shhhh." I clamped a hand over her mouth and my lips at her jaw. I didn't want visitors doing the ol' "is everything all right in there?" routine at this house party, since the place was crammed to the brim with them. Her eyes flared wide, and I sense she was not happy about what I'd just done, but again, that did not deter me. "It's just me getting rid of that ugly nightgown for you. I loathed it." I took my hand away and covered her lips with my mouth instead. She mumbled under my kisses at first, and tensed beneath me, but once she got a feel of my tongue inside her, she responded beautifully, softening under my body, letting me play my games, and take her. "I despised that gown, but I love you." I kissed down her throat to the hollow of her neck, onward over her sternum and then to right between her breasts. I flicked my tongue out and dragged it over to a nipple. She arched her back to bring herself closer. I swirled over her budded, pink nipple 'round and 'round until she was practically writhing beneath me.

"That's better," I told her. "I have to see my beautiful wife…every inch of you."

"Ethan?"

"Shhhh, baby," I soothed, "just feel what I'm going to give you."

I kissed my way down, giving a caress over her stomach as I went lower. Spreading her inner thighs firmly, I opened her up and enjoyed the magnificent view. She took my breath away, and she always had. Her pussy… No words for it. I inhaled, getting drunk on her intoxicating scent. Unique to Brynne, and utterly delectable, triggering my insta-need to have her.

I licked up the inside of her thighs, giving equal

attention to each one until I couldn't deny myself another second and had to have her sweet cunt under my lips. I started slowly with little licks along her smooth folds and worked in a circle, pointing my tongue like a tiny cock. She flexed against my mouth and rocked in rhythm as I built her up. I could do this all night, for as long as she was enjoying my feasting, or told me otherwise.

The beautiful sounds of quickened breath warmed my anxiety, melting away my torment, telling me of her pleasure. I slipped two fingers inside her drenched warmth, curling them up to slide into that special little cove, with the rough patch of skin where the magic happened.

She arched sharply, moaning under the onslaught of fingers and G-spot combined with tongue and clit. An explosive mixture. I had her coming for me in under two minutes, panting out my name just as I loved for her to do. *Total fucking perfect beauty.*

After a second orgasm brought her shuddering underneath my tongue, she pressed a hand to the top of my head. I knew what that meant. She was ready for some cock.

I dragged my mouth off her pussy and mounted up, folding her long limbs over my arms. My girl sighed at me in impatience when I lifted her backside up to meet my cock.

I chuckled at her frustration when I slid the shaft

of my cock along her clit for a few dragging strokes.

"I'm going to fuck you now, baby," I whispered, nudging forward. Fully aware, I lost a measure of my control the instant the bell end of my cock kissed her slippery heat, I went floating off into a haze of sex and lust, and superb fucking.

The tight squeeze of her grip around my cock as I slid in deep sucked the breath right out of me. From base to tip, she took me in, accepting the invasion I couldn't curb. I'd never curb my driving need to be inside her. Impossible. My only truly safe place in the world.

As the frenzy built, I felt her clamping down with each penetration of my cock into her slick quim. She started to wheeze and circle her hips to get the friction where she needed it to be. I pushed deeper with every downward stroke, and saw the look she gets when it's about to happen. Triumph. She got off on making me come just as much as I did with her.

My cock swelled in preparation for the blast.

Her eyes blazing up at me, I clasped her neck and held her in place, rotating my thumb around and down into her mouth. She wrapped her tongue around my thumb and sucked. My balls tightened and let go, a flood of sheer blinding pleasure washing over me as I emptied into her.

I did manage to move off to the side before I collapsed, coherent of the baby, and not wanting to crush.

Brynne breathed heavily against me, silently coming down from the peak, along with my cock still pulsing inside her. I drew my hand away from her neck, down to a breast, and filled my palm. I clearly felt her heart beating beneath the super-soft barrier of flesh. *My heart.*

"What was that?" she asked after a moment, her expression difficult to read as her eyes burned rather green in the lamp light.

"That was you being well and truly fucked by your man, my beauty," I teased, plumping the breast I was holding in my hand and giving her a slow grind of my hips.

"Not the fucking, Ethan. *That*, I understood perfectly when you ripped my nightgown off. I want to know why you abandoned me all night to get drunk at your best friend's wedding."

My cock withered, as I gained some clarity about what she might be feeling. There was hurt and sadness in her sorrowful eyes, and even the watery glistening of tears.

The feeling of euphoria vanished as I became aware of what I had just done to her.

I don't deserve her, and I never will.

I watched his smug grin fall away to be replaced with remorse. "Did something happen, Ethan? Did you decide that you made a mistake in marrying me? Are you—unhappy...with me and the baby...because my body is ch-changing?"

I had to ask him. He knew how I operated, and it was by truth. The thing was, I'd always felt that about Ethan. He'd always been so blunt and truthful to me from day one. I loved that about him. He told me what was on his mind, sharing his desires, helping me to understand what he wanted and needed. But this awkward detached behavior really confused and hurt me.

"Oh, baby...no! Fuck no!" He shook his head vehemently. "Marrying you was the best thing that's ever happened to me, Brynne. You think I am unhappy about you and the baby? Why?!"

He tightened his hand at my breast and loomed over me, his face very close, his dark blue eyes searching, flicking over me as if staring intently would reveal some mystery to him.

"You hurt my feelings. You left me there at the table and went off and started drinking. You never do that, Ethan. Why did you dance with Gwen and not with me?" The pitiful questions tumbled out of my mouth, humiliating me, but I couldn't help it. Blame the hormones.

"Who?"

"Gwen, the skinny blonde."

He didn't look any less confused.

"Dillon's *date*," I said with emphasis, wondering if he was still drunk.

"Ahh… Yeah, her," he grunted dismissively, "she pulled me out there, and I was too smashed, and too distracted to say no."

"This does not make any of what you did tonight *okay* with me." He needed to hear my unfiltered thoughts and know this sort of behavior would never fly.

"I'm so sorry, baby," he said earnestly, before dropping his mouth to mine. He kissed me softly; very gentle and very loving, settling into his pattern of our after-sex make-out session. Long drawn out sweeps of tongue and lips, with no other purpose other than showing me he did indeed love me. I did feel considerably better, I'll admit, but I was still confused about what had transpired tonight at the reception.

When he finally pulled back and gave me his eyes again, I sensed something big was going to be revealed.

"I love you so much, Brynne, and I can't make it in this life without you. I'll never regret our baby, and I'll never stop loving you, or our children. You're my life, and you're stuck with me. And you are the most beautiful woman in the world. In the fucking *world*! Do you understand me, Brynne?" He sounded harsh, but the look on his face was pleading.

"Y-yes." I sucked in a sob, feeling over-emotional and relieved, but still needing some answers from him. "S-so what happened t-tonight? Something happened, right?"

He settled on his side and faced me with his hand on my hip, as if he had to have physical contact with my body in order to tell me whatever he needed to say. "Yeah, baby, something happened." He pulled me against him and pressed his lips to my hair and breathed in deeply. "Remember the woman who wanted to meet you at dinner? Sarah?"

"Yes. She seemed very nice, and friendly. How do you know her, Ethan?" Sarah was a beautiful woman, and charming in conversation. I recalled her seemingly genuine interest in how Ethan and I had met. She'd asked about my due date, but it had all felt socially normal to me, nothing weird.

"She came to the wedding today to pay her respects I suppose, but she had to leave because it was too hard for her to see Neil and Elaina, and you and me, living our happy lives with people we love." His hand at my hip began to rub in a slow motion. "Sarah Hastings was married to someone who served in the SF with Neil and me. He didn't...m-make it out of Afghanistan."

"Oh...that's horrible. I imagine you and Neil were close to him..."

"Yeah. He was under my command—in my

squad."

Ethan appeared calm as he talked, but I felt that he was harboring some deeply held grief or guilt about this man's death in the war. I could only imagine whatever the experience had been for him, was horrific.

"You cared about him," I said gently, not wanting to ask questions that would hurt him further. It was better for me to make statements of fact, rather than ask for more than he felt comfortable sharing.

"Mike Hastings was the very best of soldiers. Strong, loyal—a fighter to the bitter end. The kind of soldier you want at your back when the shit goes FUBAR," Ethan said, in a faraway voice, weighted with respect and honor for his fallen comrade.

"I—I've heard you call out his name once...when you had a bad flashback..." I swept my lips to his chest and kissed right over his heart. I laid my ear there so I could hear his courageous heart beating against me. *My heart.*

He brought his hand up to the back of my head and rubbed into my hair, keeping me against him, allowing the comfort. "Mike. Yeah. That...m-memory about Mike is—is the worst one."

"You don't have to talk about him, Ethan, if you don't want to. Baby, please don't put yourself through it again just for my benefit."

"No, you should know. You're my wife, and you

should know why—why I'm this way."

I closed my eyes and braced for the explanation, knowing it would be something truly dreadful. "I love you, Ethan," I whispered.

"Mike was taken prisoner along with me. He suffered what I suffered for just twenty days instead of my twenty-two. Then they ex-executed him in front of me. They used him as a—a p-practice run f-for what they were planning to do to me."

I felt him swallow but his voice didn't change. He sounded eerily calm and I tensed as I imagined how Mike Hastings had met his death. I remembered very well what Ethan had told me once. The Taliban were going to behead him and show the world a video of them doing it.

"They used a big fuckin' knife and forced me to watch. They told me if I closed my eyes or looked away, they would make Mike suffer longer, cutting off parts of him that wouldn't kill him, but lengthen the agony and prolong the inevitable. This was amusement for our captors, in their senseless, fucked-up, pious war they are so fanatical about."

I cried silent tears as he told me of his experience, unable to say anything, unsure of what to do except hold onto him and be whatever he needed me to be.

"But I failed Mike. I tried—I tried so fucking hard, Brynne, not to flinch away, but I couldn't help it—"

He stopped talking. The silence grew deafening

above the steady pounding of his heart against my cheek, now drenched by my hot tears…for him, for his friend, for the helpless guilt he carried over things beyond his control.

"I love you, and I always will." There was nothing else to say to him.

He breathed in my hair at my temple and seemed to relax somewhat. After a time of quiet he asked me a question. It was painfully difficult for him to get the words out. I could hear the fear as he struggled to force the words past his lips. "Do you think there's a place, or a person somewhere that may help me?"

"Yes, Ethan, I *know* there is."

CHAPTER 12

23rd November
Somerset

My office was the best room in all of Stonewell Court. I was convinced of it. Rich oak panels on the walls framed the most magnificent window view of the ocean. It reminded me of *All Along the Watchtower*, Hendrix's cover of Dylan's song. *What princess kept her view here? How many servants did she have?* I surely felt like a princess in this house.

The Bay of Bristol stretched out before me, and on a clear day you could see all the way to the coast of Wales at the other end of the bay. Somerset had stunning country in every direction. I'd discovered that the inland landscape had commercial lavender fields. Miles and miles of purple flowers scenting the air, and so beautiful, your mind could barely accept what your eyes were seeing. I loved coming here for the long weekends, and I knew it was good for Ethan, too. He thrived in the peace of the place.

When Ethan and I had searched through all the

rooms of the house figuring what we would use them for, I'd known the instant we'd come into this one, that I wanted it. And the amazing thing was the impressive desk already in the room, confirming that others had thought of this room as excellent workplace long before me.

The desk was the second best part, after the view. A massive, English-oak, carved beast, but perfectly balanced with artful carvings that softened its bulk, making it perfectly designed in my eyes. I liked to imagine myself sitting in front of this splendid window view of the sea and working on my projects for the university, or just as a place to take a phone call, or surf the net.

Sheer perfection.

I sipped my pomegranate tea and indulged in the deep flashing blue of the ocean under the sky right out my window. I could sit here for hours I realized, but that wouldn't help me get anything accomplished—and I had plenty of stuff to do. I think I was moving into pregnancy "nesting" mode a little early. Ethan teased me about my nesting when he read about it in the *What to Expect When You're Expecting* he kept on his bedside table, and studied religiously. And my husband was not a pleasure reader like me. He read world and sports news, and trade publications, but not fiction. He read to learn and inform. I thought it was adorable the way he followed the website and read the book so he would know what my body was up to and what was coming. Ethan was so good at preparation and planning, and pretty much everything, but especially at taking care of me.

I sighed after another moment of daydreaming, knowing I had tasks that needed attention. Not my favorite, that's for sure. But then, I doubt wrangling computer cords is anyone's favorite. I got down on my hands and knees and crawled under the desk to see if there was a hole drilled in the back for a power cord to feed through. Somebody must have used it in the modern era I rationalized. But maybe not. I wondered if Robbie could help me. I braced my hand on the concave inner corner and pushed, backing myself out from under my desk, when I heard a mechanical click, and then the dusty slide of wood.

JOURNALS. Three of them stacked on the top of the desk. Leather-bound, gilded, and tied with a silk cord, the pages of which, shared the private thoughts of a young woman who'd lived a long time ago, in this very house.

When I'd untied the cord stiffened with age, and opened the first book, I was captivated from the first page. To the point I forgot about everything else and got lost in her words…

7th May, 1837

 I visited J. today. I shared my news with him. More than anything I would wish to have his understanding of my regret, but I know that it is out of the realm of possibilities until such a time as I meet my maker. Then I may know his feelings on the matter…

 …What shall be the price of Guilt? Just five letters in a word that buries me with its weight.

 …My bitter regret that now must always be born in an endless silence that has broken the hearts of all those I ever loved.

 …Today I also gave my agreement to marry a man who says he wants nothing more than to care for me and to allow him to cherish me.

 …So I will go to live at Stonewell Court and make my life with him, but I am very afraid of what awaits me. How will I ever rise to the standard of what is expected?

 …Darius Rourke doesn't yet understand that I do not deserve to be cherished by any man. I am torn, but alas, I am unable to deny his wishes for me, just as I was unable to deny my beloved Jonathan…
M G

Marianne George, who later became Rourke, upon her marriage to a Mr. Darius Rourke, in the summer of 1837.

The hair on the back of my neck tingled as I

looked up from the journal, and out at the picturesque view. The coincidence was unbelievable.

My book of Keats, the first edition of poems, given to me by Ethan on the night he proposed, had belonged to this same Marianne as well. How could I ever forget, *For my Marianne. Always your Darius. June 1837,* in the elegant ink scrawl of an earlier era, as an inscription? A lover's gift. I cherished what Darius had written to Marianne. So simple, yet so very pure in the sense of how he saw her. He loved her, and yet, for whatever the reasons, Marianne had felt unworthy of his love. Guilt weighed down on her. As it does for me. *As it does for Ethan.*

And now we were living in their house? I could hardly believe it. She mentioned Jonathan—the name carved on the mermaid angel statue down in garden, facing soulfully out to sea. I realized now, the statue was a memorial for her lost Jonathan, and not a grave. Because he had no grave. Jonathan had been lost out there in the beautiful and sometimes terrible sea. She loved him…and then he'd drowned. And Marianne felt she was the one accountable for what had happened to him.

She loved him…and then he'd drowned. I understood Marianne's pain better than most people could. I understood it because, I too, longed for the release of my own guilt. Probably wouldn't ever happen for me. Some things just have to be accepted even so the outcome will never change. Because the fact remained; I knew what it meant to feel responsible for the loss of someone you loved…and would never see again in this life.

Yes, I sensed him watching over me, but that didn't take away the enormous loss I felt from missing him. The hole in my heart that his death created was still a cavern. The guilt I wrestled with daily, still feeling it was mostly my fault, remained within me. I missed my dad. I hadn't realized just how much his love and support had protected me until I experienced the loss of it. I missed his presence. I missed his love. I just missed him.

Dad, I miss you so much…

As if to shake me out of my sad thoughts, I felt a kick and then a nudge. I smiled and rubbed my expanding belly. "Well hello there, butterfly angel."

My angel poked me in the ribs for an answer, making me laugh at the timing. The movements didn't feel like butterfly wings anymore at twenty-six weeks, but the name had stuck in my head. "I suppose you're telling me you want to eat, which means I need to put some food in, right?"

"Brilliant child we have, baby, and I agree wholeheartedly. You do need to eat," Ethan said behind me, draping his big hands on my shoulders and inhaling deeply. He scraped his beard along my neck as he nuzzled the sensitive spot with kisses. I leaned back into him and tilted my neck for better access, and an inhale of my own—he always smelled so amazing. My man liked to smell me, too. Everywhere. A bit kinky, but it showed how he bared his honesty with me. I liked honest. I needed honest in order to function in our relationship.

"Ahh, you've caught me talking to myself again."

"Not yourself, but little lettuce, and that makes all the difference. I don't think we need to ship you off to Bethlem Hospital just yet," he quipped.

"We have a lettuce baby this week?" I shook my head at how funny it was to me that he could memorize every fruit and vegetable on that prenatal website. He was right every single time, too. I was starting to think he might have a photographic memory. Ethan remembered everything, while I was getting "pregnancy brain" and forgetting just about everything I'd ever learned. I felt another jab. "Here, feel. Baby is kicking right now."

He spun the chair and knelt in front of me, quickly pushing my shirt up and the waistband of my leggings down, to expose my bump. I pointed to the spot where the action was happening and we both watched. It took a minute, but then the slow roll of what was most likely a tiny foot, poked my skin out as clear as day, before retreating back inside the space just as quickly.

"Awww, did you see that?" he asked in wonderment.

"Um yeah," I nodded, "I felt it, too."

He kissed over the spot very gently and whispered, "Thanks for looking out for your mum and seeing that she eats on time." Then he looked up at me with a serious expression—not stern, but not smiling either—just intense and full of emotion.

"What is it?" I asked.

"You are utterly amazing, you know that?"

I brought my hand up to his cheek and held it there. "Why am I?"

"Because of everything you've given to me. Of what you can do." He turned his eyes down again, framing my belly with both of his palms. "Creating life inside here." He flipped his eyes back up to me. "For loving me as I am."

My heart hitched in a small stab of pain at the last part he mentioned. Ethan was struggling still, with what he'd revealed to me about Mike's horrific torture when he was a prisoner. I hated to think about it, but I could only imagine how exponentially more painful it was for Ethan to remember, than it was for me to hear about and imagine. Ethan had lived it. And couldn't forget, because his subconscious forced him to relive the terror at its whim. But I was working on finding a therapy placement for him through Dr. Roswell—something he felt comfortable with, and could lead him through helpful techniques and methods to ease some of his torment. I refused to accept any other alternative for him. Ethan was going to find some relief, I was bound and determined.

"I don't want you any other way than how you are. You are just what you are supposed to be." I leaned down to kiss him on the lips, but he met me first, engulfing me in a deep kiss that left me breathless when he finally pulled away.

"Now, if little lettuce wasn't insisting upon food right now, I would have to carry you off somewhere, missus, and show you a really good time." He raised his brows at me saucily before restoring my leggings and shirt back to their original state with determined efficiency. "But, alas, that is not the case." He stood first, then helped me up by the hand, and then bringing it to his mouth for a soft kiss. "After you, my lady."

"Such the gentleman right now, Mr. Blackstone," I said as I went ahead of him. "What's the occasion?"

He smacked me sharply on the ass as an answer.

"Oh!" I squealed, "You did *not* just spank my ass, Blackstone!"

He laughed the deep laugh I loved to hear and leapt out of my reach. "I am afraid I did, baby, now move that spectacular American *ass* of yours down to the kitchen so we can feed you."

"Payback's gonna be fun for me," I said, looking back over my shoulder and narrowing my eyes.

"Promise?" he said at my ear. "What are you

going to do?"

"Oh…I don't know. Maybe something…like this—" I spun around and grabbed his crotch, finding my target easily, giving a little squeeze to his prized possessions. "A tug on your balls for a slap to my ass sounds about fair."

The look on his face was priceless. And the very surprised open mouth.

"I have you by the balls, Blackstone," I reminded him.

He laughed and leaned down to kiss me. "This is not new information to me, my beauty."

"IT'S a surprise, I told you. You have to trust me." I led her along carefully, a silk scarf over her eyes serving as a blindfold. "I want to show you before everyone begins swarming down upon us for your Thanksgiving."

My girl had decided that she wanted to do a Thanksgiving dinner at our place and invite everyone to join in the US holiday we didn't officially celebrate in England, but with such strong influence from our American friends across the pond, was certainly gaining momentum in the UK. Brynne wanted a nice house party to serve as a housewarming of sorts, so we were hosting—and would be circled in another half day. My dad and Marie were traveling up together, as were Neil and Elaina. Fred, Hannah and the kids of course, plus Clarkson and Gabrielle. We'd have a house crammed with guests and I would have to share my girl with everyone else for a few days.

I never wanted to share her.

She sniffed the air. "I smell cloves so we must be near your office?"

No more smokes in the house.

I was back to my once-a-day habit after my slip the night of the Senator's—*cocksucking bloody serpent—* ultimatum. Make that, Vice-President of the United States of America. Or he would be come January, once the new president was installed in the White House. Colt-Oakley had indeed won the US election earlier in the month by a sweeping margin. Having a hideously wounded soldier for a son was a helluva way to stir patriotism and win votes. And apparently, it was inconsequential if the same son abused young girls with his friends at parties, and made videos of it happening. The landslide was no surprise for any of us.

Brynne seemed resigned to putting her past behind her for good, and for that I was very grateful. She didn't offer much about Oakley, nor of their meeting, to me. She had said she'd felt less troubled by the visit than expected, but I hoped she'd worked through it with Dr. Roswell, because I couldn't bear the idea of her suffering anymore because of his problems. That hospital visit was hard enough on me, so I couldn't imagine how she felt having to see him, speak to him...and touch him. I closed my eyes and shoved the thoughts of Lance Oakley down and away. I breathed in my girl's intoxicating scent in front of me and focused on what I wanted to show her instead.

"You are relentless right now. I forget sometimes just how competitive you are." Which was straight-up truth. Brynne was a scrapper at her core. A girl who went in with her fists up—ready to deal a blow, or take a hit on the chin. I loved it, and thought it made her just that much hotter. "And I think it's fucking hot, baby."

She laughed softly at my last comment, the sexy sound of her making my cock bone hard and my mind race with possibilities.

"All right, we're here," I said at her ear, positioning her body exactly how I wanted so the view would be the best it could be when she saw the surprise. "And I think you should know that I've been waiting for this for six months. Six long months I've thought about this moment," I said dramatically.

"That *is* a long time, Ethan, I agree with you. Kinda feels like I've been waiting six months to get this blindfold off."

I tapped her lips with a finger, and then traced around them slowly. "Such a smart mouth, baby, and I have busy plans for it later…but right now I want you to see the surprise, so I suppose I'll take this blindfold off you now." I began unknotting the scarf as her breathing picked up the pace. My words had turned her on. "This silk scarf is sexy as hell on you, by the way. I think I should remember to use it again sometime," I whispered at her neck.

"Mmmm," she moaned very softly. Just a low breathy sound that told me a lot about her true feelings regarding the blindfold. I wouldn't forget.

"Your surprise," I said, pulling the scarf away.

She blinked up at the portrait of herself, silently observing. I wondered if she saw it as I did. The mile-long legs pointing straight up with crossed ankles, the arm shielding her breasts, the strategically splayed fingers between her legs, hair spread out on the floor to the side.

The same image Tom Bennett had sent along in an email to me, when he asked for my help in keeping his daughter safe. The captivating photograph of her I'd seen in the gallery the night I met her, and bought on impulse, not knowing the gallery required six months of display before they would release it me. The portrait of my beautiful American girl—now in my sole possession.

Utterly breathtaking.

"You finally have it." Her voice was low and soft

as she studied the huge canvas taking up the dominant wall in my office study at Stonewell.

"I do indeed."

"Having this picture of me really means a great deal to you, Ethan." She leaned her body into mine as we both looked at the image.

"Oh, yes it does."

"Why?" she asked.

"Well, this image was the first part of you my eyes ever looked upon. I saw this picture and knew I had to have it. It was just a defining moment I can't really explain properly, but one I understand perfectly."

I rubbed up and down her arms slowly, dropping my lips down to the base of her neck. I flicked my tongue out for a taste of her skin, loving how she tilted and exposed her neck for me. So generous all the time, she never ceased to amaze me.

"I had never met a collector before that night I met you," she said wistfully. "The idea that you'd bought my portrait, and then were meeting me in person…was a very defining moment for me, too. That night—you standing there in your dark grey suit—the way you looked at me from across the room—was something I will never forget as long as I live."

Her words shot straight to the center of me. "I couldn't forget that moment even if I tried, Brynne. It's seared into my memory."

"Why, Ethan?"

"Come here." I turned her so I could look into those beautiful brown-green-grey eyes of hers and rubbed my thumbs over her cheekbones. "I couldn't forget you that night because when I saw you in person for the first time…it was the moment I came alive again."

Her eyes got the glassy look in them. When she feels a great deal of emotion I see it in her, so I knew my words were something meaningful to her. They were true. Seeing Brynne that first time…brought me back to life somehow, some way, and none of it was planned or expected. It just happened that way.

"It's true. You made me want to live, at a time when I knew I'd never really thought about, or cared much about, what the future held," I repeated.

"I love you, Ethan."

"I love you more, my beauty."

Her expression changed from emotion to something else. Something just as wonderful in my opinion—a sultry, *I-want-you* look.

"So, you said something about plans to keep my mouth busy," she hummed in a low voice, her eyes darkening as the lids lowered slightly.

"Are you offering, baby?" I managed to ask without my voice cracking too badly.

She dropped to her knees on the thick Oriental carpet beneath us, and gave me the most excellent response. With her equally excellent and very busy mouth.

⸎

"BRYNNE, my darling, you are to be congratulated for an outstanding meal. To Thanksgiving," my dad toasted enthusiastically with his glass of wine, "which I say is a lovely idea that I think we should repeat every year. Make it a tradition for this family."

"I wholeheartedly agree, Jonathan," Marie began. "Yes, my sweet Brynne, it was so lovely. It's been a long time since I've enjoyed an American Thanksgiving meal as you've prepared it with the yams and the cranberry sauce. Fetches back some really happy memories for me. I am so glad you decided to bring Thanksgiving to us, and I would love to make it our new tradition, as Jonathan said." She glanced over at my dad with a look of total devotion.

I knew Brynne's great aunt was half American by birth, but had spent all of her adult life in England. Marie had also caught the eye of my father. I wasn't sure exactly what was going on between the two of them, but I had a pretty good idea. I'd know after tonight for sure, depending on what rooms they used or didn't use for sleeping.

Everyone went 'round the table in turn, giving

their toasts and acknowledging my girl for her efforts, as they should. Even Zara gave her sincere appreciation for the pumpkin pie, which reminded her a bit of gingerbread but much "squishier."

Brynne thanked them all for coming to share it with us, blushing under their praise, so graceful and humble. She was an accomplished cook, but this I already knew. She had been cooking for me as soon as we'd gotten together and I just chalked it up to my tremendous capacity for luck in getting a girl who was good at everything she did.

There were two areas of my life when I'd been blessed with luck. One of them was at cards—for a time—until I left it behind me. The other was in finding her. And that gift was for forever—until I drew my last breath.

"I have a toast," I said, raising my glass. Looking at all the faces of my family and our friends who'd come to be with us, and share in a celebration of thanks together, it all felt very fitting.

I realized thankfulness *was* my truth for the first time.

"To my beautiful American girl, for reminding us all to be thankful." I put my eyes solely on her. "But mostly me...because she's helped me to see all of the blessings in my life I didn't notice before. She's the reason I have anything at all to be thankful for." I spoke the truth out loud for everyone to hear. "She is *my* thanksgiving."

Part Three

WINTER

As the winter winds litter London with lonely hearts
Oh the warmth in your eyes swept me into your arms
Was it love or fear of the cold that led us through the night?
For every kiss your beauty trumped my doubt

Mumford & Sons ~Winter Winds

CHAPTER 13

13th December
London

I texted Ethan and wondered if he'd make it before my name was called by Dr. Burnsley's receptionist. It wasn't like him to miss a prenatal check-up. In truth, Ethan was probably more into all the details than me. He spent more time on the website and reading the book than I did, for sure. He was always telling me little snippets and factoids he learned from his research, about how our baby was doing and the developmental stages. I teased him relentlessly about being a super nerd who knew "*everything* about birthin' babies"—to quote Prissy from *Gone With the Wind*—and as long as he was the expert he could just give me all the info, saving me the work of looking it up on my own.

Jokes aside, it really wasn't like him to forget to message me, or call. I tried once more with a text. **Is there a problem? Where r u?**

I wondered if he would still meet me for lunch. We had a little routine after seeing Dr. Burnsley—lunch somewhere in the city, before he had to return to his office, which was keeping him busier than ever. He'd be leaving for the XT Winter Europe Games on an important assignment for the King of Something-burg right after New Year's. Ethan didn't seem thrilled about the job of babysitting a royal crown prince at an international sporting event, but when the king asked for him personally, I think he pretty much had no choice but to say yes. I couldn't go with him to Switzerland anyway, because flying in the final trimester was a no-go. I'd be here on my own, but it was only for a week. I planned to use the time to get the final touches on the nursery finished up. Make that, *nurseries*—plural. I had two homes to get prepared by the end of February.

I decided I would go shopping once I was finished here, with or without Ethan. Originally, I'd thought that it would be a good day to get some Christmas shopping done. Only twelve days left to pull it all together, and the presents wouldn't wrap themselves.

"Brynne Blackstone." The nurse ticked something off on her chart, and held the door open for me. "Go ahead and leave a urine sample and then I'll take your weight." She smiled sweetly, probably to counter the stink eye she usually got from pregnant women who desperately needed to do the first task, as much as they dreaded having to do the second one.

Fun times.

REPLAYING the statistics Dr. Wilson has just rattled off to me didn't really inspire a great deal of optimism for my future. One in five firefighters; one in three teenage survivors of car crashes; one in two female rape victims; two in three prisoners of war. Especially the last two items on that wretched list. What in the fuck did that say about Brynne and me? PTSD sufferers. Damaged souls who had somehow fallen into each other's lives by a twist of fate. Brynne was owning up to her demons, and worked with Dr. Roswell to find a way to cope with what had happened to her. She amazed me with her strength—very British in her methodology—just like the WWII poster the doc had plastered above his desk: KEEP CALM AND CARRY ON. Brave and beautiful was my girl. Straight-up truth.

Was there some hope for me, too? I wanted there to be. Now, I craved to find a way to be free of the fucking curse that had woven itself into the darkest caverns of my psyche. I needed relief so badly.

I needed it so I could be the husband and father I had to be for Brynne, and for our little one.

"So, I'm listening." I gave the doc my focus and

thought about why I was here with Combat Stress Psychiatrist, Gavin Wilson, at his nondescript office in Surrey, discussing the merits of a course of Cognitive Behavioral Therapy.

"The goal is not to force you to dwell on events in your past, but to gain insight into your emotional state of mind at present. This is not a "lie on the couch and tell all" type of therapy, Ethan."

Thank fuck-all for that. I took in a slow breath and felt relief at what he'd just told me. Talking terrified me. If I spoke of it, I'd go numb, freezing back in time to that place, hearing those voices, smelling the piss, and puke, and shit, feeling the cold, seeing the knife and the …rivers of blood. I'd only told Brynne a fraction of the worst part, because I'd felt so strongly that she deserved to know what I carried around, but it pained me terribly to share all of the ugliness with her. The shit was too dark, too horrible, just too fucking much for her to have to be burdened with.

"That's good then, I think. So, how does the programme work for somebody like me?" I asked.

"CBT tends to deal with the here and now—over the events during your service in the BA that led to why you're sitting here talking to me."

"My wife…she's had a traumatic event in her past, too. I worry that if I give into this—fuck, I don't even know what to call it—my worst flashback memory, then I won't be strong enough for her when she needs my support. We're expecting our first child at the end of February..." I trailed off, wishing I didn't sound so pathetically weak, but figured I should be honest with the doc.

"Congratulations to you both." He wrote something down on a legal pad. "Is your wife in therapy?"

I nodded. "For over four years. She tells me she can't imagine not having her doctor visits."

"And you support your wife in seeking treatment and help through psychiatric therapy?" Dr. Wilson asked. I had an idea of where he was going with his line of questioning.

"Of course I support her. It helps her and that's most important."

His mouth turned up on one side. "I am sure your wife wants you to have the same level of support that she has, Ethan. But the decision will have to be yours, of course."

I know she does. "So what will we do when I come here?"

"CBT recognizes that events in your past have shaped the way you currently think and behave. In particular, for you, from what you have told me, is, delayed-onset PTSD. We'll explore what is bringing your flashbacks to the forefront more intensively now versus immediately after the event." *I know why.* "And even so, CBT does not dwell on the past, we'll aim toward finding solutions of how to change your current thoughts and behaviours so that you can function better now, and in the future. It's the emotional processing of your past, rather than simply reliving it, which is key."

I nodded and absorbed his explanation. I felt ambivalent, not particularly optimistic this would work on me, but in no way critical either. I liked the doc. I especially liked his non-bullshit way of explaining things. He didn't promise a miracle. *Because there won't be one coming to you.* My miracle had been used up over seven years ago…on the twenty-second day. I knew that. I accepted the gift as I'd received it. Dr. Gavin Wilson had served in the same army as me. He was a comrade in arms of sorts. If anyone could help me, it was probably going to be someone like him.

We got down to the nuts and bolts of things and by the end of our time, I was feeling somewhat lighter about my decision. I was given a bit of homework to do as well.

CHECKING my watch as I hurried out of the building, I knew I had at least an hour of travel time ahead of me in order to make it all the way across town to meet Brynne at Dr. B's. Highly doubtful I could manage it. I patted my pocket for my mobile, and remembered I didn't have it on me. I'd been so distracted about my first visit to the Combat Stress Centre, I'd left it somewhere. *Bloody shitting hell.* This was precisely the sort of crap I did not need right now—my number-one worry. Distraction. The motherfucking worst thing in my line of work. I absolutely could not allow for distractions, or I wouldn't be able to function at my job. Impossible. All of this dredging up of phantom memories was fucking with my day-to-day routine. I should have my mobile on me right now so I could contact Brynne. I needed let her know I'd be late, or she would worry.

As I stepped into the hallway I saw *her* again—leaving another office, a different therapist than Dr. Wilson, but obviously someone who did similar work with their patients. It made sense actually. *There's your homework.* Seek forgiveness from those I believe I have harmed. My first step toward accountability in dealing with my problems would lead me to the same place as her. "Sarah, wait," I called out.

LEAVING Dr. Burnsley's office, I headed for the elevators. Still nothing from Ethan, and I could only imagine how bummed he would be that he'd missed my check-up. I would have to tease him—reminding him of all the geeky bonding time with Dr. B and the lame sex jokes he'd squandered.

I didn't pay attention to the person who got in the elevator with me because I was busy checking my unanswered texts and messaging Len to let him know I was finished with the doctor. Not until he said my name. "Brynne."

I knew who it was, though. I looked up slowly, starting from the floor. I saw his legs, both the prosthetic, and the real one, his muscled thighs, the cut body and wide shoulders, the very dark eyes, the handsome face that now looked so very different to me.

"Lance. W-what are you doing here?" My voice cracked.

"Don't be upset, please, but I saw you go in to your appointment, so I waited for you to come out."

"Are you—are you following me around London?"

"No." His eyes flickered for an instant but then he shook his head. "I was with my own doctor—getting measured for a permanent prosthetic."

"Oh." I didn't know what to say to him. Lance had lost his leg, and despite our painful history, I still felt sympathy about what had happened. It was as if my brain just couldn't turn the "empathetic" part off completely. It was still plugged in, grinding away, churning up emotions and memories from long ago. *Lance Oakley just followed me into my elevator and told me how he's been waiting for me to come out.* My appointment had lasted an hour and a half with all the waiting in the lobby, and then more waiting in the examination room. Why would he hang around for an hour and a half? I gave a mental *fuck it* and asked, "So why did you wait for me, Lance?"

"I told you before, at the hospital, but you didn't come back." He looked down at the floor and then back up at me. "I know it's way too much for me to ask, but, Brynne, I really need to talk to you. The question is, will you talk to me?"

"I heard what you whispered to me in your hospital bed, but I don't know if I can." And I truly didn't know. Part of me was curious as to why he wanted to tell me he was sorry for what he'd done. Honestly, I was completely thrown for a loop by the whole thing. Lance coming to apologize was never on the menu of possibilities in my mind. Never ever. So when he appeared before me, as he was in the elevator, looking very sincere, I was really struggling with seeing him again. I instinctively put my hand over my belly.

The elevator door dinged and opened. I stepped out and he followed me into the lobby, his limped gait very pronounced from his injury, making me feel awkward and completely confused about what to do.

"I understand." He nodded sadly. "I—I know you're pregnant…and I don't want to upset you or anything, but—" He stopped talking and lifted a hand in defeat.

"But what, Lance?" I wasn't going to let him off the hook so easily. He approached me, so I figured he should explain.

"You don't owe me anything, Brynne. I don't want to hurt you or disrupt your life, but it really bothers me that you don't know the truth about me—about what happened that night."

"Umm…well, I know what happened to me, Lance. I saw it on video." I looked away, unable to face him when I said the last word.

"I know," he said softly. "I am so sorry for hurting you, and I'd like the chance to explain myself." He blew out a deep breath. "I do know a little about what you've been through. Your mother told me some of it when I tried to contact you, but your dad wouldn't let me see you at all, and then you went away to New Mexico. I accepted that you probably couldn't see me, so I stayed away from you on purpose. I was in Iraq, anyway," he said bitterly. After a moment of silence he continued, "I—I heard about your dad's passing. I remember how close you were to him. I'm very sorry for your loss."

My goddamn tears will be the death of me. I swiped at my eyes and tried to pull it together so I could make it out of this building and not look like I'd been crying if Ethan showed up. Or Len.

In fact, Len was walking right toward me now, with the look on his face that meant my meeting with Lance was at an end.

Lance saw him too.

"I—I'm sorry, I have to go now. Lance, good luck," I said lamely. I had nothing else to give him. I felt empty and confused. I wanted Ethan.

"All right." He looked at me stoically, and nodded one time. Then he pressed a card into my hand. "Please think about it," he whispered, before turning and walking away, his uneven step a tangible sign of just how much Lance Oakley had changed in the last seven years.

❧

I told Len to drop me in Knightsbridge so I could do my shopping. There was no way I could go home at that point. I needed to clear my head and process my feelings. One thing was certain—I didn't want to share with Ethan about my meeting with Lance. It would only upset him and make him territorial, and that wouldn't do him, or me, any good. I should call Dr. Roswell though and get an earlier appointment. I needed impartial advice, and

Ethan would be anything but impartial. I still didn't know where he was or why he'd missed my check-up today, I thought glumly, feeling sorry for myself.

I went through the motions of selecting gifts for people, determinedly focusing on one simple task so I complete it. A silk robe for my mother in traitorous yellow seemed appropriate. It was really quite beautiful and she would probably love it. If I had them ship directly from the store, it might even make its way to her in time for Christmas. I didn't know how I felt about my mom right now, especially after Lance's confession that he'd spoken to her about me years ago. I wondered how that conversation had gone. Did she know something I didn't know? The niggling of doubt scratched at me like a persistent itch. His card was in my purse. His number was there. I could call him and ask, and he would probably tell me.

We'd only spoken one time since our blowout conversation. I wondered how disappointed she was that my former boyfriend's father was now the Vice President, and could realistically be the President one day. Must be a bitter pill for her. If I'd sucked up what Lance did to me all those years ago, I guess she'd hoped we might reconcile in time. I believed it was the reason she resented Ethan so much. She knew her plans were blown and there wouldn't be any fancy White House parties for her to attend. I'd been snatched away by a Brit who didn't give a *maiden queen's first fuck*—direct from his mouth—if Lance Oakley's father was emperor of the motherfucking world, let alone a US political figure. Ethan had impregnated me, and married me; even my mother could see that her fantasy was nothing but dust in the wind. Those two were like gasoline and matches ready to combust when they were forced together anyway. So sad for me. She would be my child's grandmother and couldn't stand the sight of my husband.

My phone chirped. Finally, I thought as I dug it out of my purse. *Unknown number?* **Baby I'm so sorry missed ur appt. Long story. w/o my mobile atm. This is Sarah Hasting's mobile I'm using. Where r u now? xoE**

Sarah Hasting's? I knew exactly who she was. And thought it very strange that Ethan was with her when he should have been with me. I remembered how upsetting her presence had been for him at the wedding, thus my concern about her trying to dig her claws into him to soothe her grief. I respected the military loyalty, but it wasn't fair for Ethan to suffer more because of her loss. If she was guilting him into talking about her husband I would have to set the woman straight. I felt myself bristle as I replied to his text, but remembered that it wasn't Ethan's phone that would receive my message, so I kept it neutral. But I made sure to add Sarah's number into my contacts, before I answered him. **It's fine. I'm**

at Harrod's xmas shopping. Len is here w/ me. –B

He answered me right away. **On my way to find you now. Meet at Sea Grill? E**

Well, if you say so, Mr. Blackstone, I thought, as I replied with an abrupt: **ok.** I tried to temper my irritation but something just felt off to me, and once again, my insecurities rushed to the surface to fill me with doubt.

I paid for my purchases and handed the loot over to Len who would get it all home for me. Then I arranged for gift wrap and delivery of my mother and Frank's gifts with the concierge, and headed down to the Sea Grill to wait for Ethan.

I sipped my cranberry tea in the restaurant and ruminated about my weird day. Remembering the card Lance had pressed upon me; I pulled it out and studied it. Cell phone and email on the front, along with his name and US Army contact info. I turned it over and saw a handwritten message I hadn't noticed before. *Please let me make it right, Brynne.*

I looked up and saw Ethan had arrived and was making his way over to my table, a large bouquet of lavender flowers in his hand. Shoving Lance's card away quickly, I wondered just how guilty my husband was feeling, deciding he needed to bring flowers as a peace offering.

I should appreciate his gesture, I scolded myself. Except I didn't.

"SO what happened to you?" she asked, her eyes giving nothing away as to the nature of her true feelings. The flowers were accepted and sniffed appreciatively, but we were in public and Brynne was reserved. Maybe she really felt like bashing the whole lot over my head. *You fucked up*. All I could do was hope she'd forgive me for my massive cock-up.

"I left the flat this morning sans my mobile. Sorry 'bout that."

"That is not like you, Ethan." She didn't look up from her menu when she spoke. *Yeah…you're in the shithouse*.

"No, it isn't. I'm afraid I was distracted when I left."

"And why was that?" She turned her menu over, studying it as if it were a rare book in the British Library Collection.

I desperately wished I'd had a chance for a smoke before racing over here. "Well, I didn't tell you because I wasn't sure I would be accepted"—she set down her menu and finally looked up at me—"but I had my first consultation with a Dr. Wilson at the Combat Stress

Centre this morning." Brown eyes stared at me from across the table. "Right, well...the centre is all the way out in Surrey, and I was leaving the offices to come meet you for Dr. B's appointment, and ran into Sarah. She uses the CSC as well. I was hideously late by that point, and had no way to reach you, so I borrowed Sarah's mobile—"

"—You found someone?" she interrupted, her face now full of the spark and fire I loved to see. I felt instantly better.

I nodded. "I did, baby. I'm giving Dr. Wilson a crack at me."

She reached her hand across the table. "I'm so glad. *So glad* to hear you telling me this, Ethan. It's the best news I've heard all day," she said, pulling my hand up to her cheek.

I sensed something more than my tardiness was worrying my girl. "Why? Did everything go all right at Dr. B's? Anything I need to know, Brynne?"

She pursed her lips and slowly rocked her head from side to side. "Nothing to report from Dr. B. Twenty-nine-week-old, acorn-squash baby, growing steady. All systems still a go." She gave me a slow wink.

That's my sexy girl. "So, you're saying Dr. B is still my best mate?" She laughed at me silently, loving to tease me about cutting me off. It was funny—and it wasn't. We'd just have to be more creative when the time came to drop the sex. I could stand it if I had her close by me, to touch, and to smell. Intimacy was so much more than just gettin' off. I'd learned this lesson well in the short time since I'd found my Brynne.

"Yes, he's still your friend. But, I want to know about your visit to the Combat Stress Centre." She smiled at me, completely back to her bright happy self. "Tell me about Dr. Wilson. I want to know everything."

How can I tell you everything, my beautiful darling? How? How can I ever do that to you?

I wished I could tell her everything, but I doubted I would ever be able to.

CHAPTER 14

24th December
London

"**S**he's beautiful, she's smart, she's sexy as hell, and she's brilliant with the nosh." I came up behind her and plastered myself against her body as she worked at the countertop from the kitchen. "Treats everywhere," I said, snagging a sugar biscuit in the shape of a bird and popping it in my mouth. "Sweets, and…you." I grabbed a handful of her arse and gave a squeeze as the buttery confection melted away in my mouth.

"Thief," she said.

"You love me in spite of my thievery." I nuzzled my nose at the back of her ear.

"I do, it's true. The very first thing you thieved was my heart," she said, turning to meet my lips for a sweet kiss, "and I don't ever want it back."

"Good thing, because it's all mine," I muttered before plundering between her lips with my tongue.

"And you say the nicest things to me."

"But they're all true," I said, gathering her to face me, my hands loosely clasped low at her back. "You are beautiful." Another deep kiss. "Wickedly smart." I dragged my lips down her jaw and to her neck. "So sexy you make me burn." I moved my mouth lower to cleavage that was growing by the day. "And a most accomplished kitchen-witch." I ground my hips forward into hers, giving her a good feel of exactly how much I *appreciated* all of her talents.

"ONE year ago today we passed each other in an aquarium shop, having no idea we would come to this place in our lives together." I ran my fingers over Ethan's arm as we lay sprawled on the sofa on our sides, watching the lights on the tree framed by the city lights of London. "Did you remember?"

"Oh, yeah. I've remembered very well ever since the day we figured it out. Every time I look at Simba in his tank, I remember." He rubbed my belly in a circle, his hands touching me anywhere he could comfortably reach in our position. "And especially with my birthday present, which is perfect by the way. I'm sure even Simba agrees."

"I'm glad you like her, baby. You're a hard fellow

to buy for. Dory is the perfect girlfriend for Simba though, and he definitely needed a good woman to keep him in line."

He chuckled. "Just like me."

"That's right, but you still went way overboard for my birthday. You buy me a luxury car and I get you a new fish."

"I love my new fish," he said indignantly, "a blue tang for my birthday was my greatest desire."

I laughed at his silliness, loving that my serious guy could joke and tease with me so easily. Despite his life experiences, Ethan was blessed with a wonderful sense of humor that I cherished in him. He could make me laugh as easily as he could make me burn hot. A uniquely talented man.

"So, really, today is sort of an anniversary for us when you think about it," I said.

"One year." He inhaled heavily at my neck. "I didn't even get a good look at you, but I do remember your purple hat and scarf, and of course, how taken you were by the Christmas Eve snowstorm."

Considering it was winter and we were naked on the living room sofa, I was surprised at how warm I felt, with absolutely no uncomfortable chill in the room. Hot thumping sex and a radiating furnace plastered against my backside, in the form of my husband, worked wonders, apparently. "Well, the snow was magically beautiful, and you've got to understand—a Christmas snowfall for a Cali girl is probably a once in a lifetime occurrence."

"You never know, now that you live here, it might snow again some Christmas." His lips brushed the back of my neck.

"True." I shivered under his lips making trails on my naked skin. "I also remember being jealous of the woman who got to smell you all the time, and it's funny, but I didn't look at you, either. If I had, I would've known you the night of Benny's show."

He kissed along the top of my shoulder. "Ben's show—best night of my life."

"Not for me," I said, snuggling more deeply against him. "I'm pretty sure right now is the best night of my life."

"Mmmm…you don't mind we aren't out at some party tonight being festive for the season?"

"Um, no, not at all. Besides, we'll have a full day of it tomorrow at your dad's house."

"I rather wish we'd spent Christmas at Stonewell instead of here," he said softly, one hand sliding up my torso to fondle a breast, lifting the weight and circling the nipple. "But we couldn't have done this…so, maybe not."

I laughed at his logic. "Yeah, buckets of paint and power tools pose a problem for finding comfortable places to maneuver a shag." We'd actually considered spending the holidays in the country, but the major renovations underway at Stonewell helped us make the decision to stay in London instead. Here, things were mostly organized, with the exception of the conversion of a spare bedroom into a nursery.

"I imagine I would've found a way to ravish you amid all that bulky equipment," he said low at my ear, as he thrust against my ass with a hot length of maleness wanting more of what we'd done already.

Once was never enough for Ethan, and I was perfectly fine with that. I hoped his need for me never went away. I don't think I would thrive without it.

❧

"I want this," he rasped, two of his fingers plying my back entrance with determined pressure, sending jolts of arousal firing to all of my erogenous zones.

"Yes…okay." Two words and I was finished with talking. The most conversation I could manage in my heightened state of stimulation. The anticipation of what he would do to my body sent me off into a sexual haze of need and desire, rendering me unable to vocalize much at all. I never worried about what he'd do to me during sex. No matter whatever it was, he would make it good. Ethan made sure.

"You take my breath away," he purred from

behind, where he was working to prepare me to take him in. I knew he was staring, getting turned on by the sight of me on my knees and bowed forward. I felt the slick drops of lube he pumped from the bottle to help ease the way. He was thick and wide, and perfect, but I still appreciated the lubrication.

His hands gripped my ass cheeks and spread them.

I realized what was coming at me the instant before I felt it. His glorious tongue.

Ethan used that on me first, the gentle teasing of my tight hole bringing me to a kind of helpless state where I trembled, hovering between this world and somewhere else.

He stopped with his tongue and moved into position. "You do, baby. You take my breath away." The head of his cock came against my flesh. "Every." He pushed forward, penetrating with just the tip of his penis. "Fuckin'." I felt the enormity of his flesh trying to merge with mine, the intensity of his need to sink into me, the craving I had for him to do it. "TIME," he shouted on a heavy groan, as his cock slid into place, filling me all the way to the root, his balls slapping against my sex with a jolt.

"Oh!" I gasped at his harsh, but beautiful invasion, riding through the sexual heat and sensation of extreme fullness that bordered upon pain but didn't cross into it. Just steadying myself for the real intensity that would come—once he started to move in and out of me in long, purposeful slides. I started to shake, nearly out of my mind with sensations so intense I could hardly breathe.

"Okay, my beauty?" he rasped at the back of my ear, his beard abrading my skin as he dug his chin into my shoulder to hold himself still, waiting for my answer. He sought my approval, of him, of his taking of me, of his physical domination over my body.

I would always give it to him. I wanted it so badly.

"Yeeees." I rolled my head back, unable to say more than that one word. I needed to focus on holding myself together before I blew apart into millions of pieces. Our joining felt that overpowering.

"Oh, fuck, yeah." He filled one hand with my hair and started to move within me, long careful slides of hot male flesh piercing me with exquisite deliberation. "So good, baby…" He groaned into each thrust, filling me deeply, taking me along on an erotic, lust-filled trip of sensation. "You're so beautiful…and sexy fucking amazing," he chanted, working his cock with the skill I'd come to know and love. Possessing me completely, every part of me laid bare.

I heard something else in his voice, too. A kind of desperation—a frantic desire to meld with me. A dark craving for his body to enfold mine so fully, there couldn't be any delineation where he ended and I began. His cock, fingers, tongue, his breath, his cum—his everything, wanted in.

And so, Ethan took me until he brought me to the highest peaks of my release, and held me when it broke into a billion shards of shimmering glory. He swallowed my cries with his mouth, and gave me more of him, his cock swelling to irrational hardness in preparation for the blast. He said things to me as he came, shuddering declarations of love and adoration…for me alone…as he filled me up with himself.

3rd January
London

WATCHING Brynne putting on her makeup, and I couldn't tear my eyes away. I hoped she didn't notice me watching because I didn't want her feeling self-conscious. I knew she was a little worried, because her body had changed so much. But my girl was more beautiful to me now, than ever. Our little blueberry had grown right along with her, and was now a thirty-two week-old, tiny little person, who kicked, and wriggled, and rolled around for me all the time now.

"You'd better start getting ready or we'll be late. Aunt Marie's plans wait for no man..." she trailed off, never taking her concentration away from the mirror where she was applying some kind of dark smudge around her eyes. She had on a short black lace getup that made me hard just looking, but she was only halfway dressed.

I realized quickly, it would be best to stick with the plan or we'd never make it to Dad's birthday dinner on time. So I forced myself to think of something very non-arousing, about work instead. It didn't take long. The minding of young Prince Christian of Lauenburg at XT Europe certainly helped to cool my cock. My trip was just two days away, and I dreaded leaving Brynne already. *Ridiculous fuckin' job.*

"But I'd much rather look at you," I told her.

She made a soft sound. "Well my ass is getting bigger by the second, in direct competition with my belly. I hope my ass doesn't win. At the end of this gig, I just want the baby, not the extra ass." She looked up into the mirror at me, her expression giving away little of what was on her mind. Still so mysterious, my girl was. I loved that aspect of her, though. Made me even more determined to get as close to her as I possibly could, so I could touch and taste and absorb every available molecule. My need for Brynne was still as strong as ever.

I had no doubts that would ever change, either.

"Your arse is perfection and you'll never hear me complaining 'bout a bit more of you to grab hold of." I gave her a slow wink and a lecherous grin. "From back here, you don't even look pregnant." I came up behind her, my hands sliding forward to rest on her bump. "I have to do this, to really know you've got anything here." I splayed my palms over the firm rounded swell of our baby growing strong inside her.

She leaned back and rested her weight against me. "Oh something's there all right," she said, "that you put there."

I laughed softly behind her. "I really enjoyed doing that by the way."

"I seem to remember that you did," she said dryly.

"Oh, you enjoyed it too." I slid my hands up to her luscious tits and lifted one in each hand, squeezing softly. "Now these...are a different story. They've changed a *great* deal, and I fucking love the transformation."

"I've noticed." She closed her eyes for a moment and tilted her neck, just allowing me to touch her at will. Always so giving of herself to me and my crazed needs.

"Mmmmm...you feel perfect to me, Mrs. Blackstone, and you always will."

"Did I ever tell you how much I love it when you

call me Mrs. Blackstone?" she asked lazily, pegging me with those lovely eyes.

"A few times, yes. And I'm delighted you love your new name." I grinned back at her in the mirror. "I know I love saying it to you. I know I love that my name is now your name. I love a lot of things…now."

She reached her hand up to hold my cheek, still looking at me in the mirror. "But you're getting a new name, too. We have someone coming to us soon who will know you only by one name, and it's not *Ethan.*"

"Dad."

"Yep. You are somebody's dad now." She smiled softly, a mixture of happiness and maybe a little sadness at the thought of her own father. "You'll be the best ever…" she whispered.

Brynne always amazed me in her generosity—her ability to be so lovingly giving even in the face of her grief and loss. Brave. Strong. Magnificent. I kissed her on the back of the neck and rested my chin on her shoulder, both of us staring into the vanity mirror. "I love the sound of it—Dad. I'm a dad and you're a mum."

"We are indeed."

I returned my hands to her stomach. "I love our little pineapple." I turned her around to face me and took her smiling face in my two hands. "And I love you, Mrs. Blackstone."

"I love you more," she said.

CHAPTER 15

4th January
London

The charity my father championed when he was alive sent out a notification whenever a donation was left in his name. The amount of the gift in the message I'd just read made my eyeballs bug out. I checked it again, counting the digits to make sure. All six of them.

The second shock was the message left from the donor in the comments section. *Please let me make it right, Brynne.*

Lance.

I couldn't believe what I was seeing. Lance had done this? He had made an obscenely large donation in my father's name to the Meritus College Fund? Assisting disadvantaged, but motivated kids to get a university education?

Why would he do it?

I really couldn't imagine why he would, but I knew I needed to find out. So I went to my purse and dug around in the side and end pockets until I found the card he'd given me. I flipped it to the back and read the message he'd handwritten with blue pen, just to make sure. *Please let me make it right, Brynne.*

I sent him a text with shaking hands and a pounding heart, afraid to hear what he wanted to say to me, but knew the time had come for me to know.

Ethan was at the offices, preparing for his trip to Switzerland the next day. I'd not told him about either of Lance's attempts to meet with me, at his hospital bed, and after my pre-natal check-up. I'd found the more time that passed, I just didn't want to dredge it up. What purpose would it serve? I needed to move on and deal with the here and now, instead of dwelling on the shit that had gone bad years ago.

I didn't tell Ethan, even though I knew I probably should have given him a warning. He wouldn't be comfortable with me seeing Lance alone, and he'd be over-the-top territorial to the point any meeting, including his presence, would be made useless. No, I needed to meet Lance on my own. This was *my* history. *My* past. And I was the one who needed to face up to it, and put it to rest.

So I left a short note for him on the kitchen counter instead. In case he made it home before I did, he would find my note saying I'd gone for a walk.

IN favor of some exercise, I did walk down to *Hot Java*, the coffee shop just around the corner from the flat.

Lance arrived before I did and was waiting window-side, at a table for two. He looked as he had the last time I'd seen him—completely and totally different from the boy I'd known a lifetime ago. In so many ways it was true. He was now a political celebrity, the tatted-up, war-hero son of the Vice President-Elect. He had an escort waiting for him too—Secret Service most likely, considering the terrorist risk. For someone like him, it must be enormous.

He looked miserable sitting across from me, and I wondered if he was still in any physical pain from his injury.

"I'll be heading back to the States very soon. Command performance for the inauguration." He tapped his leg with a tattooed finger. "But, I'll miss London. It's a good place to fade into."

Yes, it is. "Why did you send that huge donation in my father's name? Is it something you truly want to spend your money on, Lance?" I asked, pushing the raspberry tea bag in my mug into a mini vortex from over-stirring. No matter how much I'd thought about it, I could not for the life of me, see his motivation for the money. So, all I was left with was the unimaginable idea that he could really be sorry. *Mind. Fuck.*

Lance looked out of the café window, staring at the busy street traffic, and the equally busy foot traffic, managing the winter drizzle to go about their business. "Thank you for meeting me, Brynne. This is something I've wanted for a very long time…and also, very much dreaded." He turned his eyes back to look at me when he finished speaking.

"You said…you said you wanted to tell me what really happened that night at the party." I could feel my heart thumping erratically deep in my chest.

"Yeah." He shifted in his seat and seemed to brace himself for what he wanted to say. "But first, I want you to have my deepest apology for how I treated you, the things I did to you, for how I hurt you so very badly. I have no justification for anything that I did, no excuses, only regrets."

His eyes flickered over me, a hint of longing in his expression—for what, I wasn't sure. Longing for me? About what might have been with us?

"So, before I tell you the rest, I wanted you to at least hear that part."

I felt something strange glimmer inside of me, like a crack feathering out on a frozen lake. I couldn't speak just yet, but I managed to acknowledge his apology by nodding my head.

"You saw the video, Brynne?"

I nodded my head again and kept my eyes on my mug of raspberry tea. "Once. That was all I could watch—" My mind went black at the remembered images that flashed in my head. The other guys, me being used, the laughter, the song lyrics, the torment of my body with objects, how they spoke to me like I was a whore who wanted what they were doing to me.

"I am so sorry...I didn't mean for it to go that far," he said.

"What in the hell did you intend by filming us then?" I spat back, lifting my head. "Do you even know what that video did to me? How it changed my life? That I tried to kill myself because of it? Are you aware of all of that, Lance?"

"Yes." He closed his eyes and winced. "Brynne, if I could take it back—I just—I'm just so very sorry."

I sat there and stared at him, nearly unbelieving at what I was experiencing. For so long I'd understood my dark place for what it was. An evil deed, done to me by evil people, devoid of remorse, or even humanity for their actions. But with Lance before me, apologizing so sincerely, he didn't seem evil at all...and it was a very hard concept to accept.

"So...what *was* your intent that night, Lance? If you feel you must make things *right* with me, then I guess I'll have to try to hear it."

"Thank you," he whispered, tapping the table top

with his hand softly, rhythmically, only his fingers lifting up and down. The tattoos that decorated him covered the whole surface of his right hand—a skeleton of the bones of the hand interspersed with spider webs in between the individual finger bones.

I wondered what Daddy-O thought of all the goth ink on his son.

After a moment, he started talking.

"I was a complete prick to you," he began, "I know that, and I have no excuses, but when I went off to Stanford and found out you were with other guys when I was gone, I got insanely jealous that anyone else would have you. I wanted to punish you for it because that's how my mind worked back then." He started flicking his thumb onto the side of his coffee mug. "I got you drunk at the party with the intent of filming us having sex, so I could send it to you as a reminder that you were *my* girlfriend, and nobody else got into what was mine when I was away at college." He cleared his throat and continued. "That was the extent of what I intended for the video, Brynne. I would never have posted it anywhere, or shown it to people. It was a reminder of me…for you."

"But, those others…Justin Fielding and Eric Montrose—they were there." I couldn't look at him, so I just stared out the window at the rainy sidewalk and busy people instead.

I kept on listening, though.

"Yeah," he said sadly. "I got you drunk, but I was even more wasted, and to the point that I passed out after I…finished. Those two had come home with me for the holiday weekend and they knew I was bent on teaching my girlfriend a lesson she wouldn't forget. I told them what I was going to do with the sex video. Like an idiot. I was so arrogant I never imagined they would try to get in on it. You can clearly see on the video that after I fuck—after I'm done—I'm not there on screen again. There's a cut in the filming, and then it's just Fielding and Montrose…and you. Trust me, I watched it over and over, horrified by what they did." I looked away from the window and studied his face. He met me head on without shielding himself. I saw regret and shame in him. "Brynne, I—I never meant—"

I knew Lance was telling me the truth.

"They watched us…and then when I passed out, they took over. I don't even remember leaving you in that game room, Brynne. I woke up the next morning in the back of my car. The video had already been posted to a sharing site and it was too late. It got passed around all weekend." He hung his head and shook it slowly. "And that music they put on there…"

I tried to remember the sequence of imagery, but I'd been so traumatized by my one-time viewing of the video, I couldn't really pull up much memory of Lance's involvement at all. I knew he'd been very angry with me for dating Karl. Being an immature seventeen-year-old slut hadn't left me with good judgment skills in where I went, what I did, or whom I did it with. Sadly, I'd learned my lesson in a very hard way, but it was still remarkable to hear this new information from Lance.

"So, you didn't do it because you hated me?" I asked him the question I'd always wanted answered. It was the thing that never made any sense to me. We'd had our problems, but I had never felt hatred from Lance before that night. The video had felt like hate to me for all of the intervening seven years, and had been hard to bear because it was so confusing.

"No, Brynne. I *never* hated you. I believed I would marry you some day." His dark eyes blinked at me, regret and sadness clearly readable in them.

I gasped, unable to respond to what he'd just told me. I had no voice, so I sat there silent and stared at him, unable to do anything else.

He slid his hand forward as if were going to reach for mine, but caught himself in time, leaving his fingertips about an inch away on the table. It was so awkward I picked up my mug of tea and held it in both of my hands so I could make them useful.

"I tried to call you and see you, but your father, and mine, shut that down. My dad informed me that I would die before he allowed me to destroy his political career. He had me withdrawn from Stanford and enlisted in the Army within two days. I was shipped off to Fort Benning for Basic Training, and there was nothing I could do about it. I couldn't even talk to you to say I was sorry, or to find out how you were." He held his palm up in question. "And now with my father's political aspirations...I'm just caught up in all of it, carried along without a way out. And with him in the West Wing, I'm more trapped than ever..." he trailed off sadly.

Wow. Just wow. Never in my wildest dreams could I have imagined this reality. I didn't know what to say to him, or how to respond, so we just sat there in silence together for a minute. He didn't even know about the other sordid history connected to the whole mess— the reason behind the deaths of Montrose and Fielding, Karl's blackmail attempt, my father's murder—were all because of that video. Lance wouldn't hear it from me, either. The events had played themselves out, and it was time to put them into the ground for good. Nothing would ever change my greatest loss, by bringing my dad back to me.

I cradled my stomach protectively, needing reassurance from something pure and innocent. So much ugliness in my twenty-five years—surely I could find beauty and peace moving forward. And just like a message from above, I was rewarded with a little nudge right under my ribs as if to say, "I'm still here and I know you're my mom." *Yes, my butterfly angel, I am.*

"So, your life changed after that night…just like mine," I said after a moment.

"Yes. The choices I made that night changed everything."

WE said our goodbyes on the busy street with more of the media circus I'd experienced before, with security, and drivers, and photographers. I really needed to get back to the flat to start dinner for Ethan as this was our last night together for a week. He had to leave for Switzerland very early in the morning.

The whole meeting with Lance had been on the bizarre side of things, but I felt so much lighter with my guilt after hearing his revelation. Still ashamed of my behavior that brought me to be on that pool table seven years ago, but a great deal of the self-loathing was freed for me. I felt tremendous relief, and for the first time, felt like the feeling might actually remain with me.

"Thank you, Lance."

He looked at me curiously. "Why, Brynne?"

"For telling me your story. For some reason, it helps me to let go…of it." I rested a hand on the top of my belly, unable to explain such a private thought with any kind of clear understanding, but it made perfect sense to me. "I'll be a mother soon, and I want my baby to have a mom who can hold her head up, and know she didn't do anything wrong, that she's a good person, who did a stupid thing in a long line of stupid things."

"You are a good person, Brynne…and we all do stupid things, unfortunately. And sometimes bad things happen to us without any intervention from the stupid things we do." He looked down at his prosthetic.

"What will you do now, Lance?"

"Go back home and figure out what I can do now that I'm done with the Army. Learn to live with one leg. Maybe go back to school and finally get my law degree."

"You should do it then, if that's what you want." I smiled. "I bet the stuffy law professors at Stanford will just love all your ink."

He laughed. "Yeah, about as much as the people in D.C., but it's good to shake things up once in a while." His driver opened the car door, signaling that it was time to go.

"I think you're being summoned," I said, gesturing toward the car.

"Yeah." He looked like he had more to say as his eyes studied me. "Brynne?"

"Yes, Lance?"

"Telling you helped me, too. More than you can ever know. You deserved to hear it from me a long time ago. So thank you again, for seeing me." He sucked in a deep breath as if he was gathering strength. "You're more beautiful now than when you were seventeen, and I'm so glad I got to see you pregnant. You're going to be a wonderful mother. And I want *you* to remember that you're beautiful in spite of how we sometimes see ourselves. I'm going to remember you just like you are right now." He finished with a smile, but I could see how all the confessing was starting to get to him. This meeting had been emotional for him, for me—and now it was time for us to say goodbye to each other.

I wasn't quite sure how to respond to his many compliments, but again, they were heartening to hear from him. "I wish you well, Lance." I put out my hand. "I hope you get the chance to pursue your own dreams now."

He took my offered hand and leaned into me for a half-hug, and even a press of his cheek to mine. Then he got into the back of the limousine, the window tint so dark he was made invisible to me the instant the door closed behind him.

And just like that, Lance Oakley was gone.

THE drizzle was strangely comforting on my walk home. It reminded me of the dreary days I'd learned to get used to when the climate was still new to me. In the beginning, when I first moved to London, I missed the California sunshine. But as I blossomed in my new environment, immersing myself with school and the heavy cultural influences around me, I grew to love the London rain. So, as the drizzly drops scattered over my purple hat and scarf, I wasn't bothered a bit. The rain had always felt cleansing to me.

I walked faster, hurrying to make it home before Ethan discovered my absence, and the questions he would have about where I'd been. I knew I absolutely wasn't ready to discuss Lance with him yet. I owned the truth about what had happened to me seven years ago at that party, and re-hashing it again in conversation was not something I was quite ready to share, even with Ethan. He would have to understand that I needed to do this my way, and trust in me to make the best decision for myself. And, in many ways, for us. Ethan should understand the process now as he was finally into therapy himself. Being forced to re-live traumatic events did not always help the victim. Sometimes it hurt badly.

I pushed through the heavy glass doors of our building and waved to Claude as I headed for the elevator. I pressed the button and waited, feeling a little sweaty now that I was out of the rain. I dragged off my hat and figured I now sported mega hat-hair, and hoped I wouldn't have to ride up with anyone, to spare him or her the sight of me.

The doors opened and out came a tall blonde I'd seen before. Sarah Hastings was dabbing at the corner of her eye with a floral handkerchief, as if she were drying tears.

She stopped abruptly, realizing I'd spotted her, and it was too late to pretend I hadn't. "Oh, Brynne, hello, it's me, Sarah. Do you remember me from Neil's wedding?"

"Yes, of course, I remember you. How are you?" What I really wanted to ask her was a bit different: *Why are you coming out of my building, and were you just up with Ethan?*

I had my reasons to be wary of Sarah, though. The texts from Ethan on her phone were one annoying thing, but when she called him later that evening, my wifely intuition perked up. And now she was here at our home meeting with him? I got the feeling she was using him, or possibly something more, and I did not like it one little bit. I also knew how hard it was for Ethan to interact with her. Ethan's worst trauma had been the loss of Mike while they were prisoners. He'd been forced to watch the murder and was tortured emotionally throughout. It was horrible for him to have to re-live the events through Sarah each time she called, or wanted to reminisce, or whatever the hell she was trying to do with my husband.

She swept her eyes over me, took in my swelling

pregnant self, and much to my irritation, the messy hair and damp skin. I knew I looked ghastly. "Oh, I'm just leaving now, but I'm fine, thank you." She blinked and looked down at the ground. Her eyes were red and it was apparent to me she'd been crying.

"Are you sure? You look upset."

"Actually, I've just left your husband—there was—something I needed…to give him."

"May I ask what that was?" I asked, boldly.

"Um…I think you have to ask Ethan, Brynne, I'm not at liberty to say." She shook her head and looked pained to be standing and talking to me. Sarah Hastings resented me, and if I had to peg her further, I'd say she felt guilty about it, too. Maybe she begrudged the life Ethan and I were living together…while she had only memories of Mike.

Exactly what I was afraid of. The feelings coursing through me were unwelcome and unpleasant. I felt jealous and useless at the same time. I didn't know what to say to her so I just nodded and stepped into the elevator. Sarah had already turned away when the doors closed.

When I let myself into the flat I anticipated Ethan to be right there tapping his foot, but he wasn't. Things were quiet. It wasn't Annabelle's day so I wasn't expecting her to be around, but Ethan knew I planned on cooking tonight so we could have a quiet evening together before he left for his trip.

I checked our bedroom, thinking he might be in there packing, but he wasn't. I headed back through the great room toward the other side of the flat, when I smelled the cloves. The door to his office was closed, but I peeked in without knocking. The room was dark except for two forms of illumination: the aquarium and the burning tip of his Djarum Black.

"You're in here." My eyes adjusted to the dim lighting and caught a glimpse of his face through the shadows. He looked grim as he sat there smoking in his study. Not happy to see me. No real acknowledgment. "Is everything all right?" I asked, stepping forward.

"You're back," he said idly. He just sat there staring at me, the bright lights of the tank framing him from behind, Simba and Dory swimming peacefully among the pieces of bright coral, as he ignored my question.

"Why are you sitting in the dark?" I wondered if he would tell me about Sarah's visit. It was pretty clear that he was upset over it. He tended to go on a smoking fit after a bad dream or a flashback. Meeting or talking to Sarah seemed to bring about the same sorts of coping behaviors in him, but he smoked outside now exclusively, so doing it inside his office was my first clue that something wasn't right. I wanted him to tell me about their conversations, but so far he hadn't shared. I didn't push him, as I'd promised, but it hurt me that Ethan could apparently speak to Sarah about things that he couldn't with me. She could help him but I couldn't? I wasn't happy with how his reaching out to Sarah made me feel, but felt I couldn't complain or bother him with it because it would just make things harder for him. I never wanted to be the one responsible for bringing Ethan more hurt and stress than he already had to deal with.

"How was your walk?" he asked, stubbing out his cigarette and standing. "I don't want you in here breathing this shit."

"Then why are you smoking in the house?" His manner was so cold, I felt a shiver of nervousness catch me.

"My bad." He stalked toward me and steered me out with a firm hand to my back. There would be no resisting and no arguing, I could see that plain as day in the rigidity of his stance as he moved beside me.

We came into the kitchen where he left me to sit at the bar. He often sat there while I cooked dinner, either working on a laptop or asking about my day. But he didn't look like he wanted to chat when he set his phone on the granite countertop with a clap. He looked up at me and folded his hands. His eyes told me he was fuming, swirling dark blue and searing.

I swallowed and tried again. "Ethan, did something happen to upset you?"

He raised an eyebrow at me, but didn't answer the question. I realized he hadn't answered a single question I'd asked him since I'd come home.

"Where did you go for your walk, baby?" *He's answering everything with questions of his own.*

"I walked to Hot Java," I said slowly, but getting the feeling he already knew. "Do you have something to say to me, Ethan?"

"No, my darling, I don't, but I very much think you do." He picked up his phone and held the screen up for me to see.

Lance Oakley embracing me on the street.

CHAPTER 16

9th January
Switzerland

The young prince was quite the Renaissance man, I had discovered. He had skills on the slopes, and with the ladies as well. No wonder his grandfather was worried about him. The lad might very well be in some real serious danger here at XT Europe.

Of death-by-fucking.

The screaming shag-party he had going right now on the other side of the wall, fouled my mood even further. I was in sheer hell here—the teenage fuckathon next door notwithstanding. What I needed was to speak to Brynne and to hear her voice. The one thing might make the next days marginally bearable.

We hadn't parted well at all. A hideous row over keeping secrets. When the photos of her meeting Oakley were sent out in a Tweet, I received the alert straight away. I was utterly shocked of course, but when she got home, and I realized she wasn't going to tell me why she would go behind my back to meet the man who ruined her life and nearly gotten her killed—I lost it.

Lost. *Exactly how I feel right now, without my girl.*

I topped off my glass from the bottle of Van Gogh and took a swig. My drink of choice—when I needed it. I surely fucking needed it to get to sleep tonight if the "oh, fuck yes's" and "yeah, baby's" didn't shut off soon. Surely His Royal Highness would be shagged to within an inch of his life soon, and quiet might be a possibility. *Please, blessed Christ.*

Brynne didn't tell me anything about her visit with Oakley, during, or even after our row. I still didn't know why she'd gone to meet him. Maybe I would never know.

She just kept telling me the same thing over and over. *I can't talk about it right now, Ethan, and you'll have to just accept that until something changes for me.*

When I pushed her to tell me, she got angry and bit back with accusations about Sarah and our "private" meetings, saying I was shutting her out in favour of Sarah. Was I? I didn't think so, but then, when Brynne asked why Sarah had been to the flat to see me that night, I couldn't tell her. I wasn't ready yet.

Her face had revealed how hurt she was, but I imagined mine did, too. We'd never quite been in this position before in our relationship. Both of us standing our ground on silent issues that had shaped so much of how we were made. It bloody sucked.

I think we could have worked things out if we'd had more time.

There had been no time, though. I'd had to come to this shitting job and leave her behind, pregnant and sad, and on her own. Well, not totally on her own. Neil and Elaina were keeping a close watch for me.

My girl and I were due some serious attention to our problems when I returned, and I'd said as much to her when I had to leave very early the next morning.

She had tears in her eyes, which were red and swollen, when she nodded and agreed with me.

When I kissed her goodbye, her sweet lips melted beneath mine and her arms came up to hold me tightly against her scented softness. I hated to pull away. I had to though, and it fucking hurt me to have to do it. I had hope we'd solve our differences, and work through the doubts both of us were carrying. I wouldn't accept any other alternative.

She held my face with her hands and told me, "Come back to me." I knew her words meant more than just my physical presence. I understood what she meant.

"Nothing could ever stop me from coming back to you," I said. "Or you, little one," I whispered against her belly.

And I believed that.

THE banging that woke me was not the nice kind. In fact, whoever was doing it might need a lesson in etiquette, via my fists if they didn't stop fucking about.

"Ethan! Get up, man! We want to go for a backcountry run!"

I blinked at the bedside clock. 3:12 a.m. Stumbling out of my warm bed, I answered the door to find my young charge geared up and grinning wide.

"Now?" I barked. "You're going up now, Christian?" I might have hoped I was dreaming him in front of me, but sadly, I knew I wasn't.

He laughed, "Yeah, man, suit up. It's a dead day otherwise. We leave now and can be up at the top by daylight. I need to blow off some steam before tomorrow."

"You didn't already? What was all the shag-racket from earlier then?" It was a valid question. When the fuck did this kid sleep was another. He had the world at his feet with his money, good-looks, royal status, and celebrity. He had it all going for him. I couldn't really blame Christian for any of that, but he still managed to annoy the motherfucking shit out of me.

"That was just my bedtime story." He shrugged happily and teetered on his toes, looking wired and anxious to get going. I highly doubted he was on anything because if he was he'd be DQ'd for doping and his snowboarding career finished. I think it was just his natural exuberance…and being bloody nineteen years old. *Good Lord Bollocks. If our child is this hyper, I am fucked.* Might as well crawl into an early grave and get it over with.

I shook my head at him and rolled my eyes. "Give me a minute to get my kit together, would you?"

"Sure thing, man." He grinned again, and for the first time in my life I felt rather old.

CHRISTIAN and his entourage of four compatriots chose deep snow not far off-piste, but I didn't let that give me a false sense of security because I was well aware there were risks to doing it. I told them straight up before we set out, to have their shovel and probe kit in their packs and their beacons on them. I'd seen how people become euphoric in the backcountry, and lose sight of danger. Snowpack could change so quickly, and a span of just a few feet could have different conditions. I'd witnessed skiers on slopes right next to avalanche slides like it was a completely normal thing to do. Some of them ended up dead eventually, from just that sort of mentality, too.

"Remember what I said—aim your board towards any trees or the ridge of the mountain if you hear a roaring sound behind you." I eyeballed each one. "And don't slow your ride. Keep going no matter what."

Christian snickered, his eyes laughing at me. "Yes, Dad," he said. I noticed the colour of his eyes was like Brynne's—they changed with the light, and with different hues of clothing. It made me miss her even more.

"I'm serious. You do not fuck about when it comes to an avalanche."

THE third off-piste they chose was not a good prospect. I told them no. Too much fresh powder, with little time to settle, equaled too much risk.

The lads didn't agree and were hell-bent on going down. Lukas and Tobias called first-tracks and were off before I could call them back. Jakob and Felix started out right behind them. "Huck it, Ethan—if not now, when?" Christian shouted gleefully before he sailed down, his neon green jacket in my sights.

My choice was made for me at that point and I had to follow him.

I'm not sure who triggered it, but I heard the roar before I saw the cloud.

Bad news.

I cut toward a scrub of trees and grabbed the

biggest one I could find and held on. A churning rush of snow blasted me off the tree and sent me arse-over-tit down the mountain. I lost sight of anything, or anyone, and could only pray the lads were riding off the sides to safety.

Jolted violently below the waist, I heard a snap. No pain, just an awareness of coming to rest on a rock outcropping. An overhang which saved me from being buried by the second wave that followed about a minute later.

WHEN I opened my eyes I could see the sky, which was a good sign. Meant I wasn't buried under feet of snow. I could breathe. I looked down and discovered what the snapping sound had been about. My left boot was turned 180 degrees. I knew it was quite probable I'd sustained a compound fracture. *Fuck.* I struggled to sit up and take stock of my location.

I'd been pushed so far off the main slide, my field of vision offered nothing beyond swaths of white. Bright drops of red spattered in the snow. I felt a tickle along the side of my face, but couldn't tell through the gloves where the blood was coming from.

First order of business was to activate the beacon, so I did that, and then checked out my leg. Fucking thing was so bashed. Hiking out was not going to happen. Board was long lost from my cartwheel down the mountain.

I took a deep breath and gripped my calf. I counted to three, and twisted it to where it was supposed to be…and passed the fuck out.

SO very cold. I registered the icy temperature, but had no idea how much time had passed. Could be minutes. Or hours. Probably not hours, though. Hours up here would kill me from hypothermia. Was I dying?

No. No! I refused to believe I was. My body could withstand more than this, and had in the past. I was strong. I couldn't die. I had to get back to Brynne…and our baby. I couldn't leave them alone. They both needed me. I promised her I would come back. I wasn't going to die up here.

All I needed was to get warm. Warm. Brynne was warm. The warmest place I could imagine was Brynne wrapped around me when I was making love to her. Brynne was my warm, safe place, right from the very first. And even if my conscious mind didn't know it at the time, my heart most certainly did.

I went to where I could feel her warmth…

...I knew the moment when she stepped into the room. The real Brynne Bennett was even more captivating in the flesh than in her portrait—which gratefully, now belonged to me. She sipped from a glass of champagne and studied her image on the gallery wall. I wondered how she saw herself. Was she confident? Unforgiving? Or somewhere in between?

"There's my girl." Clarkson said, hugging her from behind. "It's smashing isn't it? And you have the most beautiful feet of any woman on the planet."

"Everything you do looks good, Ben, even my feet." She turned around and asked him, "So, you sell anything yet? Let me rephrase. How many have you sold?"

I could hear everything they said to each other.

"Three so far and I think this one's going very soon," Clarkson said. "Don't be obvious, but see the tall bloke in the grey suit, black hair, speaking with Carole Andersen? He's inquired. Seems he's quite taken by your gorgeous naked self. Probably going to go for a good palm session soon as he can get the canvas all to himself. How's that make you feel, Brynne luv? Some rich toff pulling his pud to the sight of your unearthly beauty."

I fucking wish. They get to keep it for six long months.

"Shut up, that's just nasty. Don't tell me things like that or I'll have to stop taking jobs." She shook her head at him like he was daft. "It's a damn good thing I love you, Benny Clarkson." "It's true though," Clarkson rambled along, "and that chap hasn't stopped eyeballing you since you glided in here. And he's not gay."

"You're going to hell, Benny, for saying such things," she told him as she looked over and checked me out. I could feel her eyes on me, but I kept to my conversation with the director and played it cool.

"I'm right, huh?" Clarkson asked her.

"About the jerking off? No possible way, Benny! He's far too beautiful to have to resort to his hand for an orgasm."

Oh, fuck. *I couldn't help my stare then. Impossible to look away when I'd just heard those words come out of her mouth.* She likes what she sees. *References to my cock and getting off— from her—and a whole new game plan reorganized itself in that moment. I had to meet her tonight, and that was all there was to it.*

But she got spooked and gulped down her champagne, and said goodbye to her friend.

Wait, don't go yet.

I watched her contemplate whether to hail a cab or walk. Her legs were long and fucking gorgeous, anybody could see that, and when she turned towards the station I knew she'd made her decision. I couldn't allow it. If someone was after her they'd have the perfect opportunity as she walked alone, and the thought of anybody wanting to hurt her did something to my insides I'd never felt before.

"It's a very bad idea, Brynne. Don't risk it. Let me give you a ride."

She froze on the pavement, and turned stiffly to face me. "I don't know you at all," she said.

You will, beautiful American girl…you will.

I smiled at her and gestured toward the Rover, not even very much aware of what the fuck I was doing. I just needed to get closer.

But she took a deep swallow and a defensive stance, and called my bluff. "Yet you call me by name and—and expect me to get in a car with you? Are you crazy?"

Barking mad. *I came closer and offered my hand. "Ethan Blackstone."*

"How do you even know my name?" God, I loved the sound of her voice…sexy as fuck all.

"I just bought Brynne's Repose from the Andersen Gallery for a nice sum not fifteen minutes ago. And I'm fairly sure I'm not mentally impaired. Sounds more PC than crazy don't you think?"

She tentatively reached out her hand. I took it. I grabbed hold of her and covered her hand with mine. The instant our bodies touched something happened inside my chest. A spark, heat—I don't know what, but something. God, her eyes were unusual. I couldn't say what their colour was precisely. I didn't care though, I just wanted to look at them for a long fucking time and figure it out.

"Brynne Bennett."

"And now we know each other—Brynne, Ethan." I gestured with my head toward the Rover. "Will you let me take you home?"

She swallowed again, her lovely throat moving in a slow pull. "Why do you care so much?"

Easy answer, that. *"Because I don't want anything to*

happen to you? Because those heels look lovely at the end of your legs, but will be hell to walk in? Because it's dangerous for a woman alone at night in the city?" I couldn't help looking her up from head to toe to make my point. *She must know how fucking hot she was.* "Especially one that looks like you, Miss Bennett."

"What if you're not safe?"

If she only knew why I was here. I wonder what she would say to me then.

"I still don't know you or anything about you, or if Ethan Blackstone is your real name."

Miss Brynne Bennett was a smart girl. I admired her honesty and pluck in not giving in to ride with a complete stranger, with no fuss at all. She was Tom Bennett's daughter all right.

"You have a point in that. And it's one I can rectify easily." I showed her my driving licence and handed her a business card. "You may keep that," I told her. "I'm very busy at my job, Miss Bennett. I have absolutely no time for a hobby as a serial killer, I promise you."

She laughed.

It was the most beautiful fucking sound I'd ever heard.

"Good one, Mr. Blackstone." She put my card away, and then she said something that really pleased me. *"All right. You can give me a ride."*

Oh yeah, baby, I can. *Thoughts of just how I could give her a ride made my cock sit up and take notice. I couldn't help my grin. Miss Bennett had absolutely no idea what she was doing to me with her innocent comments. If I ever got the chance to give her a ride in my bed, it would be a long and memorable one for sure, because I didn't take women to my bed. I think she could be the exception to my rule though.*

What in the mother fuck is wrong with you?! *I thought, as I put my hand to her back and steered her towards the Rover. I liked how she allowed me to do it. And I could finally smell her. Flowery, feminine, and fucking amazing. I wondered if the scent was perfume or something she used on her hair. Whatever it was, I wanted to bury my nose up against her neck and get a lungful of it—she smelled that good to me.*

I settled her into her seat and felt a thrill once I'd shut myself in with her. I had this beautiful girl alone in my car with me. She was safe and nobody was going to get to her while she walked alone in the dark. I could also talk to her, and listen to her voice. I could smell her, and look at her, admire her long legs folded in the seat beside me, and imagine how it would be having those beautiful legs split on either side of my cock…

I asked her where she lived.

"Nelson Square in Southwark."

Not the best location, but could be worse. "You are American," *I said, thinking of nothing better.*

"I am here on scholarship at the University of London. Graduate program."

I knew that of course, but I really wanted to know about her other job. "And the modelling?"

My question flustered her. Understandable, I suppose. I knew what she looked like naked. Fucking spectacular. *"Um,*

I—I *posed for my friend, the photographer, Benny Clarkson. He asked me, and it helps pay the bills, you know?"*

"Not really, but I do love the portrait of you, Miss Bennett." I kept my eyes on the road.

She did not like my questioning her. It made her defensive. I swear, she literally sizzled in her seat before letting me have it.

"Well, my own personal international corporation never came through like yours did, Mr. Blackstone. I resorted to modelling. I like sleeping in a bed as opposed to a park bench. And heat. The winters here suck!"

Oh, fuck, yeah, she's amazing. *"In my experience, I've found many things here that suck." I glanced over and pegged her glittering eyes, moving down to her lips, imagining them wrapped around my cock, thoroughly enjoying winding her up by my reply.*

"Well, we agree on something then." She rubbed her forehead and closed her eyes.

"Headache?"

"Yeah. How did you know?"

I got the chance to take another long, leisurely look at her. "Merely a guess. No dinner, just the champagne you gulped back at the gallery, and now it's late and your body is putting up a protest." I tilted my head. "How'd I do?"

She looked at me as if her mouth had gone dry.

"I just need two aspirin and some water and I'll be fine."

That's no good at all. *"When did you last eat some food, Brynne?"*

"So, we're back to first names again?"

Yes, we are, baby. *I didn't like her not taking care of herself. She needed to eat like everyone else. After a moment she said something about making food when she got home.* At this late hour? For fuck's sake, that will simply not do, Brynne.

I pulled into a corner shop and told her to stay in the car, I'd be right back. I got her a bottled water, a packet of Nurofen and a protein bar that looked palatable. I just hoped she would accept them from me.

"What did you need to get in the store—"

Not a worry. She took the water as soon as she spotted it and started drinking. I removed the pills from the packet for her and held them open in my hand. She took those too, and gulped them down, draining the bottle quickly. I set the protein bar on her knee.

"Now eat it—please."

She sighed, a long, shuddering breath that made my cock twitch again, and opened the bar slowly. But something changed in her demeanor as she took a bite and started chewing. I sensed melancholy from her when she bowed her head and whispered, "Thank you."

"My pleasure. Everyone needs the basics, Brynne. Food, water...a bed."

She didn't respond to my subtle reprimand.

"What's your actual street address?" I asked.

"41 Franklin Crossing."

I headed back on the road and in a moment, heard her mobile chirp. She responded to a text and seemed to relax a bit after that. A few moments later, she closed her eyes and fell asleep.

Having her comfortable and feeling safe with me flipped some kind of switch inside my head. I couldn't say what exactly, because it was unlike anything I'd ever experienced before. I just knew I fucking liked the feeling. I did something reckless then. I wasn't proud of what I did, but that didn't stop me from doing it. I carefully took her mobile from her lap and called my number with it.

"Brynne, wake up." I leaned in and touched her shoulder, speaking close enough to smell her natural scent. Her eyelids twitched erratically, the long lashes sweeping down onto creamy skin with just a hint of olive to it. Was she dreaming? Her lips were full and dark pink, barely parted as she breathed. A few loose strands of her long brown hair fell over one cheek. I wanted to lift it to my nose and smell it.

Her eyes fluttered open, flaring wide as she became aware of me.

"Shit! I'm sorry I—I fell asleep?" She grappled with the door latch frantically, the sound of panic in her voice.

I covered her hand with mine and stilled her. "Easy. You're safe, everything's fine. You just drifted off is all."

"Okay…sorry." She panted deeply, looked out the window, and then back to me warily.

"Why do you keep apologizing?" She seemed very rattled, and I wanted nothing more than to soothe her fears, but at the same time—I was annoyed with the strange sensation of which I had absolutely no purposeful reason to be feeling.

"I don't know," she whispered at me.

"*Are you okay?*" *I smiled, hoping I wasn't freaking her out. I didn't like the idea of her being afraid of me, but I did want her to remember me after tonight. I wanted her to trust me, too.*

"*Thank you for the ride. And the water. And the other stu—*"

I interrupted her, knowing I had to take charge so there would be another opportunity for me to meet her again. "*You take care of yourself, Brynne Bennett.*" *I unlocked the door.* "*You have your key ready? I'll wait until you're inside. What floor is it?*"

She retrieved her key from her bag and put her mobile into it. "*I live in the top studio loft, fifth floor.*"

"*Roommate?*"

"*Well, yes, but she's probably not in.*"

What was she thinking? I so wanted to know what she thought of me, if she was interested in finding out anything more about me. "*I'll look for the light to come on then,*" *I said.*

She opened her door and stepped out. "*Goodnight, Ethan Blackstone,*" *she said to me before she shut the door.*

I followed her with my eyes as she made her way to her door, used her key and went inside. I waited until I saw the light come on in her fifth-floor loft before I pulled out.

I didn't know exactly what I felt, or what might happen when I drove away from her place. But I did know this: I would be seeing Brynne Bennett again. Most definitely. There was no other option I would accept on the matter…

I smiled to myself because I didn't feel the cold anymore.

My leg hurt, but I knew it really didn't matter now. I felt warm, and I was in my safe place with my memories of Brynne, where everything was good and right. She was my light and had been from the first moment I looked upon her beauty. She'd loved me, and held me together, when I didn't think it was possible for anyone to work that miracle. We were going to have a baby soon. Thinking of our baby made me happy, but very sad at the same time. I couldn't see my child in the place where I was going. He or she wouldn't ever know me. But Brynne would tell our son or daughter about me. She would be such a wonderful mother. She already was. Brynne was good at everything she did and motherhood was no different. I knew there wasn't much time left for me. I couldn't keep my promise to her. That ripped into my heart worse than anything could. I'd promised I would come back to her. I'd said that nothing could ever keep me from coming back to her.

I desperately wanted to tell her how much I loved her, and how happy she'd made me in our time together. How I could go away, knowing I'd been loved by the most perfect woman in the world? That she was the *only* person to ever really see inside my dark soul to find me— and still made me feel like I'd won the fucking national lottery of life. It didn't hurt me so much knowing my life would be cut short. The joyfulness was in knowing she'd been a part of it.

Brynne *was* my life. The last piece of my puzzle that had finally completed me.

I just needed a way to tell her somehow, so she wouldn't worry about me. I wanted her to know how happy I was at the end of my life...because I'd been blessed with the rare and precious gift...of loving her.

CHAPTER 17

10th January
London

Neil and Elaina wouldn't take no for an answer. They had me over to their place for dinner, or came to our place every night since Ethan was away. I knew he'd arranged for them to babysit me, and I guess it made sense since they were just across the hall. Good thing I loved them both so much.

But they were newlyweds, and needed their private time together, I argued. Neil and Elaina were trying to make a baby of their own, and hanging out with me wasn't doing them much good in that department. When I said so, they both laughed at me and made cryptic comments that had me wondering if they'd already managed it and just weren't announcing the news yet. I hoped so. The two of them were so perfect together, and in getting to know them both so well, I'd learned how they'd been a part of each other's lives since they were kids. The two of them were fated to be together from the very beginning. It made me so happy knowing true love had won out for them.

Ethan's directive annoyed me, but at the same time, was so very typical of him. So protective, and caring...and cautious. I wondered how he was doing on the job with Prince Christian in the Swiss Alps. He'd dreaded to go as much as I hated him leaving. We hadn't had time to work through our hiccup, and it was the worst feeling for me.

I missed my man dreadfully, and needed him back home. I wanted to unburden everything to him about what Lance had told me. And I hoped to hear whatever Ethan was willing to share with me, to get us back to where we'd been before that hideous night we fought over things that just weren't worth hurting the one you love. Not to me. And, I know, not to him, either.

CHICKEN tacos with avocado and corn salsa, was my new pregnant comfort food. I tried to get Neil and Elaina to abandon their dinner plans with me by having it twice in one week, but they weren't buying it, saying they loved my version of Mexican food. Bless their sweet Brit hearts. Because the British rendition of Mexican sucked, in my opinion. Maybe if my career in art conservation failed, I could do street-tacos and make a killing. I laughed inwardly at the idea of Ethan ever allowing me to entertain such a thing. I could set up next to Muriel's newsstand on the street by Blackstone Security, and he could come down and have his lunch.

Neil loved cooking, so he was the one helping me in the kitchen. Elaina was off in the nursery working on the mural I'd planned out with her help. It was just a tree with birds and butterflies right now. Color and theme still to be determined, once we knew boy or girl…Thomas or Laurel.

"Do you know this was the very first meal I ever made for Ethan?" I popped a chunk of avocado in my mouth and savored it. "He brought along some Dos Equis, and ended up getting hooked on the Mexican beer *and* the Mexican food," I said.

"I know," Neil answered with a chuckle, as he added some spices to the sizzling chicken. "He talked about you *all* the time. Said you were a brilliant cook, and to give the Dos Equis a try with a sliver of lime."

"Did he?"

"Yeah. I knew he was done-for at that point. Not because of the Mexican food, mind you, but because of the beer. He left off with the Guinness practically overnight," he said with a snap of his fingers and a sorry shake of his head.

"That would be Ethan for you. He makes a decision about something, and that's that." I sighed pitifully, thinking about our unresolved "problems."

Neil stopped chopping tomatoes and looked up at me. "He'll be home soon, Brynne. There's nowhere he wants to be but right here with you."

"I know, but he left when things…weren't right between us. Do you know why, Neil?" I asked, realizing it was entirely probable he did know.

He nodded. "Yeah. I saw the photos of you and Oakley at the coffee shop. Publicity Tweets is all that was to be expected really."

"I didn't think about that part. It was just something I had to do, and when Ethan gets home I will explain everything, but it just wasn't the time for *me* right then, you know?"

Neil's dark brown eyes were very warm and understanding. "The two of you will work through it, Brynne. I know Ethan, and there is nothing he wouldn't do for you. He'd walk through fire to get back with you."

I stifled a sob and worked on the corn salsa. "Neil, what's the deal with Sarah Hastings? When Ethan saw her again at your wedding, he was really affected by her presence, and not in a good way. He told me some of what happened to her husband, Mike, and how horrible his death was to witness. I understand that part of his trauma…and at the same time, I cannot imagine how devastating it is for him to remember when he has a flashback."

"Sarah? She's all right, and I can only guess that

she has something to do with his therapy, but he hasn't said—and I won't ask."

"I understand," I said bleakly, realizing that I would just have to be patient with him, and wait until the time came when Ethan could tell me what role Sarah played in his emotional health. "Ethan told you about his therapy sessions with Dr. Wilson at the Combat Stress Centre?"

"He did, Brynne, and I am so glad he's finally getting something in the way of support. I know it's only because of you that he's been able to get himself over there."

"What happened to him was so horrible..." I trailed off, unable to even express my feelings about what Ethan had endured.

Neil stopped with the food prep altogether. "It was bad, Brynne, really bloody bad."

"I know he feels guilt, he told me he does, but why does he? Being captured and tortured was not his fault."

Neil hung his head and closed his eyes for just a moment. He paused with his head down over the kitchen counter for a long time. I figured he wouldn't tell me anything, or couldn't tell me because of strict rules within the British Army. But finally, he picked up his knife and returned to chopping vegetables, and then he started talking.

"I don't know everything, but I know enough to puzzle it together. E's shared what he could with me, and the rest I know because I heard the comms when they came through—the communications between base and squad when they're out in the field. I commanded my own team, as did Ethan. I wasn't there, just E and his men were. There were five troops, and Mike Hastings was one of them. None of them returned alive. Mike survived the ambush along with Ethan...and you know what happened there. E went through debriefing once he was returned, and he said on the day they planned to execute him, the building where he was being held was bombed into a pile of rubble. Nobody knows how E walked out of there alive. Not even he knows. He said he had no explanation of how or why he wasn't crushed to bits in the blast. It was something truly miraculous."

I held my breath as Neil explained the "why" for so many of my questions. Things Ethan just couldn't talk about. I now understood why, and it just shredded my heart for him, and what he had to suffer. "No wonder he has angel wings on his back," I whispered.

"Yeah." Neil gave the chicken another stir and told me the rest. "Mike's torture and execution was brutal, and I know Ethan feels tremendous loss and guilt. He believes because it was his call as commander, that he put them all into danger, and as a result of his decision, five young men lost their lives."

"But it was war. How can what happened be his fault?" I ached for Ethan even worse than before, and wanted nothing more than to have my arms around him, and his chest, with its fiercely brave and beautiful heart, beating up against mine.

"War is fucked no matter how you look at it. What happened to their team was indescribable really. They were lured in by a dead mother with her throat slit in the middle of the road, and with her hysterically crying son clinging to her body. He was no more than three years old. Hours of this went on and the comms kept coming in. Ethan wanted to go in and get the boy. And after many hours of haggling back and forth, he was finally given the go-ahead. But it was all a trap. The Taliban used a woman and child as decoys to take out a whole squad of elite soldiers—sympathetic Westerners, who would never conceive of such treatment to anyone or anything. It worked. Ethan went in, grabbed the boy, but he was shot and killed just seconds later, while still in E's arms. A firefight ensued and at the end of it, two innocent civilians were slaughtered, four of our own were dead, and Mike and E were captives."

"Oh, my God…"

I didn't even have words for Neil. What could I even say to him? Were there even words to be said? No…no words could make that story feel any better, no matter how many years passed. I rubbed my belly and thought of Ethan, and how much I loved him. He was so much more than I ever could have known when we first met. He was a true hero in every sense of the word, who had served honorably and suffered because of that service.

"Thank you for telling me, Neil, it h-helps me to…know."

And it really did help me, but knowing the truth was horrifying, too. I felt sick, and knew I couldn't eat the food I'd just been preparing with Neil. How did any of them eat anything ever again, when faced with the memories of wartime experiences I'd just heard? I knew how Ethan's mind worked, and I could honestly see him feeling the burden of terrible guilt over all of the deaths…how he suffered when he relived the events in dreams.

"I just love him so much. I'd do anything to be able to help him," I said finally.

"But you do, Brynne. Your love has helped him already, more than any other thing."

WHEN I was awakened early the next morning from a sound sleep in my lonely bed, I was startled. When I realized Elaina had let herself into the flat to wake me, I knew something bad had happened. When I caught a glimpse of Neil hovering in the doorway, I started crying and gripped my chest. When I heard words saying that something had happened to Ethan, I screamed.

I screamed at them both and begged them not to tell me.

Switzerland

NEON green burned into my eyes. What the fuckin' hell? I tried to push whatever it was out of my face, but it wouldn't budge.

"Ethan...oh, fuck, man. It just took us some time to find you."

"What?" I tried to focus, but the sun was shining down, and the light too fucking bright. All I could see was glare and flaming electric green—the colour reminded me of Christian's jacket as he swept down the mountain ahead of me, right before the—

"Is that you, Christian? You're all right," I babbled, "that's good." I was so relieved he'd survived I could've kissed the little shit, if I could even feel my face. The King still had his heir. Thank fuck. "Tell me, I want to know...did the other lads make it?"

"Yes! We made it, and you did too, Ethan."

Had I? Didn't feel like it at all. "But I'm up here on this mountain, and I can't walk—my leg is fucked up." I was glad Christian and the boys were okay, but I didn't see how I would get out of this mess intact, especially if it didn't happen soon. I was in very poor shape, and I knew it. I couldn't really see Christian's face, everything was blurry, and I was tired…so tired.

"I know," he said, before setting something hard against my lips. "Drink this. It'll help you."

I sucked in some liquid but couldn't tell what it was. I couldn't feel much, only exhaustion. Then I remembered what I needed to do. *More important than anything.* I pushed the drink away. "But…do you have a mobile on you, Christian? Mine's been lost. I have to tell…my wife—I need to give her—a message—"

"Hang on, Ethan, they're coming to get you. You're gonna be okay, man."

"No—I need to call Brynne. Now!" I desperately needed to make him understand.

"There's no cellular. It won't go to her."

"That's okay…it'll send once you get in range of service. Voice text—will—work…" I tried to reach for him to make him understand. "Help me, please."

"Okay, Ethan, okay. What's her number?"

I said the numbers carefully because I didn't want to make a mistake. This was so important, and I couldn't fuck this up. "Now, set it for voice…and let me talk."

Christian put the thing in my hand, which was hard to grip through the gloves, but he helped me to hold it and told me when to start speaking.

"Brynne, baby…I don't want you to be scared or sad, okay? I love you, and I'm happy right now. Very, very happy…because I got to be with you…and love you. I'll still be here, just loving you from another place, and our little Laurel-Thomas, too." I struggled to keep it together to finish my message, but it was so hard saying goodbye. How was it even possible I had to do such a thing? But yet, I needed to tell her. Nothing was going to stop me. "…you made me real, my beauty, and I love you for that, and I always will…until the end of time."

There. I'd managed it. She would hear from me one last time, and know…my truth.

Now, I could close my eyes and go to sleep. *So desperately tired…*

I floated for a time, peacefully drifting…somewhere, I don't know where. An idea came to me and I remembered about my mum. I'd get to see her again, and that was a very nice thought. I felt unusually free and weightless, as if I were being held up by…something light.

Wings?

But that's exactly what it felt like—wings holding me up, cradling my back. Silky feathers in two flowing arcs. Soft, but so powerfully strong. I realized what they belonged to after a while. They were angel wings.

I was being held by an angel.

12th January
London

COME back to me…

I'm right here, Ethan. Always. You just have to come back to me when you're ready. I'll be here waiting for you with Laurel-Thomas. We need you. I need you in order to do this. I just need you, and I won't ever let you go. I never will.

I stayed with my man at his hospital bedside. *Come back to me, baby.* Same hospital we'd come to visit Lance. I was so grateful, though. He was here with me now, and I could touch him, and see him, and the doctors could help him. Neil pulled some major strings with someone and arranged for Ethan to be airlifted to London. Ivan helped, too. I don't know what I would have done without those two. They knew people who could get things done. If Ethan were stuck in Switzerland right now, where I couldn't go to him, I'd need to be strapped down.

I think Jonathan and Marie were about to

commandeer me home but I wasn't going anywhere. They'd finally gone to get food and said they'd be back later. They could fuss and try their strong-arm tactics all they wanted with me, but it wouldn't do any good. I knew where I needed to be. *I won't leave you, my darling. I'm going to be here when you wake up.*

Even so, I couldn't do much of anything for him. The hospital had everything covered. Stitches to close the gash beside his right eye, at the top of his cheekbone. He would have a scar there now. Surgery to repair his left leg. Tibia and fibula both blown out, but they were fixed now, and would heal faster because of the pins they'd put into his bones. My man was just "sleeping" right now. He needed the deep rest so his body could regenerate.

So I sat there beside him, and called him back to me. *I got the message you left for me on Christian's phone. He was very sweet, and very worried about you. He called and talked to me because he didn't want me to be scared by the text message you sent from his phone. He told me what happened, how they wanted to take a backcountry run, and how you told them what to do if they got in trouble up there. He said they all did what you'd instructed them to do, and because of it, they were all okay. He feels terrible you were the one who got hurt—*

I felt a heavy hand come to rest on my shoulder. "They had blackberry flavor. I hope that's all right." Ivan pushed the cup of hot tea toward my hand. "Oh, and I got this for you, too." He held out a protein bar.

"Eat it, please."

Slowly, I raised my eyes in shock. His words—the gesture, was nearly identical. I looked at Ivan where he stood frowning at me. Tall and green-eyed, with longer hair—just as handsome as his cousin, but different. Ivan bore a slightly more refined look, where Ethan was blessed with a harshness that made him appear a bit more rugged. But the genetics they shared? As clearly visible as water in a glass. They were of the same blood, and of the same mind.

Ivan's offering of the protein bar brought back vivid memories of that first night, when Ethan drove me home from Benny's show—all in a split-second. I could smell the scent of him and feel the warmth of the Rover's heated seats. I could see him perfectly in my mind, the way he'd set that protein bar on my knee and waited for me to eat it before he would move the car. The "don't-fuck-with-me" attitude. And the heavy dose of persuasive dominance I couldn't deny. *Come back to me, Ethan...*

"Okay." I nodded, and felt my eyes fill, struggling to keep it together, wanting to be strong for Ethan.

"Good girl," he said softly, pulling up beside me in a chair. "He'd have a tantrum if he thought you weren't taking care."

"I know," I said pitifully, taking a bite and chewing. It tasted like sawdust but I ate it anyway, and sipped the tea. My butterfly angel needed food even if I didn't want any.

"Thank you, Brynne," he said with a gentle smile. This was a different side of Ivan I was seeing at Ethan's bedside. Ivan Everley was a devastating combination of charmingly sexy mixed with witty cynicism, but not right now. It was blatantly obvious he was worried about Ethan, too. They behaved more like brothers than cousins, I thought, and I always had felt that from the two of them. They were brothers in their heart, where it mattered.

"The first night I met Ethan he bought me a protein bar and made me eat it," I told him.

I felt the tears spill out and down my cheeks and tried to wipe them away with the back of my hand.

Ivan put his arm around me and pulled me in against his side. "He loves you so much. I know he's fighting his way back. I know him. I know how his mind works. E's fighting his way back to you right now, Brynne."

I nodded my agreement. I couldn't speak, all I could do was *believe*. Ivan's words were my lifeline to Ethan right now, and I couldn't allow any other thoughts or doubts to creep in.

So, we sat there together, and gave him some more time to come back to us.

FINALLY. I smelled her again. Her scent was in my nose, and I breathed it in. A lungful of Brynne. But how could that be? I'd said goodbye to her up on that mountain. I felt different, though.

Vastly different.

I could now *feel* my body. My hands, my toes, my head. *Does that mean…I've made it?* Oh, fuckin' fuck yes! I felt euphoria. I was alive…and Brynne was close by. It was so good…whatever was being done to me. The massaging of fingers through my hair, over and over again. Fingers I knew well. Belonging to a hand I'd felt, and held, and kissed. The hand slowly rubbed my scalp. Her hand—Brynne's hand touched me, and that was the most wonderful perfect fucking thing. I wanted to tell her how much I loved her, and that I was going to be fine, but I couldn't speak yet. All I could do was breathe her in, and savour the feel of her touching me. Somehow, by some miraculous intervention, I'd survived. I remembered the angel wings holding me when I was floating between life and death. It very much reminded me of another time when it had happened to me.

Thank you, Mum. Again.

I knew complete and total relief, and knew I

could stop struggling now…and just sleep a little more, with my girl right beside me.

✎

LITTLE kicks and nudges rumbled against my hand. I loved it. Always made me smile. I knew exactly what I was feeling. Laurel-Thomas was talking to Daddy. *You've gotten stronger, little one.* I rubbed my hand over the baby, trying to imagine which body part was which. Was that a little bum or the crown of a head? More kicks pummeled my palm, and made me laugh. It was the best damn feeling in the whole fucking world. Like a blessing—a gift I didn't expect—perfectly beautiful.

"Ethan laughed. Did you hear him, Ivan? He's laughing at the baby kicking." I knew that voice. That was my Brynne talking to Ivan.

I opened my eyes.

"It worked," she said in a whisper. "You came back to me."

Brynne's face was a mess of tears and worry. She looked exhausted with dark circles under her eyes and her hair all mussed. Her eyes were glassy from crying. But the sight of her against me so close, was the most beautiful sight my pitiful eyes had ever beheld in the whole of my life.

"Brynne…baby—" I smiled, and stared at every

inch of her face, soaking in the sight of her for a moment. "—I dreamed of you up on that mountain—to help me to get warm...and find a safe place to go. I just dreamed you, and knew things would be good, and I was happy, not afraid."

"Oh, Ethan, Ethan, Ethan..." she sobbed, burrowing into my chest and rocking her forehead back and forth. I took stock of where we were and figured it was a hospital bed, and both of us were lying on our sides, facing each other. My girl had crawled up into my hospital bed with me, apparently, so I could smell her. She'd even gone a step further by putting my hand on her belly so I could feel Laurel-Thomas kicking madly away from the inside. *Both* of them had called me back.

I looked over at my cousin and caught the words, *welcome back*, mouthed at me.

Thanks, I mouthed in return, grateful to him for helping Brynne while I was out of it. Then he grinned at me, and slipped out the door, jogging his hand to his ear in the universal "ring me" gesture.

"I love you so much," I whispered, trying to keep my own emotions in check. I brought my hand up to her chin and forced her face up to meet mine. I needed to look into her eyes first. Then, once I'd drowned myself in all their multicoloured glory, I would need to kiss her for a long, long time.

I think she was in a bit of shock because she just

kept saying the same thing over and over again.

"You came back to me."

"I did, my beauty, because *you* brought me back. You did it…and an angel helped me, too."

15th January

ETHAN was so very quiet on the ride home from the hospital. We sat in the back seat together while Len drove. He held my hand tightly, gripping so hard it actually felt uncomfortable, but I wasn't willing to pull away from him. Ethan needed to touch me, even if it was just by our hands.

His dad had called me and asked about having dinner to celebrate his homecoming, but I made an excuse to postpone for the following week. Ethan wasn't up for socializing, and quite frankly, I wasn't either. His accident had made me paranoid, and if I allowed myself to think about how close he'd come to dying, I was likely to have a panic attack. I knew that wouldn't be good for the baby, so I refused the frightening thought's entrance into my mind. For now, I just wanted him near me, where I could take care of him, and he could heal.

Ethan walked into the flat by himself using the

crutches, but on his own power. I closed and locked the door behind him, and followed him into the main room.

He stopped in the middle and just stood there, his eyes on me, a brutal rawness in his expression now that we were alone together.

"Come here," he said in harsh whisper.

I went to my Ethan.

I was swept into his arms immediately, seized so tightly against his body, I gasped in surprise. His crutches crashed to the floor with a bang when he let go of them to hold onto me. Ethan's desperation to bring me close, ruled the moment, and I understood why. My man had been traumatized, yet again, by the imminent threat of death. He'd been certain he would die up on the mountain, without ever getting a chance to see me again, or to meet our baby, or tell us he loved us, or say goodbye properly. Memories of me had been his comfort to help him through the experience, and then when he didn't die, he was thrust back into reality and forced to process that he'd survived. A total and complete mindfuck for him.

"Ethan. I'm here, baby. Let me help you."

"I need—I need to be with you," he rasped into my neck, his beard prickling my skin as he pressed in deep.

I pulled back, forcing him to look at me, and focus on my words. "Let's go to our bed, and forget about everything else for the moment. Just you and me together." A look of pain spread across his face. "And then, later, we can talk about the things that we needed to say to each other before you left for Switzerland. But right now, the two of us need to be close, and feel that for a while."

He closed his eyes for a second and then opened them again, a look of total relief in his eyes. "Yes...please." He looked down at the floor where his crutches lay sprawled. I bent to retrieve them, and handed them to him one at a time. His hardened, wounded expression softened as he took the crutches. "I wish I could tell you how much I love you...but there aren't enough words to fucking express it."

"I know."

He followed me into our bedroom and sat down on the side of the bed. This time, arranging his crutches where he'd be able to reach them when he wanted to get up again. I came to stand between his legs and felt his hands come up immediately to draw me closer. His face buried just below my breasts, his hands cupped my backside, and his nose inhaled my natural scent.

Ethan was desperately trying to crawl back into me.

I knew what he really needed was a hard and wild fuck from me, but I also knew, just as he did, that I couldn't give it to him any more than he was capable of giving it to me. We would have to figure out another way.

I stepped back until I was just out of reach, but still close.

I kicked off my flats and kept my eyes on him.

"I want you to remember the first time I was here in this bed with you—the first time we were together."

I unbuttoned my back cardigan and let it fall to the floor. His eyes followed to where I'd dropped it, and then lifted back up to meet mine. "I remember," he said.

"Then let's go back to that time together," I told him. "We were careful with each other because we were unsure about what the other person might want, or need."

His blue eyes darkened. "I could hardly believe you agreed to come home with me. I was dying for you that night, Brynne. I'd never wanted anyone as much as I wanted you."

I swallowed deeply and moved back between his legs. I reached for the hem of his shirt and pulled it up over his head.

He did the same with my dark grey dress—just lifted it up and off me when I bent at the waist to help him.

I straightened. "I wanted you just as much that first time, Ethan. Just as much." I unhooked my bra and let it drop. The almost inaudible sound of it hitting the floor ratcheted up the tension.

His eyes flared as he took in the sight of my much heavier breasts, and he reached out a hand to touch one. He traced the flesh with a fingertip in a wide circle, growing smaller with each rotation until he finished at my nipple.

He flipped his eyes up to mine. "I wanted to please you more than anything. I wanted to make you come, and hear the sounds you made when you did."

I bent down to the floor and untied his right shoe. He leaned back on his elbows and stretched out his long body, lifting his hips for me so I could slide his sweat pants down his legs and over his cast.

My man looked absolutely gorgeous, splayed out naked with his cock fully erect. I knew what I would be doing first.

I knelt on the floor right at the edge of the bed, between his legs. I asked in a whisper, "And what did I say when you made me come?" I took his rock hard cock in my hand and stroked it from base to tip, standing it straight up off his packed abs.

He sucked in a breath and lowered his eyelids in pleasure, but he answered my question. "Ethan...you said...Ethan."

I covered the head of his cock with my mouth and slid him to the back of my throat.

SHE gave me everything I needed. I don't know how she knew what that was precisely, or when I needed it, but Brynne always knew the right thing to do.

After she got me off with her beautiful mouth, I returned the favour, relishing the exquisite feel of my very warm, and very safe place, shuddering beneath my lips, and convulsing around my tongue. I heard her call my name more than a few times before I was done with pleasuring her.

Later, we fell asleep together, spooning on our sides while I was still inside her, and slept that way for hours.

Best sleep of my life—with my precious girl wrapped around me.

I didn't forget to be thankful.

CHAPTER 18

24th January
Somerset

Land Rover knew how to make luxury vehicles, and I'd learned that information firsthand. I loved my car, and now that I'd gotten the hang of driving lefty, I was venturing out more than ever before. I think sometimes, Ethan might have second-guessed his birthday gift to me. *Too late now, Blackstone.* But he'd just have to deal with it. I was the driver in the family for the time being. He had a cast he could walk on, but only using crutches. He needed a few more weeks of bone-healing time before he put much weight on his left leg. He'd still have the cast when the baby was born. Something that annoyed him greatly, I knew, but he didn't complain about it. I didn't complain either. We both knew how much of a blessing it was to have him in the cast...over the unbearable alternative of him not being here at all. Hell, I *loved* that damn, inconvenient cast.

I'd left Ethan at Zara's mercy. Tea party today. I

don't think he really minded a bit. In fact, he'd seemed quite into the whole thing, even putting on a velvet jacket and a fancy bow tie- cravat thingy. I took pictures of them together with my camera. They would be priceless keepers for sure. Robbie's wife, Ellen, had made the prettiest spread for them, iced cupcakes and strawberries, and tea, of course, with milk and sugar. I would've stayed and joined in, but I needed my twice-weekly massage more than I needed tea and cake. Especially now that I was bigger and experiencing all kinds of aches and pains. Back pain, pelvic pain, and even the occasional headache. The massages helped me so very much.

I'd been enjoying regular massages since Christmas, when Ethan purchased a decadent amount of treatments for me to enjoy. God, my man gave the best gifts. But after we'd made the decision to spend his recuperation time at Stonewell, I was in need of somebody local to help me get through the final weeks of the pregnancy. Enter Diane, who took very good care of me with her Aromatherapy and Reflexology talents, and thanks to Hannah pointing me in the right direction.

I pulled up to her little shop called *Treats*, and parked on the street. The historic village of Kilve was tiny, but complete with a seventeenth-century coaching inn called *The Hood Arms*, a thirteenth-century church named *St. Mary's*, and its famous fossil-laden shore at *Kilve Beach*. It looked like an old postcard to me, and was so very peaceful. I think both Ethan and I instinctively understood that the peace of this place, combined with its natural outdoor beauty, was exactly what we needed, and doing us more good than anything else could. We planned to stay at Stonewell until mid-February. So, we'd be in London, where Dr. Burnsley was standing by with his superior medical experience, to deliver our Laurel-Thomas, hopefully by my due-date on the 28th of February.

As I walked to enter Diane's shop, a beautiful young dog got up from underneath the sidewalk-table where he'd been sitting. He wagged his tail enthusiastically and hunkered down to greet me in that universal way dogs have of showing you they are friendly. "Well, hello there, handsome." I bent down and pet the top of his head, the fur thick and dark around his face, but more amber on his chest and belly. He wasn't a small puppy, but more like an adolescent dog, and he was definitely a *he*. I knew his breed—German Shepherd—and thought he was absolutely beautiful. "What's your name, gorgeous boy? Are you waiting for your owner?" I spoke to him as I rubbed through his silky fur, loving the color of his golden eyes. He licked my hand and leaned into me as I gave him some attention, wondering why he had no leash or collar on him. Surely he belonged to somebody.

He looked at me solemnly when I stood up to go

inside the shop for my appointment. "I have to go in now, fella," I said.

He barked once as if he were saying, "*Don't go...*" It rather broke my heart to leave him.

"NOW I need a very long nap, Diane. God, that was wonderful." I complimented her and rolled my neck, breathing in the aromatic oils she used at the shop. As I handed her my card to pay, I heard the bark again. And there he was, staring in through the glass of the shop window, wagging his tail at me.

"Looks like you have an admirer, Brynne," Diane chuckled. "I bet he'd go home with you, if you allowed him."

"He would?" But what about his owner? "Who does he belong to?"

"He's a stray. Just showed up a few days ago, and has been lingering around the shops for scraps. It's so sad what people do to innocent animals. Especially the big ones, as he will be when he reaches his full growth. The larger dogs get abandoned, dumped on the side of the road." She shook her head and grimaced disgustedly. "Arseholes ought to be abandoned to the cold with no food or shelter, and see how they like it." Diane looked out the window at him. "I've been putting out some food, as has Lowell from next door because we don't want him to starve, but he really needs a home, and a family. A big dog like that needs open space where he can run." She winked at me with her pretty hazel eyes. "He would make an excellent guard dog and protector. I imagine your husband would very much approve."

"LET me do all of the talking, okay?" We shared a look with each other, his round golden eyes lifting up to hold mine as if he understood me. The new leather collar and leash looked good on him. And he was fluffy and clean now, thanks to Diane pointing us in the direction of the pet supply and groomers, where her son, Clark, just happened to work. With Clark's helpful assistance, I chose dog food, a bed, dishes for food and water, and even some doggy chew-toys, while he was being bathed and groomed. Then Clark loaded everything into the back of my Rover, and waved cheerfully to me as I drove away. And just like that, the decision was made.

The drive home was fun, and I don't think I ever stopped grinning once. I had a furry passenger sitting in the front beside me with a seat belt strapped across his chest. My dog. I could tell he loved me already.

Nothing left, but to drop the bomb on my husband.

"I need to figure out a name for you," I said to him as we went in search of Ethan and Zara. His toenails clicked on the wood floor as he walked beside me. I swear he was on his best behavior, trying to show me what a good dog he would be. I wasn't worried, I just didn't know what Ethan would say when I showed up with a big German Shepherd, and announced I'd be keeping him.

I was about to find out.

I could hear them before I went in, and knew what they were doing before I saw the evidence. They were playing a game that Zara loved, and Ethan, probably not so much, but he was a good sport about it. *Pretty Pretty Princess.* I'd loved the game, too…when I was little. There were photos of my dad wearing the crown and other jewels, happy as could be, indulging me in playing a ridiculous little girl's dress-up game just because it pleased me. *You were so good to me, Daddy.*

And there was Ethan sporting a turquoise necklace and matching earrings, battling Zara for the win. "Ah ha, the black ring is gone!" he boasted across the table from Zara, in her blue and yellow party dress.

"But you don't have the crown," she smirked, poking her finger into the frosting on her cupcake and licking it off.

"I probably will win it, though," he teased, "I think I'd look good in a crown."

Zara giggled at him, and my heart just melted into a puddle of goo. I knew Ethan would be such an amazing father. Just watching him interact with Zara was a beautiful thing. It made my heart so happy, I needed to rub my belly to remind myself everything was still real. Yep, that was a miniature rump underneath my hand. I grinned as I worked out the position of head vs. legs and decided that my butterfly angel was upside down. It was fun to figure things like that out.

Sometimes my new life felt more than a little unreal. So much had changed in such a short time. But, moving forward was my only option, and desire. With Ethan's commitment to me, his devotion and love, and our child, how could I want anything else?

My companion whined softly beside me. Ethan and Zara looked over and spotted us. I checked Ethan's reaction, and decided to just stand there, and smile. Hoping for the best, and waiting for him to figure it all out.

⨎

"YOUR doggy looks like Sir Frisk," Zara informed me.

"And who is Sir Frisk, may I ask?"

"A dog in a painting at my house."

"Really." I was very intrigued by this information. I'd checked out most of the art at Hannah and Freddy's

Hallborough, but I didn't remember a dog painting.

"I'll show you when I go back home. It's a very good painting of a dog, Auntie Brynne." She nodded her head seriously, and petted him all the way down his back, in long, careful sweeps. "And he looks just like him," she reminded me.

My new dog must've thought he'd died and landed in doggy heaven, as he lay at Ethan's feet with a very dedicated little girl working over his freshly washed fur with lots of soft stroking. I don't think he could've been coaxed out of the house if our lives depended on it.

"So, while I'm fighting to take the crown in this game, you're collecting stray animals and bringing them home?" he asked dryly, giving me the added tilt of his head with an eyebrow raise. And so devastatingly sexy doing it, I could lick him.

"'Fraid so, Blackstone," I shot back confidently. "He's a good one."

"Well, that's obvious, my darling. He chose you, so he must be good," Ethan said, bending down to rub under his chin. "Are you going to protect your mistress and keep her from danger, young sir?" He spoke earnestly to the dog, eye to eye, man to man. "Hmmm? Because, it's a very important charge, but somebody's got to do it. If you want the job, it's yours."

I laughed at how sweet he was about everything I tried to do. Could there be any man on earth more perfect than my man? Highly doubtful. "So you approve of him being our new guard dog here in the country?"

"I do, my beauty."

"WHAT a beautiful dog. Oh, my God, he looks just like Sir Frisk." Hannah bent down to pet him and held his face as she studied him thoroughly. "He could be his descendant."

"So everyone keeps telling me. I want to see this painting."

"I'll show you," Zara said, grabbing hold of my hand.

Ethan stayed in the kitchen with his sister. He wasn't quite up to navigating marble staircases like the one at Hallborough just yet. "You take good care of your mistress, young sir," Ethan told the dog in a serious tone. "And you be careful, too," he told me, with a pat to my belly, and a kiss to my forehead.

"I will." I put my hand to his cheek and mouthed, *love you.*

"Me too," he whispered. That was my Ethan, still controlling and protecting even while semi-mobile and using crutches. He was determined to be off the crutches by baby time and just have the walking boot. I knew he was disappointed he couldn't do some of the things he wanted, but he hadn't uttered a single complaint. Broken legs heal.

Zara took us to the guest wing of the house. The part they used for the bed & breakfast, which was why I hadn't seen the portrait of Sir Frisk before. I'd been to the gallery, of course, which in stately homes such as Hallborough, was simply an elegant room in which to showcase the private collection of art the family had acquired over time. Hallborough's gallery had quite a few marble sculptures, and some lovely paintings, but I'd not spent a lot of time over here studying everything in minute detail. I hadn't had the time, and had been working on my own garden and decorating projects at Stonewell.

She stopped us at the end of a hallway, with doors on either side opening into guest rooms. Right above a carved table hung a large painting of a German Shepherd in rich detail, almost photographic in its execution. I immediately thought of the camera obscura and figured the artist must have employed the use of one to do this portrait. The subject did, indeed, look like my new pet, in coloring and in body shape. A gold plate had been made and attached at the bottom of the ornate frame with the title of the work *Sir Frisk* engraved into the brass.

"Well, that is something, now, isn't it?" I grinned at Zara. "They do look almost exactly alike."

She giggled. "Said so, Auntie Brynne."

"I like the name. Do you like it, Zara?"

She gave me a serious nod. "That's his name. Sir Frisk," she said with authority, as if the decision had been made from the beginning. "He can play with Rags and they will be best friends."

"What do you say, Sir Frisk?" I asked him. He lolled his tongue out happily, and cocked his head at me. "I can call you Sir for short." I scratched him under the chin and I'm pretty sure he was in doggy love with his new life regardless of what we would be calling him. But still, he should have a regal name to go with his gorgeous bearing. "Sir Frisk it is then," I announced.

Just then I felt the baby kick. "Oh, baby's moving," I said to Zara. "Do you want to feel?"

"Yes, please." I brought her little hand to just under my shirt and pressed it flat down. Her eyes grew wide and she got excited. "I feel her moving around. She likes Sir Frisk and she wants to play with him."

I laughed at her antics. "Well, we don't know if the baby is a girl. It might be a boy I'm having."

Zara ignored that possibility and said, "It's a girl, Auntie Brynne."

"How do you know?"

She shrugged. "Because I want a girl baby."

Leave it to a child to tell you how things should be. Since we'd met, I'd learned Zara had opinions on things. On lots of things. And she had no qualms about expressing her opinions, either. She was, quite simply, lovable down to the hairs on her head. No matter what the sex of my baby, Zara would be the best cousin ever. I felt really happy at that thought.

Then my second surprise.

I took another glance at the painting, *Sir Frisk*, because there was something about it that was very familiar... Something also told me I knew that artist's hand. I'd worked on other things very similar. When you conserve art, you spend many quiet hours with a painting and you get to know the artist even though they've been dead for a long time. You see how they set down the images they create, and their process becomes recognizable the longer you spend with the works.

Was it possible?

I looked closer and scoured the bottom for a signature. The glaze had darkened over the years, partially obscuring the lettering, so it wasn't easy to make out, but it was there. The letters were also made smaller than typical for the particular artist I had in mind. But I knew what I was looking for. I could smell victory when I made out the letter T followed by MALLERT—before the rest was hidden by the edge of the frame. My heart pounded deeply as I realized what I was staring at. A previously unknown painting, of a very handsome dog named Sir Frisk, painted by the skillful hand of none other than the celebrated, Tristan Mallerton, creator of

Lady Percival, and hundreds of other masterpieces. *Jesus Christ, what else do they have in this house?!*

I so needed to call Gaby and tell her this fantastic bit of incredible news.

6th February

BRYNNE was so beautiful. I was admiring from the bed, where I had a great view of her in front of the mirror as she brushed out her hair. She'd always been beautiful to me, but my connection to her now was so much deeper than it had been before. More inner feelings. My accident had broken through the really impenetrable part of me, when I was faced with saying goodbye to her up on that mountain in Switzerland. Everything seemed to reset, or realign, within my emotional grid. So the horribleness of my past was now made less important, because of what I had with her. Brynne, and our life together, was the most crucial part in making me the man I had become up to this point in my life. It was a hard concept to explain in words, but I knew how I felt, and it was a great deal *better*—like I could get beyond the events that had shaped so much of me in the past decade, and finally put them in their place. And leave them there.

This included Sarah Hastings for me, and Lance Oakley for Brynne. Peace, for lack of a better term, had been made and accepted within the constructs of our relationships with those people. For me, I'd made apology to Sarah about my part in Mike's death, and as difficult as it'd been, it was crucial in letting some of that guilt go. That's what she'd given me the day before Switzerland. Forgiveness. Dr. Wilson seemed to know what he was doing when he assigned homework. I was giving the therapy my best go, and hoping for the best, too.

Brynne had her own reasons for meeting Lance Oakley and hearing his version of things. I might not believe a word of what he'd told her was the truth, but I also knew it didn't matter what I believed. I'd never seen the video of her and him, and I never would. Brynne was the person in charge of her destiny, and she was the one who called the shots when it came to her emotional healing. If what he'd revealed helped her to feel better about herself, then I was in full support of it. I couldn't deny that I was fucking thrilled about Oakley being gone from London, either. That cocksucker would have been a massive problem for *me* if he'd decided to stick around and be her new *friend*. I could be reasonable to a point, and he would be fucking well past it.

In the end, both Brynne and I learned a valuable

lesson about trust and respect for the parts of us that needed to stay separate. And that nothing was more important than the other person's happiness. She loved me, and I knew that, just as she knew how much I loved her. I tried to show her every chance I got.

"What are you thinking about?" she asked, as she came out of the bathroom dressed in a filmy nightgown I could see right through. *Much better than that ugly thing I destroyed.* She'd grown curvier, but her frame was still the slim shape as before, and except for her belly and breasts, she looked mostly the same to me. *My beautiful American girl.*

"Nothing but how beautiful you are." I held out my arms. "Come here, baby."

She smiled her half-smile and crawled up into bed, carefully pulling back the sheet and blanket to expose me. I don't think the state of my cock was a surprise for her, either. It still worked just fine even if I couldn't stand, or carry her when we were in the heat of fucking. My leg would heal in time though, and I would eventually get back to normal with how I liked to make love to Brynne.

"I thought so," she purred, before hiking up her nightgown and straddling me. She sat down right over my rock-hard length, her legs splitting open so the folds of her pussy kissed the length of my cock.

I thrust up against the slick heat of her and

groaned from the contact. "Oh, fuck, you feel so good."
I grappled with the hem of her gown and pulled it up
over her head, tossing it away. "That's much better," I
told her, roaming my eyes over her naked body. I could
never get tired of looking at her, pregnant or not, she
captivated me. I dipped down to a breast and sucked the
nipple into my mouth as she started rocking up and down
the shaft of my cock.

She pushed her tits against my mouth so I could
work both of them over good, sucking and biting the
nipples until they were tight and hard, and she was about
to come from sliding her clit against my cock.

"You want to come, baby?" I met her eyes and
saw the slack-jawed desperation in her expression. "Tell
me what you want, and I'll give it to you," I told her.

"Ahhh…I want to come with—I want your cock
in me when I come…right here." She rotated her hips
and really worked her sex over me good, the scent of her
arousal in the air making me burn hotter. Then she lifted
up onto her knees and took my cock in her hand.

Oh, fuck yes!

She moved slowly down and impaled herself on
me.

Felt so fuckin' good I growled from the pleasure
of the hot grip of her inner walls clamping around my
convulsing cock. I took her mouth and plundered it with
my tongue, sweeping around in a circle as deep as I could

go. I always wanted to be inside her in as many places as possible. Something drove that need in me, and I only knew I was compelled to be that way with her and couldn't rein it in. I also knew she loved me to be that way.

I settled my hands beneath her bum and we started to go at the fucking in earnest—me thrusting up and lifting, her riding up and down my cock with a little squeeze of her muscles and a twist of her hips. We made it last as long as we could, slowing down just enough to keep us on the edge. I let her keep the pace she liked. We'd be at this for as long as she wanted. I was always all about pleasing my girl, and thought she was so goddamn sexy when she got desperate for my cock and didn't want to wait for it. I loved working her up into a fuck-frenzy to pull us both over the edge when it was time for us to fall.

She reached her hand around and found my sac, squeezing my balls and my cock simultaneously, flipping my switch.

And propelling the pace of our fucking into overdrive.

"You're so fuckin' perfect, baby. My cock feels so good inside you! I want you like this forever. I'll never stop crawling up…inside…YOU."

"Don't ever stop, Ethan. I don't ever want you to stop."

"Never, baby...I'm doing this for the rest of my life."

I brought a hand forward to find her soaking clit and circled it as she continued to ride me. Tonight I wanted to come with her—both of us at the same time. It was important to me. I wanted to feel her spasms when the top of my cock shot off inside her. I wanted to swallow her cries when my tongue owned her mouth, and I savoured the sweet flavour of her.

Of course, I had to stop eventually, after I'd made her come, screaming my name. And after I'd poured everything I had deep inside her. It was the meaning behind our words that were significant, not the literal definition. I would never stop loving Brynne, and fucking wildly at times was definitely part of demonstrating that love. We had always been on the same page with the sex. Thank the gods for whichever one of them blessed us in that sector. I was under no delusions about how unusual and rare it was to find someone so compatible.

I lifted her off my hips, settling her on her side so we could face each other. I still needed to be able to look into her eyes and kiss her afterward. She was sleepy and soft from climaxing, and I worried that maybe what we'd just done was a little too much, and too rough for her more advanced stage in the pregnancy.

"Was all of that okay, baby? Maybe we shouldn't

have been so rough at it." I traced her lips with my finger. She opened her mouth for me and I slipped my finger in between her lips. She closed them in on my digit, wrapping her warm tongue around it, sucking gently. I felt my cock twitch and start to harden up again. *Not happening, you fucking Neanderthal. You can't.*

"Mmm hmm, don't worry. I feel wonderful right now," she murmured with her eyes barely open. "I needed that orgasm. Badly. And I love you…"

"And I need to kiss you now," I said, dipping my lips to hers, our heads resting on the pillows.

So I kissed my girl, and told her all of the things that were important for me to say to her, and necessary for her to hear from me, until we fell asleep, tangled together, our bodies touching wherever we could comfortably connect.

I felt something different. Utter contentment…and peace. It was the first time I could ever remember feeling that way, and I prayed it wouldn't be the last.

CHAPTER 19

7th February
Somerset

"That would be the last of the deliveries from London, Mrs. Blackstone. I'll have to assemble the crib tonight when my helper has some free time." Robbie winked at me. His "helper" would be Ethan, who wanted to be part of putting the crib together.

"Oh, I know, Robbie, he's been reminding me about it. I'm sure he's been reminding you, too. Ethan just wants to make sure the crib is assembled correctly so it's one-hundred-percent safe. It's the security-guy thing in him. It crosses over into all aspects of our lives, as I am sure you already know," I said sarcastically.

Robbie laughed and headed out, but he turned back before he left the room. "Does Sir Frisk need to have a trip outside before I have to head out?" he asked me.

"I don't know, maybe he does, although he looks pretty happy where he is right now." I peered down at

Sir who was sprawled out on the new rug, blinking up at me with his gorgeous golden eyes, and asked, "Do you want to go outside with Robbie?"

He didn't budge. And I was certain he understood my question. My Sir was super smart, and he loved me best. *Doggy love for the win.*

"Guess not right now, Robbie. He'll let me know when he needs to go out, and I want to take a walk later anyway."

"Very good, Mrs. Blackstone."

I returned to my mural painting for the nursery after Robbie left. He and his wife, Ellen, took really wonderful care of Stonewell, both when we were here, and when we were in London. Robbie had grown a soft spot for Sir Frisk too, which was a nice thing, as he would always stay here. None of us could imagine confining such a creature to a London penthouse flat. It just wouldn't be right. I'd miss him very much though, and we planned to go back in another week so there were no chances taken with me going into labor early. Ethan was paranoid about it, and as usual, I let him have his way.

This mural was of the sea instead of a tree. Some of the elements were still a question until we knew if we had a Thomas or a Laurel. I smiled as I worked on some of the white cloud shapes, remembering how Ethan interrogated me this morning about the paints I was using for the project, and *were they water-based, non-toxic mixtures?*

He was always so cautious about everything, but I knew it was just because he loved me so much.

He'd been worried last night after the mega-amazing sex session too, which I thought was unwarranted. I felt fine, and from all that I'd read in the literature about pregnancy and birth, sex was perfectly safe for couples as long as there weren't complications, and you felt up to the task. Well, I certainly did. And Ethan always was "up" for it. I think we were both really desperate for the intimacy and closeness after our scare with his accident. Nothing prioritized life faster, or more effectively, than the *near death* of a loved one.

We'd come too close to losing each other. I shuddered at the thought and went back to shading fluffy white clouds over a sparkling blue-green sea.

SIR hovered on his haunches, ready to spring the second I let his favorite rag bone fly. "Go get it, boy." I let it go, putting my high school shot-put skills to use. He tore off to find it in the natural plantings at the edge of the lawn, happily rooting around and enjoying himself. I sat on one of the garden walls and waited for him to come back.

Feeling a little bit of backache earlier, I'd hoped an easy walk with the dog would help, but it hadn't. The dull pain was still there, and I wanted a hot drink. I pulled my sweater shawl closer to ward off the chill. It was wintertime after all and I was grateful for the dry day, but checking out the dark clouds above, it looked like it would be raining in another hour or so.

I called Sir back over to me, and stood up to go back inside the house. The weirdest sensation of heat hit me between my legs. It lasted for about two seconds before it didn't feel warm anymore. I was wet down there. A lot wet. Like I'd pissed my pants, but I knew I definitely had not.

I freaked for a moment, afraid it could be blood, but when I touched the area of my leggings, my hand came away clear and wet, not bloody. I put my fingers up to my nose and smelled it. Not pee, just wet... Water...

Shit!

I figured there was a very good chance my water had just broken.

Double shit!

RUNNING Blackstone Security from Somerset was really working out quite well. I'd put in the same communications system I had in the London flat, and conducted my business in the same way as before. Neil was running the executive offices in town, and keeping the cogs running smoothly to the point I don't think I was even missed. I'd have to give some serious thought to what my role would be in London for the future. The idea of staying here at Stonewell for more than just weekends was an appealing one. I knew Brynne loved the country, and had even been in contact with her art advisor at University of London about organizing some evaluative study of the paintings at Hallborough. After the discovery of the *Sir Frisk* painting belonging to Mallerton, she'd been thoroughly charged up with discovering what other secrets might be hiding in the old house. She told me there was plenty of work there to keep her busy for years, if the proposal was funded.

The sound of a barking dog assaulted my thoughts. Incessant, non-stop, frantic barking. This wasn't like Sir at all. He was usually fairly quiet, which was a trait I liked about him. He was a good dog, but what I was hearing sounded like he was agitated. I wondered if somebody was outside on the property.

I stood up from my desk and used the crutches to head over to the window. My study overlooked the back gardens and then the coastal sea beyond it.

I could make out Sir, barking frantically in the direction of the house with his head pointing up at the sky.

He was beside Brynne.

She was sitting on the garden wall holding herself between her legs.

Her light grey leggings were stained dark at the insides of her thighs—

Fuck. NO! NO! NO!

"FRED, what's going on? Tell me something useful!" I had my brother-in-law by the collar and pulled up to my face, feeling like my heart would explode in another minute or two.

"Stop manhandling the doctor so he can deliver your baby," he said calmly, pushing me off him. "Go with Mary Ellen. She'll get you scrubbed for theatre. You're about to be a father, you big nob."

"Caesarean section? Really, Fred?" I croaked.

"'Fraid so, brother. The baby is in a breech position and we can't risk a foot-first birth for Brynne. She's not built for it." He slapped me on the back hard. "She's going to be fine. Stop worrying me and go get ready." Fred left me in the hall and disappeared into a door marked for staff only.

I gulped and followed Mary Ellen, hoping I didn't pass out before I got to wherever she was leading me.

"Where have they taken my wife?" I asked.

"She's being prepared for the surgical theatre

right now and getting her epidural. Dr. Greymont will walk you through the process as he does the procedure. You'll be able to watch the whole thing, and talk to your wife throughout." She smiled kindly. "Congratulations, Dad."

"Really."

Was that myself speaking? It didn't sound like my voice to my own ears. Why did I keep saying *really* like a moronic half-wit? I think I was in too great a shock to process much of the events of the last two hours. After Sir had alerted me to Brynne's situation in the garden, I'd called 999. While we waited for the ambulance to show up, I called Dr. B's service in London, as well as Fred, in a complete panic about what to do and where to go. Then the motherfucking horror ride, with Brynne in the back of an ambulance all the way to Bridgwater Hospital—over thirteen, long, rolling, country miles. So much for planning. No posh London hospital, or society doc, would be delivering our baby after all. The worst part had been not being able to carry Brynne inside the house to wait. I had to hobble around like a fucking gimp with no idea of what was happening to her as they whisked her away for evaluation. The baby wasn't due for another three weeks at least...

"Mr. Blackstone?"

"What?" I turned to the voice and blinked.

"You need to remove your clothes and put these

on, even the hat. Then you'll wash your hands and forearms according to wall plaque directions, and when you're all set, you'll meet me just through there." Nurse Mary Ellen pointed to where I was to end up. "I'll take you into the theatre and you'll be reunited with your wife, and you'll watch your baby being born." She looked happy.

"Oh…real—all right." Again, surely the bloke who was speaking in such a pathetically weak voice was some other person, and couldn't possibly be me.

Mary Ellen grinned some more. "Deep breath, Mr. Blackstone."

"But is everything going to be all right? It's too early for—"

She tilted her head and told me in a no-nonsense tone, "Babies have their own ideas about when to come. Nothing to be done about that. Your wife is in the best possible hands. Dr. Greymont does this all the time, but I'm sure you already know that." She looked at me oddly, probably figuring there was more wrong with me than just my busted leg, before she left the room so I could change.

I don't know how I walked into that operating theatre because I was fucking scared to, but at the same time, I needed to see Brynne and reassure myself she was okay. The room was cold and there was a strong antiseptic smell that hung in the air. I went to where everyone was gathered, limping slowly without my crutches. One thing I'd decided—I was walking into this on my own two legs, fucking busted or not.

"There he is," Fred said, giving me a thumbs up.

"Ethan?" Brynne called out.

I closed my eyes in relief at the sound of her voice, and made my way to her. All I could see was her face and the main portion of her stomach. Everything else was swathed in blue medical drape. "I'm here, baby." I leaned down and kissed her on the forehead. "How are you?"

"I'm fine now that you're back here." *I love you*, she mouthed.

Funny, how I felt exactly the same. All of the stress and panic sort of melted away as soon as we saw each other and could be together. Brynne was so strong, and brave. She looked completely ready for what was about to happen. And…so beautiful. If she could do this, then the least I could do was stay conscious. How did I ever find this amazing and remarkable woman? How did she ever fall in love with me? *Lucky bastard.*

"I love you more," I said.

"Ready to become Mum and Dad?" Fred asked cheerfully.

Yes.

"RIGHT, you can look now, if you like, E." Fred said in a methodical tone, which told me he was focusing on the job at hand, as he should.

I'd kept my eyes on Brynne's while he did the incision, stroking her hand with my thumb, knowing there was no way in hell I could watch a blade slicing into her perfect skin. She was so calm, and matter of fact about everything. No apparent fear of any kind; just a solid determination to get on with it and see this to its conclusion. *She is so amazing.* Women on the verge of giving birth had some serious mojo in the way of resolve and bravery, and it was utterly spectacular to see Brynne this way.

The sound of monitors beeped in the background, against the clicking of medical instruments and the jostling of her body on the table as they worked their way closer to the baby.

"I can't feel any pain, Ethan. Just pulling and pushing. Feels weird, but I'm good." She nodded and smiled at me. "I just want to meet our baby now."

"Me too, my beauty. Me too."

"Out we go," Fred said with firm authority.

I peeked over the drape and saw a cap of dark hair emerging from Brynne's belly, then a scrunched-up face looking furiously outraged at the rough treatment of being dragged into the world of bright lights and loud noises, then miniature shoulders and arms slipped through the opening, and then…the rest of a tiny little body. The whole process took probably about ten seconds in total.

And just that quickly…she was finally here with us.

LAUREL Thomasine Blackstone was born on the 7th of February at precisely three forty-four p.m. She weighed six pounds, four ounces, and was nineteen and three-quarter inches long. She came into the world with a healthy cry, and some pretty, dark curls on her perfectly shaped head. The last two came from her father, of course.

My butterfly angel was a beautiful little girl who would look to me to care for her, and help her to grow, and to love her unconditionally, along with her father, who would do all of those things for her, too. He would do them well. Because Ethan Blackstone was a wonderful man, with a beautiful heart, filled with so much love for me, and for our daughter.

I cried tears of happiness and joy when they put her into my arms for the first time. I couldn't take my eyes off her, even though I was so exhausted I probably could've slept for a day straight. I wanted to look at her little hands, and fingers, and toes, and feet instead. And I did—for hours. Her nose, and eyes, and rosebud lips, and cherub cheeks were pretty captivating as well.

When she was born, Ethan saw her before I could, because of the drape shielding everything from my view. He looked back at me and told me we had a daughter.

And for the first time since I'd known him, I saw tears in my Ethan's eyes.

14th February
Somerset

"JUST a minute, little one, Daddy's got to get you dressed, and then I'll take you to Mummy. You must be a good girl, and stop wriggling—and let me put your arm— oh, for fuck's sake—I can't get this silly thing on you. It's completely stupid," he sang to her in a soothing voice. "So we'll just wrap you up in a blanket instead. Yes we will…"

The most beautiful sounds of Ethan talking to Laurel in the night made me hold my breath so I could hear every whispered word, every baby sound, every rustle of the diaper changing, and the frustrating struggle of him trying to worm her into a fresh sleeper. Ethan did all of it because he wanted to, because he embraced fatherhood in the way he embraced everything in his life. With complete attention, loyalty, and dedication to those he loved.

I'd discovered something else about my daughter in the short time since she'd been born. She was a daddy's girl, just like me. Ethan's voice comforted her when she was fussy, and lulled her off to sleep when she was tired. He was the Laurel-whisperer all right, and it made me hope my dad could see her, or know about her, somehow…wherever he was in the vast universe.

"Ahh, you're awake," he said as he limped across the room toward me, cast still on his leg, holding our baby against his chest. My beautiful man, in all his sleep-mussed glory—all six foot three inches of him, his fine physique, and hard, carved muscles—holding a tiny bundle like it was the most precious treasure on earth. I wanted a picture of them together.

Thankfully I kept my camera on the bedside table, so I picked it up and snapped a photograph.

"That's going to be perfect." I smiled at him as he put her into my arms. "Thank you for changing her for me."

"Of course," he said, settling himself back into bed beside us. Ethan had helped me so much in the first days when I came home from the hospital. The incision from my C-section still hurt and the pain meds made me sleepy. So he'd gotten into a routine of getting up and bringing her to me for feeding in the night. He waited until she was finished, and then put her back in the bassinet again. Sometimes he'd burp her for me, too. Once he'd gotten the hang of things, he was really good at handling her, with one exception. His big hands and fingers didn't work too well with putting her into tiny outfits with mini snaps and closures.

"So you had trouble with the sleeper again?" I said, as I opened the flap on the nursing bra I now wore around the clock. Wearing it was better than waking up in a puddle of milk.

"Yeah. It's hard to get her arms into the sleeves."

"I know. I heard you." As soon as Laurel smelled the milk she started rooting for my nipple. Her little bow lips latched on and she started to suckle, her tiny hand fisting above my breast. "I heard that sweet little f-bomb you sang to her, too."

"Shit," he muttered. I looked over at him and laughed. "I'm going to have to work on that with her. Sorry. My mouth is filth."

"I love your mouth, but yeah, it is filthy, and this little angel will copy everything you say and do. She's her daddy's girl."

He looked happy at my prediction, his blue eyes lighting up in a smile. "You think so?" he asked softly.

"I know so, baby."

"I love you both so much," he said slowly, his simple words full of deep emotion, and heartfelt truth. He brought his lips to mine and kissed me lovingly, and then he leaned back into the pillows and watched over us both.

⧫

DAWN was breaking as I woke. I was alone in our bedroom. When I saw the lavender roses, I remembered the day and smiled. Valentine's Day. Our first one, in fact. I looked at what had been left out for me by my romantic husband.

Beneath the vase of flowers, an envelope was propped beside a black velvet jewelry box. I opened the box first. It was another vintage piece from his family's collection no doubt, and it was beautiful—a filigree butterfly pendant with a large ruby for its body. So perfect for me. I slipped the chain over my head and admired it. I would love wearing this necklace as a reminder of my butterfly angel.

I reached for his letter and read it.

My Beauty,

Every day since the first day, you have made my life worth living. You make me wake up every single day knowing that I am a blessed man. With you, I am real. You made me real when you walked into that gallery and looked up to see me. You are the only one. The only person ever able to really see me. I want to spend every day of the rest of my life loving you. That's all I want, all I need.

Forever yours,

E

Brushing the joyful tears from my face, I got out of bed, and went to find my loving husband, so I could thank him for his precious gift.

28th February
London

"DO you know what today is?" I asked from my spot on the rug.

"Of course I know. I'm good with dates," she said smugly.

"All right then, what is today, missus?"

"It's Laurel's original due date, mister."

Not a surprise to me that she knew. Brynne remembered the important things. Our baby girl was three weeks old today, and growing like a weed. She had gained nearly a pound too, which was a good thing, because she was simply too tiny when she was born, in my opinion. But she was a strong little nurser. A fighter, just like her mum.

Right now, the two of us were indulging *Mummy* as she organized us for a photograph she wanted. Brynne was becoming quite the photographer, and took pictures of Laurel and me all the time now. This particular shot was one she'd seen on a pinning site and showed to me, asking if she could recreate the scene with our baby once it was born. Today was the day, apparently.

The first step had been to nurse Laurel into a milk-coma. Then Brynne strategically placed her on my back while she was asleep, so my tattooed wings appeared to be hers, making her look like a little baby angel. She already was anyway, so why not have a photograph of her as one?

"How do we look?" I asked, her camera clicking away.

"Like a smokin' hot daddy with a newborn baby sleeping on his back," she sassed.

"Somebody needs to have her mouth kept busy, I think."

She laughed at me. "I hope that's a promise you're going to keep later," she said sexily.

"My cock heard that, baby," I teased, expecting some kind of sarcastic rebuttal in return. But the thing with Brynne was that she was not terribly predictable. And really fuckin' quick on the draw with comebacks.

So, usually, when I thought I had the upper hand in a verbal sparring? She swooped in and trumped my hand. Did it *all* the time.

I heard her catch her breath, though. Made me wonder if she was thinking about my cock, and if it was making her consider *other* things. I sure thought about it, but the reasonable portion of my brain realized she was still healing from a major surgery. I'd just have to wait until she let me know she was ready.

"I am finished here," she said, abruptly, setting her camera on the table. "And someone is ready for her crib while she sleeps it off." The baby was lifted away, and then the clack of the door as she left the room told me I was alone.

I rolled over onto my back and stared up at the ceiling, thinking about how changed my life was from a year ago. The man from last year was two months away from receiving Tom Bennett's email. He was somebody I didn't even recognize anymore. And thank Christ for that, because I had no desire to ever return to such an empty life.

The door opened again, and in Brynne walked, interrupting my reminiscent ramblings.

Understatement. Of. The. Year.

She stood over me with sexy eyes that looked rather green at the moment, and slowly reached for the hem of her shirt.

I felt the breath empty out of my lungs.

She lifted her shirt up and over her head, and dropped it on the floor. Then she shimmied out of her soft leggings and flung them over her shoulder. Left in nothing but some skimpy pink knickers and a bra, she looked nearly the same as she did before she'd become pregnant, with the exception of her scar and a magnificent set of tits that were even more spectacular now.

I put my hands behind my head and grinned up at her, unable to come up with anything particularly clever or witty to say, but mostly because my mouth went dry when she reached behind her back and unhooked her bra.

My beautiful girl let me know, and showed me, yet again, what a rarity I possessed in her love, as she had from the very first.

Rare.

Brynne's love was something rare—a gift.

A precious gift I'd been given, by some divine twist of fate that had brought her into my world...and changed everything about me. About how I saw things, about what I dreamed for the future, about my capacity to move beyond the shadows of my past.

Brynne's love changed absolutely everything.

Part Four

SPRING

Take me down, take me down by the water, water,
Pull me in until I see the light,
Let me drown, let me drown, in you honey, honey,
In your love I wanna be baptized.

Daughtry ~Baptized

CHAPTER 20

26th April
Somerset

It was a simple wedding held in the garden, overlooking the sea. The bride and the groom looked very happy, as they should. I winked at Brynne, admiring how delicious she was in her periwinkle lace. The same dress she'd worn the night of the Mallerton Gala, and now getting double-duty as a bridesmaid. She shot me a wink back, along with one of her sexy half-smiles.

Hannah's dress was rose coloured, and looking at her reminded me of photographs of my mother. I often wondered what that was like for my father to see in his daughter, the spitting image of his wife, as she would have looked when he lost her. He'd kept his thoughts on the matter private over the years, so I imagined whatever they were, would stay that way.

Today was for celebrating something new, and for that, I was so grateful, because after finding Brynne, and learning what it meant to love someone so deeply, I finally understood the depths of what he'd lost, and why it had taken him three decades to move on to a new love.

Today was that day for my father, and he was able to finally make the move forward…with his lovely Marie.

ONE of my biggest surprises was the dramatic change in someone I had absolutely no hope would ever come around. But, stranger things have happened, I suppose. Didn't matter on my part, of course, but for Brynne it was critical, and if I was being completely honest, good for my daughter as well.

Watching my mother-in-law holding Laurel captivated on her designer-clad lap, was proof that her heart did indeed beat, and wasn't made of stone as I would have sworn it was. She looked…like a real grandmother.

She actually sought me out during the reception, which shocked the hell out of me when I least expected it.

"Ethan?"

I turned to meet her inquiry with as neutral a stance as I could manage.

"Laurel is getting fussy and Brynne told me to bring her to you. She also said that Laurel is her daddy's girl." She handed my fitful daughter over.

"Right," I said, adjusting Laurel facing outward against my chest how she liked, and rocking her tiny body gently from side to side. "Thank you, Claire."

"She's absolutely beautiful, just like Brynne," she said softly.

I nodded in agreement but didn't know what to say to that, so I kept quiet.

"Thank you, Ethan."

"For what, exactly?"

"For keeping my daughter safe, and for loving her so much, and for making her so very happy."

I felt my eyes grow wide, not believing what I'd just heard.

"Oh, and for this little miracle right here." Claire took one of Laurel's hands and kissed it, before turning to go back to sit beside her husband. I couldn't envision myself ever getting on with Claire very well, nor forming much of a relationship with her. I didn't want to be unforgiving, as much as…remembering the many times she'd hurt my beautiful girl so badly, and not ready to let all that go just yet. But for Brynne, and now for Laurel, I would have to try.

***

THE two of us went to our special place. I'd figured out early on, when Laurel was cranky and tired, she was soothed by gentle words and the stimulation of simply looking out at objects of beauty. So while the wedding partying was still raging, I slipped away with my little princess and took her into the house. Along the way, we stopped to look at things of interest like paintings on the wall, or flowers in a vase, or the view of the sea shining out from one of the windows.

When we went through the door to my study, she kicked her feet and made a cooing sound as if telling me to hurry my arse up and get there already.

She made me laugh at her baby antics, and she was only three months old. How would things be once she started talking? *Oh God…or walking?*

I inhaled and couldn't find the scent of my clove cigarettes anymore. This was very good. I was determined to make it off them this time. I hadn't had a smoke since Switzerland, and no longer craved the scent of the spice. I liked to think my therapy was helping me to disassociate the smokes with being alive. I had real reasons now.

"There it is, little one. Your favourite." Laurel kicked her legs out and cooed at the portrait of Brynne in my office. "You know that's Mummy, don't you?"

She gurgled happily and gummed two of her fingers.

"Did I ever tell you about the first time I saw her at the art gallery?"

Two little kicks hit my abdomen in quick succession.

"She walked into the room and headed straight over to this very portrait hanging on the wall, and stared up at it. Mummy didn't know it at the time, but I'd already bought the portrait for myself." I laughed softly. "Crafty Daddy, I know, but I simply couldn't help it. It was the way she looked at me from across the room that caught my attention. And she was so beautiful. So beautiful…"

3rd May
Somerset

"NOW that it's my turn behind the camera, I think I can see your attraction to photography, baby," Ethan told me, as he used my camera to snap multitudes of photographs I couldn't wait to see. My naked back faced the lens, but Laurel faced Ethan over my shoulder. I didn't know how much longer I could hold out posing for him, though. There was only so much I could do with a squirming three-month-old in my arms.

Ethan laughed softly through the shutter clicks. "I see you, Princess," he said to Laurel.

"What is she doing, besides trying to leap out of my arms?" I asked.

"Oh my God, she's smiling so much. It's like she's posing for the camera."

"Well, I'm sure she knows exactly what you're doing with that camera. She's seen it pointed at her constantly since she was born."

"I know, but she just looks so happy right now," he said.

He snapped some more pictures of us. The photos were his idea. He asked me if he could do them and I agreed, of course. There weren't many things I could deny him, and this was something he'd asked for specifically, just for him. He'd asked me shortly after I told him I was finished with modeling. I know my announcement pleased him. Ethan had accepted the nude modeling before, because he'd had no input in my choice for doing it. Now, he'd been given the opportunity to respect my decision to give it up. He was still the same, deliciously possessive, handsome, dominant, and sometimes irrational man I'd met exactly one year ago, and the idea that no more male photographers would see me naked, was a clear-cut positive for him.

Why did I give up my modeling?

Quite simply, I had no need for it anymore. The things that defined me were so much more than physical, and I'd changed and grown throughout the past year while discovering that knowledge about myself. And I'd learned to love.

But most importantly, I'd allowed myself to be loved.

I don't think any of the good that happened to me in the past year would have occurred if not for Ethan. I believed that with all of my heart. Nobody could have done for me what he did. Only Ethan's love could have found its way into my desolate heart. Only Ethan's love gave me the security I needed to trust again, and to love myself again.

Only him.

"Of course she's happy. She's looking at her precious Daddy."

EPILOGUE

28th May, 1838

I have written of the weight of my guilt many times upon these pages. Moments when I was consumed so greatly, I could not see a future of any kind ever becoming a possibility. A heavy burden, carried for years until one person helped me to cast it away. I know there will be times I feel guilt still cloaking me, but for the first time, I have some clarity of forethought to understand how my burdens did nothing to help any of those who have been lost to me.

Darius saved me from myself. Of this, I am very aware. Without his love, I am certain I would not breathe to this day, nor would my heart beat within my breast.

There is great beauty in the simplicity of giving oneself to another in trust, and allowing them to hold you up. My Darius taught me this lesson. From the beginning, he could really see me. I believe he is the only person to ever see inside my soul. A rare gift, which has served to give back to me—my life.

He gave me our precious Jonathan, and also the gift of serenity in letting my J. go. I now know J. is at a peaceful place, where what transpires in this earthly realm, is but a speck floating along in the oceans of time. In the hours of the darkest kind, Darius has ever been my light. My lover who saw inside my battered soul and freed me.

M R

I set down the journal and looked over at the mermaid angel statue facing out to sea. Brynne loved it from the first time she saw it. The unusualness of the design was compelling, but now that we knew the story behind its creation, it was much more than an appealing piece of carved stone decorating the garden wall.

I'd read this particular passage many times. I probably had it close to memorized by now. The private thoughts written by a woman who lived in this house nearly two hundred years ago. Found by Brynne in a secret drawer of an old desk. When she showed me the journals, I read them, of course. They were a novelty, a glimpse back in time of daily life in the same house we now lived. This one particular entry stuck with me though. It was relevant.

I'd figured out from the very first time I read it,

the name *Darius* could be exchanged for *Brynne*, and it became my truth.

In the hours of the darkest kind, Brynne has ever been my light. My lover who saw inside my battered soul and freed me.

THE END

FROM the AUTHOR

If you enjoyed this book, please consider leaving a **spoiler-free** review on the platform of your choice. You have my grateful thanks and appreciation for your time.

It wasn't easy to write *THE END* on the previous page. In fact, I can't even say that this is absolutely and finally the end for Ethan Blackstone and his American girl, because I never know the answer to that question, and I try very hard not to become a liar. I always say if I have more story for them, I will write it. But, for now, they should be left to their hard-earned HEA. They certainly deserve it after all they've been through. There will be more stories coming for some of the other characters you've met here, though. *winks* I bet you can guess. If you are interested, I have a discussion group on Facebook for people who have finished reading, called:

DISCUSS Rare and Precious Things by Raine Miller
https://www.facebook.com/groups/209180052623315/

For those of you who are curious about the journals of Marianne in this story, you can turn the page, and read an excerpt from *The Passion of Darius* to see if my historical romance is to your liking. Darius and Marianne's story was my first published book, and very special to me for many reasons. Tying their love story into **Rare and Precious Things** was a joy, and I hope you will read further.

I have nothing but endless thanks to my readers, who inspire me daily with good wishes and encouragement, or just to drop me a line and say how much they enjoyed a particular portion of a book. Your enthusiastic support inspires me with new stories to keep us all busy for a very long, time. I am indebted to you. Raine has the BEST fans on the planet. Truth!

To my dear hearts at *NS* and *SC*, I couldn't do this without your friendship, love, and daily commiseration. Truly, I would be a blubbering, hot mess 24/7. Love you so much.

I wish for all of you, a wealth of good stories, well told.

xxoo R

Please join us here for daily fan fun featuring news and chat for all of my books:

The Blackstone Affair Fan Page on Facebook
https://www.facebook.com/groups/blackstoneaffair/

Find me on **TWITTER** @Raine_Miller
Sign up for the blog here: http://www.RaineMiller.com

A word about PTSD and Combat Stress...

In my Blackstone Affair series, you've read about Ethan and his struggles with flashbacks and night terrors resulting from PTSD, coming from his wartime trauma.   These experiences can have a devastating effect on daily life and relationships, as they did for Ethan in my books. For many soldiers, their fight goes on, long after their military service ends, some, for the rest of their lives. Statistics show as high as twenty percent of enlisted personnel may suffer from PTSD. There is help.

USA
http://www.ptsd.va.gov/
http://ptsdhotline.com/
UK
http://www.combatstress.org.uk/

A Blackstone Affair, historical prequel. If you've read my contemporary series, you know all about Ethan Blackstone and his American Girl, Brynne. **The Passion of Darius** is a part of their story.

Somerset, 1837

'Ti amo, mia cara'
The fine art of persuasion.
Darius Rourke and his burning passion for a woman.
The gentle Marianne…as beautiful as she is mysterious.

When presented with an opportunity to make her his bride, Darius takes it, and knows Marianne will finally belong only to him. Or will she?

Marianne carries a secret. Something she believes will prevent her from ever being worthy to be loved by any man—even the masterful Darius, despite the fact he captivates her utterly.

A look… A caress… A kiss… A brooding sensuality. A lushly passionate tale of lovers entangled in the discovery of each other's sins and secrets. As Darius and Marianne embark upon a journey together, they will find that learning to command is just as important as learning to surrender.

A man who knows what he wants…
A woman who needs him in order to know her worth…
'Ti amo, mia cara'

CHAPTER 1

The Declaration

Somerset Coast, 1837

Darius chose his seat strategically every Sunday. Close enough to catch her scent just from sitting behind her in church. He waited for it, knowing what would come, for he was familiar with her choice of perfume. The soft essence of violets floated to him, its delicate sweetness stirring and calming both at once. Savoring the instant when he could draw even the tiniest part of her into himself, Darius indulged in the simple pleasure of breathing her.

Her neck was his favorite. He loved to look at the place where her coffee-colored hair swept up with just a few strands escaping. Indulging in wild dreams about her, he imagined how she'd look with all those glorious waves spilling down over her pale, naked flesh. Of how he would brush it aside and put his lips to that spot he so desired to know. He thought of the triumph of possessing her totally. Of her soft, pliant body beneath his hard, commanding one, accepting him inside when he took her.

Wanting her so badly was nothing new. He'd known the feeling for a long time. Marianne was perfection in Darius's opinion.

Marianne might be perfect, but her father was an idiot. Mr. George was a weak man. He had turned to drink after the death of his wife, bringing them to the brink of ruin with his drinking and gambling. At the pace he was going, Darius figured her father's descent would sit well with his own plans regardless. Being a patient man, Darius didn't think he would have to wait much longer. Her father would see to that for him.

THE hair on the back of her neck tingled and she knew. His eyes were on her. Again. Marianne looked around as soon as the service ended. Yes, indeed. He stood there staring—his dark eyes calling her to meet his gaze.

Her father nodded politely at him. "Mr. Rourke, good day."

"Mr. George. Miss Marianne, you look well today." Mr. Rourke greeted both of them warmly, but his eyes rested only on her.

"Yes, sir, my Marianne is very fine. She takes after her mother, God rest her soul." He crossed himself. "I daresay there's not any more beautiful to be found in all of Somerset," he boasted.

Marianne wanted to crawl under a pew in mortification. Why did Papa say such things? His thinly disguised attempt to throw her into the path of a wealthy gentleman such as Darius Rourke was grossly inappropriate. She felt her neck flush with heat.

"Papa, please!" She pulled at her father's arm to lead him away. Offering a sympathetic look to Mr. Rourke, she mouthed a silent, "I am sorry," for her father's boorishness before turning to leave.

"What? Can a father not want the best for his child? He admires you! It would serve you well to encourage him, lass!" He practically shouted his opinions at Marianne as she led him out to the churchyard. Mr. Rourke would have to be deaf not to have heard.

"Shhh, Papa!" She vowed silently to skip church next Sunday for she didn't know how she could face Mr. Rourke after this horrifying display.

Something compelled her to turn around. And Marianne knew exactly what would be waiting when she did.

Still standing in the same spot, tracking her, Mr. Rourke smiled, his perception all-knowing, as if he'd been assured she'd turn back to him.

Oh, dear God! I must be in hell.

At least a decade older than her, Mr. Rourke was a quiet man, possessing an air of mystery that hinted at the level of intensity to his character, but remained properly veiled under the gentlemanly comportment of his station. He conveyed a subtle influence in most of his dealings with others, not entirely discernible in anything he said or did, but recognizable nonetheless. Marianne thought him handsome. With his noble features, he attracted the notice of many women. Tall and broad shouldered, he filled out his fine European suits brilliantly. His skin held a darker cast than was typical for an Englishman, a golden hue that complemented the dark hair and eyes perfectly. He was simply beautiful.

But male beauty aside, Darius Rourke wasn't for her. No man was for her.

Marianne couldn't fathom why he would even show an interest. Her upbringing had been respectable enough, a gentleman's daughter, but their situation had declined perilously in recent years. Her dowry had long since gone by way of drink and cards. Papa had seen to that. Marianne shuddered, thinking about the debts Papa incurred on his forays into town.

Still, whenever their paths crossed, Mr. Rourke made a point to pay her specific courtesy and deference. He was never anything less than a gentleman in his behavior towards her, but Marianne detected an undercurrent. There was something about his attentions that unsettled her. Thoroughly. Like he could peer right inside her and know her every thought. When he cast those flashing dark eyes of his in her direction she felt exposed and vulnerable, on the verge of being devoured. By him.

He might even be more aware of her "need" than she thought, from the way his gaze could penetrate. After an encounter with him she always came away feeling a little shaken, breathless, and confounded.

***

IT took the passing of another month before Marianne's father ruined them completely. This pleased Darius for it worked into his plans rather seamlessly.

Darius summoned father and daughter to his home under the guise of a summer picnic. With lunch *al fresco*, and then strawberry picking, he figured an opportunity would likely result. There would be others attending as well, of course, friends and neighbors, Mr. Jeremy Greymont, the Rothvales, the Bleddingtons, and the Carstones.

Darius felt himself harden just from the thought of spending so many hours with her so close. It was becoming a challenge for him to control the urges. Yes, Miss Marianne George would be here at his home this day, and he knew the time for waiting was over. She was coming for a picnic, true, but he had other plans in mind for his Marianne.

Yes, mine.

Darius could not help the sway of his heart. He wanted Marianne and only her, for he found her to be perfect, meant for him in a way that prevented him from considering any other but her. He dreamed about her constantly. Dreamed of making her his, of claiming her, making love to her, envisioning his body all over her body, of being inside her. His dreams of Marianne were always erotic and very vivid. These and similar thoughts of Marianne George obsessed him.

He'd only come back to Somerset a mere six months ago, after being away for years. Darius had thought he might have put his infatuation for Marianne George aside during the long absence, but that'd proved false the second he'd laid eyes on her again.

Waiting for her had been a challenge while she grew up. And through the years he'd ever admired her, she was forever in his head, tempting him mercilessly. Now she had grown up a most beautiful woman, unattached to any man and ready to be plucked. He thought her silky, dark hair, blue eyes, and lush figure magnificent, but there were other reasons for the attraction.

She did not throw herself at him, as many other

young ladies tried to do. Marianne George was a complex young woman, and Darius was sure he understood the reason. There was more to her than youthful beauty, much more.

She had fire in her waiting to be stoked. This he could tell. He also suspected that submitting to him, to his dominance, would appeal to her. He'd noticed that he could make her look at him when he stared at her, and that she definitely waited for his gaze. The looks she returned mesmerized him. Her eyes smoldered, like burning embers waiting for a rush of air to fan them into flame.

Darius was certain. The dominance would be lovingly bestowed of course. If Marianne craved it, then he needed to be the one to give it to her. He would offer to her that which she desired.

MARIANNE'S cheeks burned hot. She could only imagine the deep color of her blush. Sitting right next to her, she could sense Mr. Rourke's eyes staring because her neck tingled. Nothing new there. This game they'd been playing had gone on for weeks and needed to cease. Today.

She braved a glance. His black eyes glittered at her. He smiled as if he'd expected her to look. She grasped at anything to say and came up with very little except, "The day is lovely. You picked a good one for your party, Mr. Rourke."

"Yes…so lovely," he answered, his eyes roaming over her.

She got the impression he wasn't referring to the weather and felt supremely stupid. She would do better just to keep her mouth closed before more half-witted nonsense left it.

"I'm so happy you're here, Miss Marianne. I hope today is just the first of many visits."

She shook her head. "Oh, I don't—"

"I say it's time for the berry picking! They're sweetest when the sun is high," Miss Byrony Everley announced her opinion to the group.

Marianne thought her dear friend's interruption especially timely.

"Byrony! It's Mr. Rourke's party and for him to say," her mother admonished.

"No worries, Lady Rothvale," he said, rising from the grass. "I am not in the least offended, and I venture that Miss Byrony's suggestion is a good one." His voice turned rich and his words slower. "I'd hate for the full sweetness of the strawberries to be missed." And then he looked right at Marianne's mouth.

Oh, dear God! Marianne swallowed hard, thinking she was in very deep trouble.

"'Twould be a tragedy to pass up the sweet." He held his hand down to her. "Shall we?"

She couldn't refuse him. Not in front of everyone. Mr. Rourke was her host, and it would be rude not to defer to his desire to accompany her. Marianne put her hand out and felt it clasped in a warm grip. Maybe more than warm. His skin was hot—melting hot. He pulled her effortlessly up to standing, right at his chin.

Damn her if she didn't look up at his rich, brown eyes again. What in the world was wrong with her? She didn't want his attentions! Darius Rourke rattled her soundly. He had a way of making her forget why she couldn't receive him. She supposed the time was nearing that she'd have to tell him so. But for right now she calmly accepted the basket he handed over to her and watched as he got one for himself, and before she knew it, was being led with the others, down the path to the glade with her arm wrapped through his.

Idiot!

DARIUS felt he could be in heaven, or possibly as close as he would ever get. For the moment, he had Marianne all to himself. Slowly, he'd steered her away from the others to where he thought the quietness might relax her a little. Darius didn't fool himself. He knew she was wary of him and realized that if his plan were to work he'd have to earn her trust.

He found Marianne mesmerizing and could just watch her unendingly. He admired how graceful her hands were, watching as her fingers gently pushed aside green leaves to search for the heart-shaped fruit. She parted her lips just a bit whenever she found a cache of berries hidden beneath the greenery. The pleasure of observing as she ate a few of the berries had been the definite high point. Marianne had a beautiful mouth.

"Oh! A blackberry vine has pushed in over here," she said.

Darius came right to where she peered into the tangle, standing just behind her shoulder. "They grow as wild as weeds, sprouting up in new spots each year, so I'm not surprised." A few errant curls had come loose, and there was a bit of leaf right above her ear.

Delectable.

He wanted his lips right above her ear so he could flick out his tongue and get a taste of her. What would she taste like? He had to force himself to respond coherently. "But it's a tad early for blackberries yet. By the end of July they'll be bursting with sweet juice. You'll come back then," he told her.

Her spine stiffened, and she faced him. Little creases marred her brow. "Mr. Rourke, you mustn't presume that I—"

"—only an invitation to pick berries, Miss Marianne, and only if you wish it," he said smoothly. He disarmed her with his response. He could see it happen and knew the second she regretted her comment, as clearly as if he could see inside her head.

"Of course it is." Her blue eyes swept down. "Please forget I said anything."

Impossible to forget anything about you.

He reached out his hand, helpless to restrain himself. Darius was going to touch her. She saw what he meant to do, though, and reacted by backing right up and away from him. He followed her anyway, deftly plucking the small, dry leaf from her hair.

He held it up to show her. "You had this trapped in your hair."

"Ahhh," she breathed out, looking relieved. "Th—thank you, Mr. Rourke. We should probably go back now," she said softly, her eyes fluttering down once again.

The urge to take her further into the berry thicket and kiss her senseless flashed as a possibility, but sanity overruled it.

"As you wish." He offered his arm. They had not taken even a step before the rending of fabric sounded below them.

"Oh blast! The brambles have caught me!" She turned, reaching for the thorny vine imbedded in her skirt.

"Careful! You don't want to get—"

"Ouch!" she cried.

"—pricked."

The basket dropped to the ground in a rush as she gripped her injured hand, palm-up.

"Here, let me." He took her hand for inspection. A large thorn was indeed buried in the pad of her index finger, the black strip a garish invader on such lovely skin. "I'll get it for you. Hold still and squeeze your finger on the sides as I remove it." She followed his directions perfectly and hardly winced when he pulled the thorn away. A bead of dark blood chased the thorn, welling up red on the pad of her finger.

Darius couldn't help what he did next. His mind and body were operating independently of the other, and he just reacted without conscious thought of how he would be perceived. Before he knew it, he had her hand drawn to his lips and was sucking the blood away. Earthy spice met his tongue and the merest moan escaped him. Her horrified gasp followed his moan. She jerked her finger away.

"Mr. Rourke!" she scolded, frowning at him before dropping down to retrieve the strawberry basket.

He couldn't hold in the grin and bent down to help her with the berries. "Sorry. I assure you I am no vampire."

She looked up at him sharply. "You don't look very sorry. About being a demon, I'm sure I couldn't comment."

She was flustered and irritated with him and so utterly adorable it required everything he had to refrain from pulling her against him and taking her mouth. In her present state he might just get a smack if he did though.

"Just trying to close the wound, and I am indeed sorry for your injury," he told her. "Now, if you'll stand still, I'll get this vine detached from your skirt."

Her soft breathing came faster as he worked on the blackberry thorns. She obeyed and stood still for him, but her lush body trembled mightily in response underneath all those layers. God, it would be good between them—all the sex. He told himself to focus on the goal. It was time to tell her.

"At the conclusion of the party today, I've asked your father to stay. I have some business to discuss with him, and I'd like for you to be present as well, Miss Marianne."

She nodded once in agreement. "We must go back now, Mr. Rourke." He could tell she had been pushed as far as she would go…for now.

"Of course we must." He smiled down at her.

She didn't speak again for the rest of the party. That was fine. Darius could enjoy her simply by having her near…for now.

"THOUGH your amount of debt is ruinous, Mr. George, I have a solution. It will be much preferable to debtors' prison, I think."

"What can I do for you, Mr. Rourke?" Mr. George slurred, probably half-sprung from all the wine he'd taken during the day.

"Give your consent to Marianne's marriage to me." He saw the shock in her expression at his proposal. Her eyes rolled up, her lips parted, and her breath grew shallow. *Perfect.* "Your debts will be paid, an allowance provided you, and Marianne will be settled respectably, protected and cared for as my wife."

"Of course, Mr. Rourke, you may have *my* consent. She'll marry you," Mr. George agreed eagerly.

"No! Papa, you cannot make me!" Marianne faced Darius, her lovely blue eyes sparking at him. "Sir, I have no wish to marry. A decision I have made long ago. I am not suited for marriage. Your offer is flattering, but I will not be able to accept you."

The thrill is already beginning, and you are so wrong. You are perfectly suited.

Right now, her regal stance, glinting eyes, and flushed cheeks all combined into one glorious vision. Her throat rising and falling with anxious breathing, causing strands of silky hair to flutter about her head, transfixed him. He wanted to press his lips to her neck and draw her to him. She might say she didn't want it, but he believed she did. She just needed some convincing, was all. He could do that. The art of persuasion was a skill he possessed in abundance. Darius instinctively knew the way to get to her was through her father.

He changed his voice, directing it only to her. "Miss Marianne, would it not be easing to put your troubles aside? Let your cares and worries be placed into the hands of another? Into *my* willing hands? I would never wish for you to feel you had been coerced or forced in any way to do something that you could not reconcile yourself to. My offer is an honorable one. It is time for me to marry, and I greatly admire you."

He paused at seeing her swallow hard, her neck pulsing in the hollow below her jaw. "I believe you are aware of that, and I also believe you would be the perfect partner for me. I approve of the manner in which you conduct yourself and your...disposition. There is no avarice in you."

He turned to look disparagingly at Mr. George. "Your father's debt is grave though. In a matter of days you will be out of your home, forced into debtors' prison. But such a horrifying fate doesn't have to be yours. I hate to think of you being subjected to such harsh conditions. And yes, Marianne, you would have to go, to look after your father. Is that what you would choose? Prison? Over marriage to me?"

He asked his questions gently, knowing exactly how to appeal to her need for direction and guidance at this moment of self-possession. "I think you want to marry me, don't you, Marianne?"

"Sir, why would you do this?" Marianne shook her head unbelievingly.

Because I must have you.

"You suit me, Marianne. You are beautiful and elegant, and know your duty. You always do the right thing, because you are good, and you never want to disappoint."

She looked at him. So silent, solemn, and utterly magnificent.

He whispered the last very softly. "Don't disappoint me, Marianne."

CHAPTER 2

The Acceptance

When she heard him say, "Don't disappoint me," Marianne realized he knew. Somehow Mr. Rourke was aware of her desires. He'd watched her for so long, he'd puzzled her out. He knew what words to say and how to phrase them. And Mr. Rourke seemed to be the kind of man prepared to persist until he got his way. She realized this as well. He sought to compel her and tell her what to do. He wanted dominion over her. But Mr. Rourke was wrong about one part. Not always did she do the right thing. Sometimes she did wrong. Very wrong.

Marianne felt the walls closing in. The air in the room seemed to grow heavy as he stared into her eyes. She couldn't do this. It wasn't right for her to want—

"Mr. Rourke, I cannot accept your offer. It is— it's not possible for me to be your—"

She stopped and shook her head at him, and then even had to turn away. She had almost said it out loud for God's sake! It simply wasn't possible for her to be a wife.

She wasn't fit for the role. Matrimony would not be her destiny, and it'd be best if she made that fact clear to him right now. He wouldn't want her anyway if he knew what she'd done. Darius Rourke was a man of wealth and property and needed heirs to pass it along. He must have a wife sensible in mind and capable of rearing his children, and that person certainly wouldn't be her. She must not even consider such a notion.

If she allowed him to bore into her eyes a second longer, she'd lose her resolve. She had to get out of here. Her instincts screamed at her to get away from him and his commanding presence before he spoke another word! He was too good at coercion. Their little dance around the berry patch earlier had proved just how good he was. And the problem was that she liked when he directed her. Far too much.

"Papa, we are leaving." She took her father by the arm and led him out. At the door, she paused, feeling a cold shiver rattle up the back of her neck.

"You disappoint me, Marianne." His voice had a hard edge now. That Darius Rourke did not like being told "no" was of little surprise.

Marianne froze, closing her eyes, praying for strength. Without turning back, she whispered, "I am sorry, Mr. Rourke. I just cannot—" Stumbling on through the doorway, she fled his house, pulling her father along with her.

AS soon as his guests departed, Darius took paper from his desk and began to write. He was calm but resolute when he called for his steward and gave instructions for delivery of the missive.

She'd surprised him with her refusal. This time. He wasn't really all that concerned though. There were means at his disposal to be more persuasive. This was something he could do. If it meant winning her, he could do just about anything. Yes, Marianne George may have just turned him down, be he'd felt, no, *seen,* a crack in that armor she covered herself in. Darius would be more successful next time, getting under her skin, forcing her to acknowledge him, to accept him. He would have her acquiescence. No other alternative was tolerable.

MARIANNE looked around the room. The destruction of her life was clearly visible and she wanted to weep. But that was just self-pitying indulgence, wasn't it? And she could truly say that the wreck of her family was all her fault anyway.

Papa was sprawled out on the chaise, foxed to the gills. The eviction notice he'd read, crumpled on the floor. A bailiff had served it into her hands this very day.

Three days was all the time they had. In three days he'd return with officers of the court to see they were taken to the Marshalsea in London. She picked it up and read it again. Unpaid debts were a crime under the law. Papa was a…criminal. There was only one creditor listed and that seemed odd, and the name was not one she even recognized.

Grasping at any solution, she thought about a way out. Maybe Lord Rothvale might be inclined to help. He was influential and very kind. She'd known him all her life, and his daughter, Byrony, was one of her best friends. She threw up her hands in frustration. What was she thinking? She could never impose upon friends in such a way.

Marianne left the house. She had to get outside and go look at the ocean. Her legs felt weak as she made her way, but the closer she came to the majestic expanse of brine, the stronger her resolve grew. Once the glassy blue of the water was in her sights, she breathed out a sigh. The sea soothed her and always had. It comforted in a way for which there was no substitute. It had always been so for her. She made her way to the rocky shore, seeking that which would ease her, until she was leaning against a large rock at the mouth of the jetty. She allowed herself to remember.

Shame was the worst of it. She wasn't worried

about what they'd have to endure in the Marshalsea. It was the shame that killed her. That and the cruel fact of knowing even if they went to prison, it still wouldn't change anything. Jonathan wasn't coming back to her. Papa wouldn't be restored to his former respectable self. Mamma was gone forever. The ravagement of her life was complete, and nothing was going to put it back to rights. She mourned the loss and realized suddenly the ache and despair of knowing she'd never be free of her guilt.

She wouldn't even have this—the comfort of the sea. That would be the hardest part to give up. She let the tears come and tried to memorize every sense in moment. The smell of salt and seaweed, the whip of the breeze chilling the tears on her cheeks, the sounds of the churning water and flapping of her dress, the variant colors of blue.

Can you hear me, Jonathan? We're going to be leaving…soon, and I won't be able to come here anymore. I'm so sorr—

"It doesn't have to be like this, Marianne."

Marianne snapped her head around and then quickly down, brushing at her tears with a knuckle. "Mr. Rourke! You startled me, sir." She turned away so he couldn't see her face. Why had he come out here? Had he seen her and followed?

"I apologize for startling you, but not for my

words."

Marianne didn't answer or acknowledge his apology. She just kept staring out at the sea. The wind and the waves buffeted the rocks below, as they had done for eons. *Jonathan?*

"I saw that the bailiff paid you a visit and I know why he was there."

Of course he knew why. The whole village probably knew already. Any words of acknowledgement still refused to come from her mouth. What could she possibly say anyway? Frozen in place, she continued to do what she'd been doing before he'd come out here to confront her. She faced into the wind and churning surf and stayed silent.

"My God, Marianne. Prison! You'll have to live in a filthy prison! A dirty, defiled, infested prison, miles away from your home and that which you've known your whole life!"

I know.

She nodded imperceptibly, still unable to look at him. "Did you follow me out here just to throw that in my face?" She spoke toward the sea and thought it very cruel of him to voice it even though she'd been the one to reject him and he was probably still angry.

"No. I did not," he said more gently.

"Then why are you here, Mr. Rourke?"

"To remind you that it is in your power to stop

this madness, Marianne. You can stop it. You know what you *could* do. The question is—will you do it? Will you?" His voice burned through the ocean breeze.

Oh, dear God! Could she have heard him correctly? He still wanted her? Even after she'd refused him? A proud man like him, willing to offer again, even in her low situation? Unbelievable. Still she remained frozen, afraid to look.

"Look at me, sweet Marianne. Show your beautiful face to me."

She started to breathe heavily. A warm flush penetrated and began to tingle through her. He had moved closer and was now standing right behind her. So close she could smell the spice of his cologne.

"Do it. Turn around and look up at me. You want to, Marianne. I know you do," he whispered, near enough that his breath kissed her neck.

He was right. She did want to. Turning to face him, a warm heat flooded between her legs. She saw him inhale as if to scent her. A curl of a smile lifted on his mouth and his eyes burned.

"You've been crying." He fished out his handkerchief and pressed it gently to each cheek. "I don't like you crying. And I think I know why you were." He leaned down closer. "Let me take care of you. Your father, too. You'll want for nothing." He tilted his head, honing in on her. "Marry me."

Telling her what to do didn't seem to be a problem for him. He smiled and slowly nodded, willing her to accept him. He was boldly telling her to agree, but did it in such a way that she *wanted* to agree. Lord, he was handsome! A lock of glossy black hair slipped down over his forehead, and she had the urge to reach out and smooth it back. What would his hair feel like?

Mr. Rourke had her ensnared without a doubt, and he was very skilled at seduction. Marianne accepted that resisting him was a futile enterprise on her part. Her desire was far too formidable of a beast to conquer. It felt enormously relieving to yield to him. His lilting voice, like cool silk brushing over warm skin, told her exactly what she wanted to do.

And if she was honest with herself, she could admit to the pure comfort to be had in embracing his dominance. Soothing. Relieving. Oh, yes. Feelings she had never allowed herself to indulge in. He would be *good* for her in that way. And more importantly, a marriage with Darius Rourke would enable her to save Papa. This marriage would provide a way, albeit insufficient, to partially atone for what she'd done.

Resolving to accept his offer before she might change her mind, she straightened her posture. A shiver and a breathy sigh escaped at the thought of belonging to him. The way he looked at her. Imagining what he'd do with her! She was certainly a mouse caught in the paws of an indomitable, pouncing cat. And when the time came for the cat to devour the mouse, Marianne prayed she'd not regret her choice.

"Mr. Rourke, I—I do agree. I'll marry you."

"Yes?" His eyes lit up with glittering sparks at her answer, spurring her to speak resolutely.

"I will."

Marianne would not forget the look upon his face when she gave him her agreement. Darius Rourke looked very…pleased, which, again, mystified her as to why he found her so attractive. She prayed he wouldn't regret this decision any more than she might.

<hr />

THAT'S my good girl. You want it. I was right about you.

He took her hand and brought it forward. His lips kissed the cool skin of her hand as his thumb caressed over her elegant fingers. The essence of her flesh so close threatened to overpower his senses. Darius let the desire seize him—the tightening down low as the blood hardened him to iron. God, it felt good. He could stand here staring, breathing in her delicate scent, nibbling her skin, forever and never get tired of it. Just having her close felt like a reward. He kissed her hand a second time, lingering a little longer with his lips, drawing in her natural essence through the softness of her silky skin.

"You have made me *very* happy, Marianne. Let's go tell your father the good news."

Her luminous blue eyes looking up moved him deeply. She was beautiful to him. And now she'd be his. He would be the one—the one to discover her secrets.

Anticipating how he would take her the first time made him lightheaded. Her innocence required a gentle hand of course. And he would gladly give it. Darius would be so very careful with her initiation into the pleasures of the flesh. But still, his need to know her was nearly uncontainable. In his imaginings, he experienced lurid visions of possessing her beautiful body in so many ways, of satisfying his desires finally, after years of wanting her.

MARIANNE sat down that night and began to write. The journal had been given to her by her mother. One of the last gifts she'd ever received from her before she was gone. Mamma had said it was admirable for a lady to put down her thoughts in a journal. Marianne thought of what she had agreed to this afternoon, and once again, could not see how she would manage to be all that her future husband believed she would be.

7th May, 1837

...Today I also gave my agreement to marry a man who says he wants nothing more than to care for me and to allow him to cherish me. He looks into my eyes and touches a part of my soul in a way that terrifies me, yet at the same time draws me in deeper to understand his motivation. I believe he can see into part of my secret. He understands me, because his words cut right to the essence of my problem, leaving me no choice but to give in to his demands.

So I will go to live at Stonewell Court and make my life with him...but I am very afraid of what awaits me. How will I ever rise to the standard of what is expected of me? I am not worthy, and I fear my carefully guarded heart is in great danger of being shattered beyond the ability for it to continue to beat within my breast. Darius Rourke doesn't yet understand that I do not deserve to be cherished by any man. I am torn, and yet he is persuasively persistent in continuing to assure me all will be well, and to trust in him.

I find myself unable to deny Darius in his wishes for me, just as I was unable to deny my beloved Jonathan...
MG

CHAPTER 3

The Kiss

Marianne realized Darius felt entitled to demand a little more since she was now his betrothed. Their engagement had been announced, but it would be three weeks yet until they married. As her fiancé, he could call upon her and sit next to her in church. And he took full advantage of those opportunities. He held her hand and kissed it, walked with her, and often sent her letters and gifts.

"I have something for you, Marianne." He presented a slim, leather volume into her hands.

Opening to the title page, she smiled when she saw the inscription he'd written. *To my Marianne, From your Darius.* She hardly knew what to say. Did Darius think of himself as belonging to her? It was a very intimate thought, and Marianne felt a thrill of pleasure at him believing in it.

"John Keats. His poetry is beautiful. I will enjoy this very much. Thank you, Mr. Rourke."

"I think you want to call me Darius." He nodded

slowly at her. "And now, you want to kiss me, Marianne." Still nodding, he smiled knowingly.

He told you what to do, and now you must do it.

Her breath grew heavy, her heart sped up, but she tilted her mouth toward his. Pushing up on her toes, her soft lips pressed against his firmer ones, and she felt the heat, a shuddering slice of arousal that shot right up between her thighs. A yielding breath escaped before she broke contact of their lips. She kept her lips close to his though. Marianne lifted her eyes to his burning ones.

"Darius," she whispered. Just that short union of lips was shattering, and not nearly enough. He smelled divine, his cologne carrying a hint of exotic spice mixed with fresh linen and...heavenly male. To be so close to him stirred her blood. She let herself be drawn in easily and wondered what else he might ask of her. A shiver brushed over her shoulders and down her spine.

"Say it again."

"Darius..." His name coming off her lips was lovely

His eyes flared as he descended for another kiss. This time his mouth moved on hers, warm and soft, but commanding. He nipped at her bottom lip, pulling it into his mouth partway, like he wanted to devour her. She was going to allow him. Unable to resist, she leaned into his kisses, letting him tug her into his mouth, wondering where this would lead.

Darius didn't demand anything more though. At least, not today. He stopped and just smiled, looking pleased when he brought the back of his hand to her face and stroked gently.

"You are something so perfect, Marianne."

No, I am something so definitely not!

WHEN his elegant carriage came to collect her, there was an envelope lying on the leather seat.

Dearest Marianne,

When you go today to be fitted for your wedding clothes, I have arranged for you to select new gowns and assorted garments from the modiste in town. She is French, and will guide you in selecting those items I wish for you to have. Dressing a woman is like framing a beautiful work of art. You, my dear, are the art, and so you must be framed, magnificently. Madame Trulier will have some things ready to take home with you today. Wear them for me, Marianne. I cannot wait to see you dressed as I believe is your due.

Yours,

D. R.

Reading his letter, she became flushed. The thought of Darius picturing her body in want of clothing was very intimate and made her heated. He always did that to her. His words, the looks, the smiles, the barest touch, all served to enflame her until she was unable to think or do anything other than what he asked of her. Darius understood her. Now, when she looked at him, she didn't see a man that was not for her. Rather, she saw a man she wanted to please. She needed to. Compelled to do those things that satisfied him, she was bound to do what he asked of her.

Darius made her feel special in a way she had never experienced before. He cherished her in words and in deeds. Giving in to him felt comforting, and more importantly, safe. He would make sure she did the right things. If she followed his directions she wouldn't be able to make terrible mistakes. Marianne couldn't afford to make another one. Another mistake, like the one with Jonathan, would be the end of her.

Measuring tape in hand, Madame Trulier looked Marianne over carefully. Stripped down to her chemise, her body seemed to be met with approval.

"You are blessed in your figure, my dear. I can see why Mr. Rourke is so enchanted by your charms. We must arrange to show you off to your greatest advantage. Your fiancé was quite specific in what he wants, especially in regards to *dishabille* dress and undergarments. Mr. Rourke said only French silk for your chemises, stockings, and corsets. We shall please him, hmmm? You will be lucky to have such a husband—one who takes an interest."

Marianne chose from those garments suggested by Madame Trulier. There were morning gowns, lounging wrappers, and gorgeous undergarments. Day dresses, evening gowns, riding outfits, and cloaks. Madame insisted on several nightdresses sewn of the sheerest fabrics—beautiful, but capable of concealing little. Marianne felt the blushing heat fill her again when she pictured herself wearing them for Darius.

"He chose this shawl for you. You will take it with you when you go," Madame Trulier announced.

The heavy shawl was a work of art in sea-blue Indian silk, woven in an intricate design, shot through with violet, lavender, and dark purple, iridescent threads. Marianne loved it. The dancing fringe swayed delicately when she caressed her hand over his striking gift. Suddenly swamped with the desire to wear this shawl for Darius, she wanted him to see her wearing it and know she had done it for him, to please him.

I am unable to resist his allure and he well knows it.

RAINE MILLER

RAINE has been reading romance novels since she picked up that first Barbara Cartland paperback at the tender age of thirteen. She thinks it was *The Flame is Love* from 1975. And it's a safe bet she'll never stop reading romance novels because now she writes them too. Granted, Raine's stories are edgy enough to turn Ms. Cartland in her grave, but to her way of thinking, a tall, dark and handsome hero never goes out of fashion. Never! A former teacher turned full- time writer of sexy romance stories, is how she fills her days. Raine has a prince of a husband, and two brilliant sons to pull her back into the real world if the writing takes her too far away. Her sons know she likes to write stories, but have never asked to read any. (Raine is so very grateful about this.) She loves to hear from readers and chat about the characters in her books. You can connect with Raine on Facebook at the **Blackstone Affair Fan Page** or visit her at **www.RaineMiller.com** to sign up for updates and see what she's working on now.

TITLES

The Blackstone Affair

NAKED BOOK 1
ALL IN BOOK 2
EYES WIDE OPEN BOOK 3
CHERRY GIRL BOOK 3.5
RARE and PRECIOUS THINGS BOOK 4

Historical Romance Prequels

The **PASSION of DARIUS**
The **UNDOING of a LIBERTINE**